# A FRIEND FOR OTTER

Jesse and Ván Medlong

Published by Inkshares, Inc., Oakland, California
www.inkshares.com

Edited by Delia Davis & Ryan Jenkins
Cover design by Senetra Busbee
Interior design by Kevin G. Summers

ISBN: 9781950301492
e-ISBN: 9781950301508
LCCN: 2022945495

First edition

Printed in the United States of America

*To all the young readers who find friends in books
and dream of imagining some of their own*

# FOREWORD

Ván and I began writing *A Friend for Otter* together in 2015. When we started our adventure with Otter, Ván was an avid reader, only eleven years old, and went by their first name, Sylvia. One day, not long before that, Ván told me they wanted to write a book. I remembered how I loved to read as a child and how my favorite stories inspired me to want to write. But when I sat down and tried to start writing my own book back then, I soon grew frustrated, and the process lost steam. My desire to write compelling stories ran headfirst into my lack of understanding of the discipline of writing. So when I heard Ván say they wanted to write a book, I decided to teach them that discipline and, I hoped, spare them the frustration.

*A Friend for Otter* is a collaborative project. Ván and I formulated the story together. Ván was responsible for creating the people and places of Imbria, the world where our story takes place. Ván completed worksheets describing characters and places in detail, and each worksheet was an assignment in handwriting, punctuation, and grammar. I was responsible for drafting. All along the way, we worked together to ensure the story stayed true to our joint vision.

I promised Ván that, if we saw this project through to completion, we would publish our book one way or another. Thanks to Inkshares and our readers, that's what we have done. It took more than five years. And by the time we finally typed *The End*, we had come a long way from an eleven-year-old coauthor who gave our characters names like Otter, Pickle, and Cherry. Out of respect for that young author who was, however, we have kept all those original details.

We hope you enjoy our story as much as we enjoyed creating it. Maybe our journey will inspire you to create stories of your own. So please join us—and Otter—on an odyssey across Imbria. May it be everything you imagine it will be.

~ CHAPTER 1 ~
# OTTER

HER HANDS MOVING nimbly across her work, Otter peered out the factory window at the other children as they played in the park with their imaginary friends.

Otter never saw the other children except through that window from the narrow gray space where she toiled. When she walked to the factory in the morning, and from the factory at night, those children were in their homes with their families, and the world was dark and still.

Otter didn't have a family of her own. Neither did she have her own imaginary friend. Although she admired the great variety of imaginaries she saw running and dancing and wrestling and tumbling with the other children, none was perfect. She wanted an imaginary very badly. But she wanted hers to be perfect. So she waited. And she worked.

She looked momentarily down at the libertyslipper in her small, calloused hands. It looked just like all the others. Otter had sewn together dozens of libertyslippers already today, joining the bits of silk and magical hide as the conveyor belt slowly but continuously delivered them to her. Compared to the belt's sleepy pace, Otter sped through the process. No one else in the factory could assemble libertyslippers as quickly as Otter. This was perhaps because no one else in the factory had been doing it as long as she had. Assembling libertyslippers could be dangerous work, so assemblers didn't usually last long enough to become experienced. But Otter was always careful—she had to be.

She placed the finished libertyslipper back onto the conveyor belt beside its mate and, for a moment, watched the pair of them glide away from her toward the packaging workers' station in the next drab room down the line. Otter glanced again out the window as she waited for the next batch of material to arrive. And she thought of what it must be like to have her own imaginary. Or to play in the daylight.

"Enjoying the view, *Odder*?"

Otter's thoughts of other children and imaginary friends burst as if pricked by the reedy, nasal voice of Mr. Pickle, the factory's peevish manager. Any remnant of her daydream washed away as that voice erupted in an impish, self-satisfied giggle at the tired pun Pickle frequently made of her name. With an equally tired lack of amusement, Otter lifted her gaze to meet the face producing that giggle.

Mr. Pickle's pale face was dominated by its central feature: his nose. His face was, in that way, not unlike the town of Junkton, whose central feature was the factory that supplied the entire world of Imbria with libertyslippers. Both the town and the face were dominated by hulking, unsightly structures at their centers. For all intents and purposes, Junkton *was* the libertyslipper factory. For all intents and purposes, Mr. Pickle's face *was* his nose.

Several high-pitched squeals chirped from behind Mr. Pickle as his imaginary, Greeble, echoed the gangly manager's giggle. "You are *so* clever, Pickle," Greeble gasped between twitters. "Clever, clever, *clever!*"

Greeble was a startling sight to the unaccustomed. As tall as a short adult, he was easily the largest grasshopper most people had ever imagined, let alone seen. His greenish-brown antennae twitched with delight at the chance to praise Mr. Pickle. The duo were a perfect match. Both wore gaudy pink shirts that clashed with the neon-yellow pinstripes of their matching jackets. And both their heads seemed to be attached to their necks by loud plaid bow ties cinched tightly beneath their chins. If Greeble weren't a giant grasshopper, the only way to distinguish him from his real companion would have been the clipboard clutched tightly to his segmented, insectile chest. Well, that and Mr. Pickle's nose.

Heedless of the tense discussion, libertyslipper materials continued down the conveyor. Otter interrupted their lazy procession automatically, plucking them from their repose. Then she put her shears to work trimming the jagged edges from the narrow, rough-cut strips. Her hands never slowed in their work as her expressionless stare bored into Mr. Pickle's nose, focusing on the delicate veins etched on its pale, dimpled surface like a map. Greeble she ignored completely. For a brief moment, Otter was overcome with the notion that she might imagine a friend to devour them both in a single, salivating chomp. But she restrained herself, as was her habit.

Annoyed at his inability to stir a reaction in Otter, Mr. Pickle scowled over the blob of his bold proboscis and jabbed his fists into his bony hips. "You know, *Odder*," he said, again emphasizing the distortion of her name, "it's quite impolite to ignore someone who is talking to you."

Otter continued to stare.

Mr. Pickle's left eye twitched and his feet shuffled, slowly at first but with increasing agitation. Yet the girl's intent silence refused to crack. Fidgeting, he smoothed the five or six long, greasy hairs that stretched desperately across his head, like the decrepit remains of a thatched roof doing its heroic best to shelter the massive nose beneath it. Still, nothing.

"*Ooh*, Pickle," chirruped Greeble. A spare arm nudged his real's ribs as the oversized grasshopper's eagerness all but bubbled out of him. "Maybe *that's* why it's got no imaginary. Maybe it's not a *loner* after all." Pickle's shoulders shook with a tiny, involuntary shudder at Greeble's mention of loners. Few people liked to think too much about the pitiful souls whose imaginations could form no imaginary.

"Maybe," Greeble continued, "its personality is *sooooo* unpleasant that its imaginary just up and ran away!" And at this, the big bug's mandibles produced another spasm of mocking laughter, with Mr. Pickle's thin giggle in close pursuit.

Otter's head turned to regard Greeble. She generally ignored Pickle's ingratiating imaginary. But she made an exception now at her amusement that this giant bug would refer to *her* as *it*.

"Actually," she said with only the faintest hint of a smile, "I've never imagined one." She paused briefly for effect. "That means I *could*, if I wanted to, imagine a giant shoe to stamp out any *pests* I might find around here." Her smile grew ever so slightly. "*If* I wanted," she repeated archly.

Greeble choked on his laugh. Had he been human, Otter was certain the color would have drained from his face. As Greeble struggled to recover, Otter set aside one completed libertyslipper and began to assemble the second in the pair.

With a horrified gasp, Mr. Pickle's beady eyes widened until his sleepy lids all but disappeared. Reaching over to place a hand on Greeble's trembling shoulder, he soothed the great grasshopper in hushed and tender tones. "Don't you listen to that nasty little . . ." But his words trailed off as he recalled the fact of Otter's existence. Mr. Pickle whipped his thin neck around to face the dirty-cheeked girl standing before the conveyor belt's perpetual snaking. The force of that sudden movement left his bulbous nose jiggling for an extra second after the rest of his head had come to a stop. The unusual nasal display did nothing to relax Otter's smirk.

"Didn't your parents ever teach you," Mr. Pickle hissed through clenched teeth, "if you haven't got anything nice to say, you shouldn't say anything at all?" Then his beady gray eyes glared around his nose, and his pale, thin lips curled into a cruel sneer. He again smoothed his isolated strands of hair, but now with an air of smug satisfaction. "Oh, that's right," he intoned with mock pity. "You haven't *got* any parents."

Otter's tiny grin, a rarity on her lips, deflated. This seemed to satisfy her antagonists' desire for a reaction. Greeble's sobs melted into babbling eddies of giggles until a chorus of chortles had completely replaced the tears. "That's *right*, Pickle. Its nasty little personality probably chased *them* off too!"

The libertyslipper in her hands now done, she placed it on the conveyor belt and continued looking after her matched pair of tormentors as they turned their backs to her and walked away, laughing over her many misfortunes. When the lanky factory manager and his giant insect had disappeared around the corner, Otter turned again to look out the window.

The other children were gone.

The day's last rays of sunlight had begun to retreat and—as they always did—the children had retired with them. An empty swing swayed gently in the deserted park. All else was still.

The darkness growing outside the window was slowly turning back the light from inside the factory, bringing Otter's hazy reflection into focus on the dusty panes of glass. She tilted her head slightly and examined the face that returned her gaze. Otter rarely made time to look at herself, although her restraint was aided by her lack of a proper mirror. But now she looked.

Awkward unease drew her brows together as her emerald-green eyes probed the unsmiling face that looked back. Her thick black hair was bound tightly away from her face, allowing her gaze to wander unimpeded from the almond shapes of her eyes, over her high chestnut-colored cheekbones, and down to her prominent chin. Otter was surprised to see her cheeks and forehead were smudged here and there with dirt. Seldom seeing her own face, she had little occasion to discover how unclean it was. Equally surprising was that she found her face kind of pretty, in its own way—even with the dirt. If others also found her pretty, they had never told her so.

Otter's attention snapped back to the conveyor. Another batch of material had meandered to her. She tested the shears with a few swishing snips through the air and set once more to trimming the strips of magical hide. This time, as the narrow scraps pulled away, Otter held one up for closer inspection. It was slightly wider than the others—just wide enough to permit careful needlework on each edge. A tiny gasp caught her breath. Realization dawned in her mind. *This is it*, she dared to think. *This is it.*

Otter's head swiveled, her eyes probing the room's every shadow and nook in search of unwelcome eyes. Satisfied that her privacy was complete, she reached her hand into the front pocket of her overalls and pulled out a tight, crumpled wad. Carefully, almost lovingly, she unfolded the tiny package until she held in her hand a sad, misshapen libertyslipper sole.

A gap left one edge of the little sole unfinished, and to this edge she began sewing the scrap of libertylion hide. Next she added odd scraps of silk, otherwise destined for disposal, to form uneven sides for the misfit libertyslipper. A small loop, wide enough to accommodate a hooked finger, was the final touch, sewn onto the back above the soft shoe's heel. Otter snipped the thread and then looked down at the oddity in her hand.

This libertyslipper was *not* identical to all the others. Pieced together from dozens of disparate hide strips and scrap silks, the libertyslipper in her hand seemed a mockery of the flawless footwear Otter had spent her short life feeding to the insatiable assembly line. Otter had waited so long to hold this single item. Now that she held it, she scarcely believed it was real.

*This is it*, she thought again. *Tonight is the night.*

Ever so carefully, Otter folded the motley libertyslipper into a tiny triangle. Slowly, she replaced the triangle in the pocket of her overalls. And then she went back to work.

Hours later, a steam whistle's scream signaled the end of Otter's shift. She cleaned up the pile of libertyslipper scraps she'd amassed that day—those she had not claimed, anyway—and shoved them down the chute to the incinerator that rumbled tirelessly within the factory's depths. She tidied her station as she always did and set up her supplies for her return the next day. As she always did.

But tomorrow would not be as it always was.

Struggling to rein in her pace, she picked up her dented tin drinking cup and tossed it into the matching tin pail before seizing the pail's handle and taking leave of her lonely workstation. With a deliberately casual air, she turned calmly toward the door. Hoping to attract even less attention than usual, she walked down the hall, the smooth slab floor cool on the soles of her bare feet, past the grubby night-shift children shuffling in to replace Otter and her day-shift compatriots, and through the libertyslipper factory's main exit. For the very last time.

The cool night air washed over Otter's face, bathing her senses in all the scents of the night. She looked up at the weak starlight cast by the constellations of late spring, made dim by the factory's glaring lamps. She stood there inhaling and exhaling slowly and wondering how starlight would look far away from the factory. *Tomorrow,* she thought as her legs began to move her once more, *I won't have to wonder.*

Her calm gait carried her down the concrete walkway that led from the factory to the Junkton Home for Unwanted Children. The Home, as people often called it, was little more than a barracks to warehouse the factory's many child laborers. Children without families to care for them or worry after them made ideal workers in a hazardous occupation. If one day a worker happened to not return home from the factory, no one was bothered with mourning. It was just one less unwanted mouth to feed.

The Home lay in the sprawling shadow of the factory's stark, unadorned walls. But even its proximity to that cold industrial giant could not make the Home seem inviting by comparison. It was run-down and poorly kept. In winter it was drafty; in summer it was stifling. And it was the only home that many of its residents—Otter included—had ever known. Otter hated the Home almost as much as she hated the factory. Maybe more.

At the Home's only door sat Blotch, the entryway's rotund guard. His contemptuous gaze slid over her as if he'd discovered some foreign and unappetizing debris in a dish he hadn't cared for much to begin with. Thick, dirty fingers scratched absently at his grease-stained shirt, and he spat lazily on the ground before Otter.

"You almost didn't make it," Blotch snarled with his gravelly voice. "A few more minutes, and you'd've been locked out and working another shift." He spat again, this time striking the ground just beside the spiked, scaly beast that slept beside his chair. The beast raised its head to examine Otter with a look of bored hunger. It was a frightful animal, resembling something between a reptile and a bulldog, and its temperament seemed to confirm that blend. Blotch's imaginary suited him well. Man and beast both sneered in quiet anticipation at the dirty orphan girl standing before them.

Otter didn't make a sound. She didn't look up. She barely allowed herself to breathe. All she wanted was to get in and to her bed without any trouble. Blotch was vicious and unpredictable. Sometimes silence enraged him; other times, only the silent could avoid his wrath.

Today seemed to be of the latter sort. "Well," he growled. "Get in, then. You're the last one in tonight." Resigning itself to having no sport from her today, Blotch's monstrous green imaginary lowered its head back between its massive claws and attempted to recapture the slumber the girl's arrival had chased away.

Otter slunk silently past. The door squeaked on its heavy hinges under her hand's pressure and then on its way back as it swung closed once more behind her. No sooner had the door shut than Otter heard the resolute clunk and click of the heavy lock's tumblers turning with Blotch's key. A moment later, the low rattle of iron chains confirmed that the door would not open again until it was time to file back into the factory shortly before Junkton saw its next dawn.

The dull padding of Otter's bare footfalls echoed like tiny muffled claps through the Home's dank halls. Deep into its crisscrossing passages her feet carried her, past crowded room after crowded room of the factory's young workers as they slept or readied for bed. Finally, the winding passageway ended at the Home's deepest recess, where Otter turned in to the last barracks room. Her bottom bunk was one of four identical bunks, each with an identical top bunk sagging low above it.

The other seven children in her room were already snoring softly, their threadbare sheets and itchy, woolen blankets rising and falling in slow, disjointed rhythm. Their various imaginaries—dull, stunted products of dull, stunted imaginations of children reared in a factory—lay in seven rusty cages lining the room's discolored walls. The cages were hardly large enough for a respectable dog. It said something of the children's thorough habituation to their grim environs that none had ever conceived of an imaginary these humble pens could not accommodate. One cage alone sat open and empty, unused for all the years Otter had lived in the Home. She very much doubted that her imaginary would fit in such confines as these. But she would reserve judgment even on that count for the time being.

Focusing her attention back to the task at hand, Otter tiptoed across the quiet, musty room. Careful not to wake her slumbering bunkmates or their unconscious imaginaries, she set her lunch pail on her ratty top sheet and crouched to reach beneath the bed. The sagging mattress brushed the top of her hand as her fingers groped for the loose board she knew was there. Finding the board at last, she pried it gently up and set it aside. Otter reached into the narrow breach the board's removal had revealed. Her breath caught in her throat when at first her fingers found only air. But her lungs once again resumed their work as, a moment later, her hand grasped the clothbound bundle she sought.

Removing the bundle without drawing a breath, as if the slightest jolt might scatter it like ashes, she laid it on her bed beside the lunch pail. Slowly she unwrapped the bundle, checking each item within one by one.

She had squirreled away several small packages of stale bread crusts, hard cheese, and dried meat—essentially all that meals in the Home consisted of. These she counted and recounted, knowing that their sum might number her days as well.

A slight, deliberate prick of her finger tested the point of a bent sewing needle she had rescued from the trash. And a firm but cautious tug tested the strength of the tough thread that had been destined for incineration along with the waste scraps from her assembly line. Otter was always on the lookout for useful items that no one would miss. Needle and thread had been her constant companions at the factory; it only made sense that she might need their help beyond its walls.

She also checked the edge of the tiny pocketknife she had saved up for and bought from the Home's tiny store. The other children spent their paltry earnings on cloying sweets or on cheap toys that fell apart after a few minutes of play. But Otter had wanted the knife since the first time she saw it, knowing that this day would eventually arrive.

The inventory continued: a handful of coins, a few rubber bands, a thimble, two short pencils. Next she withdrew *Surviving in the Wilderness*, the dingy, dog-eared book she had read and reread until she knew every letter on every page. The Home had few books, all donated by local charities, or dumped from the refuse of secondhand sales. Most were worse for wear, and none were the sort to appeal to the average child. Their bland titles were especially uninteresting to the Home's exhausted laboring children, who were taught to read only so they could understand signs and instructions necessary for efficient factory work. Otter had never even picked up *Knitting Projects for Imaginaries* or cracked the spine of *Learning to Love Loners*. But this book she had read in her every spare second—though her spare seconds were few and far between. Lovingly, she set it apart from the other items in her pack.

The final item she removed was another tiny triangle of mismatched hide and silk. This she inserted with its companion in her pocket. She supposed she could have set them both on the bed beside her other things. But the thought of leaving them out, open to some hypothetical eye's casual observation, tickled her neck unpleasantly, causing the fine, curly hairs there to stand out as if they too were alert for spies in the darkness.

Otter gathered up her other belongings and rewrapped them in the old cloth that had bound them under the floorboard. The book she kept out. Gingerly, she picked up the old volume, turning several pages slowly to feel them between her fingers one last time. Then she walked over to the lone shelf, tilted against the wall to the left of the room's leaning entryway, and placed *Surviving in the Wilderness* alongside the handful of dreary titles already there. Having committed every word of it to memory, she knew the book could do her no more good. Perhaps some other child would someday find hope in its yellowing pages.

Inhaling deeply, Otter returned with resolve to the pack on her bed. She hooked the lunchbox and the pack to her rough belt, double-checking them each to ensure that they wouldn't come loose. There was only one thing left to do.

She reached into the pocket of her overalls and cautiously unfolded the unsightly libertyslippers she had hidden there, taking pains not to mishandle these powerful—and dangerous—devices.

Squatting low, Otter slipped her bare feet cautiously into the libertyslippers. Having rarely worn anything on her feet, even the best-crafted shoes were bound to feel odd. These libertyslippers, however, were pieced together by the dictates of necessity, and they were decidedly uncomfortable on her feet. Slowly, she rose to her full height, ignoring the discomfort around her toes. Fixing a steady gaze on the dirty wall of the only home she had ever known, she approached it until her nose nearly touched.

And then Otter walked through the wall, disappearing into the night outside.

~ CHAPTER 2 ~

# ESCAPE

OTTER BLINKED FROM within the pitch-blackness that seemed suddenly to envelop her head like a sack. Gradually the murky details of her surroundings emerged from the thicket of shadows all around her. Only then did she realize she'd been holding her breath, frozen where she'd first planted her feet, yet unable even to think of the place where that was. Inhaling deeply, she braced herself and took her second tentative step into the dimness outside the Home.

The night was cool—much cooler than when Otter had left the factory. The compound's towering structures obscured the artificial lights that blazed from atop the factory's walls. But the absence of glare was not enough to coax out the shy twinkling of starlight, so she saw none of the constellations her book had predicted for this part of Imbria in springtime. The night itself had grown darker as well, so darkness prevailed from above and below.

The Home's drab stone exterior loomed menacingly behind her. It was a prison and, at the same time, a monument to the life Otter was leaving behind. Before her, a plain of cropped, dry turf stretched out toward the invisible horizon. The factory compound abutted Junkton's edge on one side, and Otter knew the fence that marked the boundary of both town and factory stood far across the parched yard ahead. But no hint of the fence was visible in the blackness that surrounded her. Otter could not cover the distance between the outer perimeter and herself without first removing the libertyslippers. The ill-fitting shoes would slow her as effectively as shackles. If she were to fall while wearing them, she would not stop at the ground.

Otter shuddered as this thought transported her back to her first day of work inside the factory. An older boy named Crim was strutting about, explaining to the newbie how things were. "This is how the libertyslippers work," he had said as he pulled them over his own much-smaller shoes before walking back and forth through the assembly line's conveyor with a flair. But he was careless. Satisfied that he'd made enough show of the libertyslippers' power, he turned to his audience and, with a cocky grin, asked, "Any questions?"

And then he leaned on the conveyor.

Before Otter could blink, his hand passed through the line as though it were little more than vapor. And with that, Crim was gone.

The soles of the libertyslippers had stared up at the conveyor from the floor, but Crim was nowhere to be seen. In a desperate attempt to save the boy, Otter had grabbed the slippers and tried to pull him back up. The slippers came up easily in her hands, but empty. The girl had stood there, horror-struck at what she held, knowing then that Crim would never return. That was when she first realized just how dangerous libertyslippers could be. Otter was given charge of Crim's line the following day.

Still clutching those empty libertyslippers in her memory, she could not dare keep them on her feet all the way across the courtyard and through the darkness. One misplaced step and she would be done. And her escape along with her.

Otter lowered herself into a cautious squat, inching downward until her trembling fingers could just reach the libertyslippers on her feet. She peeled the first slipper completely off her foot, pulling it carefully by the loop of fabric above her heel. The loop was an essential part of the magical footwear. As Otter knew well, libertyslippers were indifferent to where on a person's body they were worn, and only their soles made physical contact with the ground. The small silk loops alone made removing the slippers possible without the risk of meeting Crim's tragic fate.

Once she had both slippers safely off, she folded them and placed them back into the front pocket of her overalls. For a moment she marveled at the strange sensation of grass poking up between her toes. Otter's bare feet had trod gravel and pavement many times; this was their first time on living turf.

With the libertyslippers off, Otter turned her attention to her surroundings. Odd sounds skittered and crawled from every direction in the darkness. Noises belonging to creatures heard but unseen crept into Otter's ears, as though the sounds themselves were alive. She had often been between the factory and the Home after the curtain of night was drawn. Yet never before had she been truly *outside* after dark.

A passage from *Surviving in the Wilderness* flitted across Otter's mind: *Many animals are active at night and dormant in the day. Typically, such animals have keen senses adapted to the dark. Many are predators.* She tried not to imagine what kinds of predators might be making those sounds as her cautious steps carried her forward into the blackness.

Otter's anxious creeping continued in seemingly endless monotone until, suddenly, her breath caught, and she pulled up short. Something unexpected rose up from the ground before her. Backing up to get a better look, she saw the black iron bars of a fence towering over her and the yard, crowned in sinister spikes. For a moment she considered donning the libertyslippers again and walking right through this obstacle. But something gave her pause. She leaned in to get a closer look.

To her surprise, the bars were far enough apart that she could have squeezed between them even without the libertyslippers. Releasing a breath she'd not realized she was holding, Otter knew that these bars could not have been put there to keep Junkton's workers in. Curiosity furrowed her brow invisibly in the night. A few more steps backward, however, and the mystery resolved. The iron bars marked not the outer perimeter she sought but instead formed a separate enclosure *within* the compound, like some sort of cage. *To keep what, exactly, in?* Otter wondered. Squinting through the bars, she soon found out.

Just beyond the lattice of iron lounged a pack of immense beasts, their enormous maned heads resting on massive paws. Dense mats of fur covered the creatures from the tips of their long limp tails to the rounded ends of their paws, where even in this low light Otter saw cruel claws protruding and contracting lazily beneath the animals' chins.

Otter had seen few animals in her life, even if she counted the imaginaries playing outside her window. Certainly she had never seen anything quite like these. But judging by their mass captivity in Junkton, and by the vaguely familiar look of their fur, she suspected these were libertylions, the magical creatures whose hides provided the material for libertyslippers.

Staring at their menacing paws and teeth, Otter was sure these creatures could devour her in three bites without stretching their jaws. Yet as she continued to stare at the caged brutes, she thought the eyes looking out from those giant heads seemed somehow . . . *sad.*

The libertylion pen faded into the dark distance on either side. Otter couldn't even guess how long going around would take. Thinking again of the libertyslippers in her pocket, she briefly considered walking straight through. But she didn't dare. Although Otter knew very little about libertylions, *Surviving in the Wilderness* advised one to avoid any large animals encountered in the wild. And these were magical creatures, whose powers she did not comprehend. Maybe their magic would allow them to touch her despite the slippers. And although she might have imagined it, Otter thought the creatures had a hungry look about them. No, to go through their pen was foolish, pure and simple. With a heaving sigh, she turned to her left and began her trek around the cage.

Eyes forward, feet marching ahead, Otter felt her shoulder blades draw together with an itch. She had the eerie sensation of invisible eyes following her like a shadow. She looked back over her shoulder to the enclosure and let out a gasp.

Dozens of libertylions now followed her along the fence line, their forlorn, longing eyes silently pleading with her.

What were they doing? What could they want? Having no other plan, Otter pretended she could not see them and turned stiffly back to her walk. She pretended neither to know nor to care what lurked behind her. But her gait had drawn tight and quick, practically broadcasting her hope that feigned ignorance and invisibility were the same.

Several seconds or minutes later—Otter couldn't tell which—the urge to look again became irresistible. The libertylion pack had ballooned. The girl froze in her tracks, her jaw hanging open. *What*, she wondered, *could they possibly want?*

"You wouldn't want to eat *me*," she whispered plaintively. "I'm too skinny. And I'm dirty. And," she added almost as an afterthought, "there isn't enough of me for all of you."

The libertylions' wounded expressions were untouched by her pleas, and the beasts only stared at her all the more intently. One pushed its face to the fence's bars until its great muzzle protruded slightly between them. Its teeth, each longer than the blade of her pocketknife, dripped and glistened with saliva even in the dimness. But the lion's eyes remained sad. Seeing this, Otter couldn't help but think the creature had no interest in her as a meal.

"What is it, then?" Otter could hear a slight edge of panic in her whisper. She had no time to waste in making her escape—let alone for talking to caged animals that might want to eat her. "If I knew what you wanted, I'd give it to you," she said.

As if their heads were all connected by hidden gearworks, the libertylions' eyes shifted in unison, carrying their gazes as one to a place just behind the girl.

With a sense of mounting dread, Otter turned slowly toward what the beasts seemed to want her to see. Her eyes involuntarily shut as she came completely about. She could not imagine what might be lurking behind her that so captivated these sad monsters. Bracing for the worst, Otter forced her eyes open to behold—

A wheelbarrow.

Several wheelbarrows, actually.

A long row of wheelbarrows ran along the enclosure's near side like a separate, intermittent fence line. Some were nearly empty, their rusted bottoms covered only in dew and handfuls of leaves and twigs. But most were piled halfway or higher with dark lumps that Otter could barely distinguish in the night's scant light.

Hardly able to squint any further without closing her eyes, she could just make out beyond the row of wheelbarrows what seemed to be a small, thin forest of massive trees with towering, featureless trunks.

The nervous girl craned her neck in every direction to see whether anyone was in sight besides the lions. She saw no one. But that didn't mean they weren't there. At only a short distance, the darkness was nearly absolute. Her only comfort was that anyone else who might be concealed in the folds of night's cloak would be as blind as she.

Having reassured herself as best she could that the coast was clear, she approached the nearest wheelbarrow and reached nervously in.

To her surprise, her fingers met fist-sized fruits covered in bumps and dimples. She gave the fruit in her hand a soft squeeze, and its supple skin gave way, letting her fingers sink deep into rich, ripe flesh. A gush of sticky juice soaked her hand, trickled down her wrist as she raised it for closer inspection. She turned her confusion back to the giant cats.

"You want . . . *fruit?*" she asked.

The libertylion that had stuck its nose through the fence made a sound that was to a roar what a whisper is to a shout. Although she could not say why, Otter was sure this noise meant yes.

Relief and surprise washed over her, carrying with them the sharpest edges of her fear. On one hand, she was reassured that the libertylions didn't want to eat her. On the other, she was quite surprised that these terrifying animals would eat *fruit.*

As a test, she took one of the dense fruits in her hand and lobbed it at the bars.

The libertylions' eyes followed the fruit's arc through the air and, as it hit one of the cage's iron bars and fell to the earth with a wet thud, the beasts reached their great paws between the bars and scrabbled to seize the fruit until it had been pulverized and slurped clean from between their furry digits. As soon as the ravenous licking had stopped, all the animals' sad eyes came to rest once again on the girl.

Otter stood agape at the violent confirmation of her guess. That settled it. She had made up her mind.

With a final futile look around for anyone else who might see, she pushed the wheelbarrow to the fence. The libertylions backed slightly away, an edge of anticipation cutting through their sadness. With one great heave, Otter upended the wheelbarrow, sending its contents tumbling onto the ground in front of and through the fence's bars.

The libertylions immediately pounced. They fell upon the fruits, and the night was saturated by the sound of their fanged mouths mauling the juicy lumps.

Otter returned with another wheelbarrow and dumped it beside the first. Then she dumped another. And another. She began to take pleasure in knowing that, whatever she was doing, she wasn't supposed to be doing it. Junkton's "authorities"—those overseeing the factory, the Home, and the libertylion farm—wanted the fruits in the wheelbarrows just beyond the lions' reach. These were the people whose children played just outside her window as she and the Home's other young residents toiled. These were the people who regarded child workers as an expendable commodity—the people who were relieved to find the libertyslippers undamaged after Crim vanished into the floor. And if *they* wanted these fruits safely in the wheelbarrows, then Otter wanted them spilled out, piled up, and devoured.

By the time she was done, a dozen wheelbarrows lay on their sides as an avalanche of fruits spread between the bars of the libertylions' prison.

Occupied with their ravenous gorging, the lions paid Otter no further mind. Still, she kept her eyes fixed on them for a time as she backed away from the cage. Satisfied that the lions were happier eating fruit than eating a little girl, she turned back to her imminent escape.

She walked a long way in the darkness. At times, Otter worried she had strayed from the right direction, or that she had misjudged Junkton's size and would now not reach the border before the sun rose to betray her.

*And if I'm caught*, she thought, *I'll certainly be punished.*

Just when despair began to slip its tendrils around her heart and then rise as panic in her throat, she noticed that the darkness engulfing her path was no longer empty. Something lay ahead. Something tall.

It was the fence. The *right* fence this time, she noted with relief.

The fence surrounded the Home, the factory, and most of Junkton, deterring the more adventurous factory children from wandering too far from their work. On the fence's opposite side rose the countless immense trees of Oakwood Forest, their tops disappearing into the night's black heights. What little starlight the night could spare was snuffed out completely in the spaces between the mighty trunks.

Otter had learned from *Surviving in the Wilderness* that the great forest had once taken up most of the countryside surrounding Junkton. Even when that book was written, the forest had been vast and ancient. Some of the forest's trees were older than memory. Junkton's first inhabitants had cut and burned and built the town from Oakwood's living flesh to make a home for the mighty factory so those who could afford the costly libertyslippers could have them on demand.

Staring into the forest was useless. Otter could discern none of the terrain or geography she had memorized from *Surviving in the Wilderness.* Even if the night had not hidden the wooded terrain from her, she doubted it would bear much resemblance. Written many decades earlier, the book depicted a land long gone. Yet even here in the dark, she could see that some part of Oakwood remained wild and unconquered.

From her pocket she removed the libertyslippers and cautiously donned them once more. Mindful of her step while wearing the magical shoes, Otter tiptoed toward the fence. Exhaling with an audible huff, as if pushing out the last of Junkton's air, she stepped through the bars of the fence as though they were fog.

Deeply she inhaled her first breath of true freedom.

Her next free act was to squat, warily but wasting no time, and peel the rough hide shoes from her feet once more. For only a moment, her mind lingered wistfully on the added security of being able to pass through walls. But she would not want the added dangers that come along with that ability. Deliberately she folded the libertyslippers back into tiny triangles and placed them again in her front pocket.

The fence at her back, Otter now stood among the mighty sentinels of Oakwood Forest, though she could hardly make them out. Reaching into the pack at her side, she found her tiny knife. Its smooth surface comforted her, as though rubbing its wooden handle released courage hidden within it.

Setting her jaw firmly, Otter advanced into the dark woods.

And dark they were! Only moments in and Otter could barely see her hands as they groped from tree to tree. A few minutes more and her eyes might as well have been closed. With tiny, tentative steps, her big toes probed the leaves and roots of the forest floor for anything sharp or hard she might step on. Otter shuffled blindly ahead, one hand waving before her to check for invisible obstructions, the other holding the knife close to her side. Her steps were slow and deliberate. As her fingers scraped a tree's rough bark, she stopped and cut a gouge into its trunk. She could not be sure that her path was straight, but her knife's marks in the trees would at least allow her to find her path again in the light of day.

Otter counted fifty trees with fifty marks and then stopped. She could have carried on till dawn, but she was afraid of going too far off course if she had misjudged her bearing. Tonight she had only to get far enough away from the fence so that no one from Junkton could easily discover her when the sun rose. Blotch or someone like him would look for her in the morning, but the search would be short and shallow. Other children occasionally escaped, and little time or effort was spent recovering escapees who would be unlikely to survive long on their own. There was no need to bother; the flow of laborers to the factory never seemed to run dry.

She felt around the last tree's great trunk, trying to determine which side was opposite from the fence line. *Hidden from the fence line*, Otter thought. Having made her best guess, she lowered herself to the ground, unhooked her lunchbox and pack from her belt, and placed them on the ground before curling up beside them at the tree's base.

The chill in the air, which had smelled of freedom when Otter had first stepped into it and filled her lungs with it, now seeped into her bones as she lay on the forest's leafy floor. The woods around her were invisible. So was the low, continuous chatter of whatever creatures shared Oakwood with her. At times, she thought she saw dimly glowing eyes spying down on her from the soaring ceiling of branches.

Shivering, Otter closed her eyes against the dark. Hidden sounds echoed for a long time in her ears before exhaustion overtook her and sleep finally descended on her first night of freedom.

\* \* \*

Delicate fingers of pale light gently worked Otter's eyes open.

Rubbing away the sleep from her eyes, she rolled over on the forest's thick carpet of leaves and stretched with a stifled yawn. Most of the sounds of night had fallen silent, and cheerful birdsongs now filled the air. Cold droplets of dew—*That's what it's called*, Otter recalled—burst pleasantly on her cheeks. Otter had awakened as a free girl. A faint smile lit her face in leisurely stages, like the sun slowly emerging from behind a meandering cloud. Freedom certainly seemed to be an improvement.

Rising stiffly to her feet, Otter took in her environs.

The wild landscape buffeted her from all sides with colors such as she'd never seen. Vibrant green leaves stirred conspiratorially in the breeze. The sky's vivid blue stretched out above her with imposing persistence, as if to demand that its beauty be noticed and acknowledged. Nothing like these bright hues could be found in the Home or the factory, nor seen on the barren tract connecting them in the dusk of Otter's daily commute.

She pulled her gaze from these wonders and back down to her immediate surroundings. The gouges she had made were easy to spot, even in the dawn's low light. Looking back along her path, she could no longer see Junkton's fence. In the opposite direction, Otter was surprised to see daylight pouring into Oakwood Forest, illuminating a floor strewn with leaves and teeming with tenacious green life. An uneven wall of majestic tree trunks cut the sun's beams into alternating slats, as if to stake out the border between what lay ahead and the adjacent, shadow-shrouded terrain she had covered last night. Otter had rarely seen the sun except through the grime of her window, and its relentless brightness forced her to squint and shade her eyes. *Why is the forest so thin here?* she wondered, recalling the innumerable trees she'd marked in the darkness. At the moment, though, she was hungrier than she was curious. She would find out soon enough, she thought. But first, breakfast.

Opening her lunchbox to eye the bread and cheese within, Otter reached in and allowed her fingers to twist off and withdraw stingy portions of each. Frugality was essential. The next time she would have access to more supplies was a matter of pure speculation. The logical reminder soothed her mind, but it did nothing to quiet her belly, which rumbled with dissatisfaction over a breakfast that was tiny even by her usual standards.

After she had collected her things and taken quick stock to ensure she had lost nothing during her flight, Otter walked to where the light bathed the forest. The sunlight, she found, flooded in from that direction because Oakwood Forest abruptly ended. She had planned to hike for many hours through the vast woods. But Oakwood had turned out to be far less vast than she had expected. *Surviving in the Wilderness* was old indeed, and its author knew nothing of how subsequent human activity had pruned the map.

As Junkton had grown, the woods had receded. Once, Junkton was a mere island in the ancient forest's sea. Now Oakwood Forest was more like Junkton's outermost layer, a flimsy eggshell containing the dirty industrial town it once dwarfed. Eventually, Otter imagined, even this modest strip of untamed wilderness would be gone, and Junkton would burst through the wooded shell whose broken pieces would soon be discarded and quickly forgotten.

*That's why it took so long to get to the fence*, Otter realized. *The distance from Junkton's center to the fence has grown while the distance from the fence to Oakwood's perimeter has shrunk.*

She turned in place for a moment and took in the dappled sunlight as it danced playfully along every surface; the tiny, scampering animals chasing their kin from branch to branch;

the pleasant, chaotic songs of the birds welcoming the morning. The idea that all this might perish so that Junkton might bulge saddened Otter in ways she had trouble understanding. But she could not free Oakwood Forest from Junkton as she had freed herself. So she carried on.

Otter emerged from the shadows of Oakwood's trees, blinking in the raw rays of the early morning sun. A narrow ledge of grass—dry and shorn, like the lawn that coated Junkton's surface—lay between her and a colorless expanse of hard-packed dirt and stone that slunk with inanimate contempt back toward Junkton in one direction, and forward toward the horizon in the other. A weather-battered sign on one side of the great earthen scar warned travelers of their imminent entrance into Junkton. On the other side, an equally decrepit sign gave this new place a name: Dirt Road.

Staying just off the road to avoid other travelers, Otter began walking away from Junkton. She hoped to never see it again.

## ~ CHAPTER 3 ~

# ON DIRT ROAD

JUNKTON WAS LESS than an hour behind her when Otter realized she had made a terrible mistake. Bringing her dented cup was a wise decision, to be sure. It would have been wiser still if she had something with which to fill it. Her scraps of food, dry and hard, would sustain her for some time, but every bite would worsen her thirst. She tried not to dwell on how desperately she would love a drink as she walked along that bleak and seemingly endless road. But the minutes stretched into hours, and thirst occupied more and more of her thoughts.

Still Otter kept her eyes on the horizon for any warnings of approaching traffic. A growing cloud of dust or the deep growl of an engine would send her scrambling off the road to take cover behind the low mound of earth banking Dirt Road. Only when silence had again settled with the dust would her head poke back up to be sure the threat had passed. This process she repeated dozens of times until it became an unthinking routine. And all the while, her thirst whispered reminders of itself in her mind, first in the lowest of tones, but persistent, and increasingly harder to ignore. With the sun now climbing high in the sky, Otter allowed her thoughts to wander in the hope of momentarily forgetting the slow searing of her throat and mouth.

Otter thought of the *other* children—not the children working in the factory, but the children on the playground outside her old window. Many a day Otter had intently watched them from within her dismal workspace, the clanking and whirring of the conveyor providing an incongruously monotonous soundtrack for such a lighthearted show. The other children's parents were important people, the people who *ran* Junkton. Junkton's important people spent their days imagining ways to squeeze more productivity and profit from Junkton's humming industry and its tiny workers, even as their own children played carefree. Someday, the children of Junkton's important people would grow up to *be* Junkton's important people. Did they think of her and the other children, she wondered, a mere stone's throw away, toiling invisibly so important people and their children could wear fancy clothes and spend their days playing with their imaginaries?

And what imaginaries they were! Through the haze of her smudged factory window, Otter had seen imaginary friends in such variety that it boggled the mind. Some children rode on the shoulders of gentle giants or on the backs of great elephants. Other children swooped and soared all day, cradled in the claws of monstrous birds. Still others chattered idly away with vividly colored parrots, bats, frogs, or insects perched upon their shoulders. Some children's imaginaries were hideous, hulking monsters, while others were adorable, covered in luxuriant waves of fur. But despite the extraordinary array of possibilities, Otter had never seen an imaginary that was right for her, that was quite *good enough*.

Otter had thought of her someday imaginary, an imaginary that would, in fact, be good enough, more times than she cared to consider. Captive in the confines of the factory and the Home, Otter had known she would never find an imaginary worth imitating. If the imaginaries outside her window were unsuitable, those belonging to the other children of the Home were far worse. Few had even a single memorable trait. Gray and poorly defined, they were fit for picking up what their reals had dropped or otherwise helping with mundane tasks. But little else. The workers' imaginaries, slinking forth from such paltry imaginative substance, were hardly more than extra hands to their tiny reals. With their every breath those pitiful creatures strained the word *imaginary*—but they stretched the word *friend* further. Nothing of the sort would do for Otter. That was why she had little choice but to leave the factory and Junkton altogether. At least, that was part of the reason.

Otter had refused even to consider imagining a friend until she had seen enough life to imagine one that would be perfect in every way. She could never do that in Junkton. And so she had no choice but to leave, to strike out into the world, to search Imbria far and wide for those traits she would someday assign to her perfect friend.

*My only friend.* Her brow wrinkled absently at the thought. But the need to drive herself ever forward chased such thoughts from her mind.

Dragging her tired feet down Dirt Road and trying to think of anything besides her creeping thirst, Otter was briefly overcome, and not for the first time, by the dread that she would be unable to make an imaginary, that she might be a *loner*. Loners, Otter had heard, were a sad lot indeed. No amount of imagining by a loner would cause an imaginary to materialize. Having always refrained from even trying to imagine a friend, Otter could not be sure she wasn't a loner herself. Many times in her short life, she had come within a breath of giving in and imagining the best friend she could, just to see *whether* she could. And every time, she had talked herself down, refusing to give in to the temptation. If she was a loner, Otter told herself, she would find out when she was ready. She would bring to life either the perfect imaginary or none at all, but nothing in between.

Junkton's thick smell had not fully relinquished its grip on the air beyond its borders, but the grass had shed its severe trim and now grew wild and long with neglect. Before long, the dull blades of greenish brown grew high enough to tickle Otter's chin. The scenery otherwise changed little, paying no mind to the small stranger in its midst. Only the sun's gradual journey across the sky proved the passage of time in the vast country-side through which the road endlessly cut. To Otter's eyes, were it not for the occasional copse of tall spindly trees dotting its environs, Dirt Road seemed less like a living landscape and more like a static image of grassland and highway played on an endless reel.

As the day ground on, Otter's thirst found a comrade in hunger. Each lurching step forward brought a fresh cramp from her grumbling stomach. The hunger gnawed at her, con-suming the strength from her legs and back even as they carried her deeper into its maw. Famished though she grew, she never lost sight of the need to conserve her scarce supplies. If oppor-tunities to replenish lay ahead, the deserted countryside offered no clue of them. And she knew that eating would only make her thirst just that much worse. According to *Surviving in the Wilderness*, a person could go for days without food. But water, the book had made clear, was another matter. Thirst could end her journey long before her hunger could take a serious toll.

Once or twice, she considered flagging down one of the cars driving intermittently by and asking a driver for help. But so far Dirt Road had run directly from Junkton without splitting or meeting another road. So anyone driving on Dirt Road was either going to or coming from Junkton. Otter would not entrust the fate of her odyssey to *anyone* who had business in Junkton.

Otter's thirst and hunger grew in tandem like twins as the sun mounted the sky and then, cresting, began beating a slow retreat. With more than half the day vanished, the endless rhythm of Otter's footsteps had begun to slow as her mouth dried and her belly rumbled. And with her every leaden step, the sun's unrelenting heat beat down on her harder. Exhaustion, hunger, and thirst had become her constant and unwelcome traveling companions.

Things grew only worse as the horizon slowly reeled the sun in. Swarms of tiny biting insects leaped up from the grass and buzzed about Otter's head. She swatted violently when their shrill humming tickled her ear or as the insects dove hungrily into the dark skin of her exposed face and neck. But she struck herself more often than she dispatched the elusive bugs. Soon, small swollen bites itched her from head to toe. Her arms grew tired of swatting. She grew tired of her own fruitless smacks against her skin. And her legs grew tired of walking. A dull ache had crept into her feet, legs, and back as she walked, and her hip had grown numb as the constant bouncing of her pack banged in synchronicity with her stride.

As fatigue began to blunt Otter's will, she no longer bothered to defend against her tiny flying attackers. She wished desperately for somewhere to hide from the swarm. But swarm or no swarm, she would need shelter before night fell.

Otter made a decision. Turning sharply to her right, she waded into the sea of tall grass flowing forth from Dirt Road. She had her eyes on a spot ahead where the waves of narrow leaves appeared to thin. Eventually she arrived at a spot where a small island of rock interrupted the grass, jutting from the earth like the peak of a mountain whose bulk was concealed beneath the ground. She squinted at the surface that climbed before her as she mustered her strength to clamber up the island and put some distance between herself and the biting swarms below. Once at the top, she sat abruptly down, and a heavy, exhausted breath escaped her lungs with a sigh.

The sun seemed to gain motivation as it sank. The rapidly lengthening shadows were a reminder that time would not wait on the likes of Otter. Sitting still for the first time in hours, she shut her eyes to the world for only a moment. But her neglected stomach, having none of it, growled in complaint as if to tell her that, thirsty or not, tired or not, its patience had run out.

For only the second time since her escape, Otter pulled out a few tiny pieces of hard cheese. Her jaws worked the morsels slowly as she pulled the knife from her pack. Her belly still groaned, not to be placated by these meager offerings, but she dared not eat more freely until she found a place to replenish.

*Whenever that might be*, Otter worried involuntarily. She wondered for a moment whether this had all been a terrible mistake. The faces of her tormentors, Greeble and Blotch—and of Crim, her brief compatriot—floated across her mind. Banishing her unwanted doubts, she gathered up her resolve.

Knife in hand and jaw set, Otter slid down from her perch to brave the hungry swarms once more.

Her feet marking out a path of expanding circles in the grass, Otter collected great handfuls of the reedy leaves and, with a hissing *pffp*, her knife quickly cut each handful loose from the ground. Each of these she set aside to make room for the next. *Pffp, pffp, pffp*, her knife worked deftly through each successive bunch faster than the one before. Although her hands were unaccustomed to this task, they were no strangers to work. Her years of toiling in the factory until she could have pieced libertyslippers together in her sleep had made repetitive manual work almost second nature to Otter.

Before long, she had amassed a considerable stack of the long grassy blades.

Satisfied at last with her harvest, and sparing only a brief glance at the fast-receding sun, Otter landed with a decisive thump as she sat down on the lowest edge of the rocky out-growth. Her fingers began an oddly familiar dance across the grass leaves, like a new variant on a dance they'd always known. They reemerged from beneath her nimble touch expertly woven from many into one. The leaves, which at first had splayed out uncontrollably in every direction, grew into a mat, her hands imposing discipline on the long green blades. The small mat grew from one corner outward until it was fully formed. Then she set it aside and began another. The words of *Surviving in the Wilderness* flowed across her mind like libertyslippers glid-ing down the conveyor. Gaps dotted the crosshatch of the mats, which were not nearly so neat as those described in her beloved text. But they seemed more than passable, especially for a first try.

Otter put the finishing touches on three more mats as the horizon slowly swallowed half the sun. A cloud of dust, indicat-ing traffic on Dirt Road, spread like a thin film over the sun's half disc and spread out across the line that separated Imbria from the sky. Otter's eyes followed the dust warily. Its motor-ized source sped past, but the cloud in its wake lingered before fading into the twilight, though not before the sun surrendered another quarter of its surface to the horizon's hunger. Knowing she had little daylight left, Otter returned her attention to the grass mats.

She twisted several handfuls of the remaining reeds together, binding them with their kin to form flimsy rods, which would serve as makeshift supports within the mats. These she threaded into the rough weave before dragging the mats up to the highest flat surface on her rock island. The last few loose blades she used to bind the mats together into a simple lean-to tent. Two mats formed the floor; one mat formed a wall on each side. The ends remained open like the mouths of a tunnel. In one spot, the reed joints refused to hold, but a couple of her rubber bands were up to the job. Standing back to examine her handiwork, Otter allowed a small, satisfied smile to briefly soften her face.

Otter did not relish the idea of setting up camp here. The higher ground might be visible to anyone passing on Dirt Road if they looked hard enough. The biting bugs left little alternative, though, so she had to trust in distance and darkness to keep her hidden from sight.

Her task complete, she scanned the island's surroundings one last time before the horizon swallowed the sun's orb and, with it, the final rays of daylight. Here and there a stubborn copse of trees continued to cast a dark silhouette in the deepening dusk. Beyond these, the otherwise featureless grass plains to one side, and the gouge of Dirt Road running through the earth to the other, were rapidly disappearing into shadow.

And then there was only darkness.

Otter lay curled up beside her belongings on her simple shelter's woven grass floor and shivered. Despite her exhaustion, sleep came slowly. The mats were both flimsy and drafty, and the wind cut through them even as it shook them against her with every gust. The night's chill settled over the land, cutting into her and causing her dark skin to prickle with bumps. As dreams finally overtook her, Otter thought she heard the sounds of wild animals snuffling and stalking through the grasses. A final shiver shook the girl's tiny frame at the thought of what might be lurking around her, perhaps waiting only for her to nod off. But even that unsettling thought could not keep its head above the exhaustion flooding over her. Moments later, she was asleep.

Like a paddle on a waterwheel, the sun slowly emerged from Imbria's surface opposite to the one into which it had disappeared. The songs of birds and crickets encouraged its graceful ascent. Otter's eyes fluttered open as the sun's rays insinuated themselves insistently between her eyelids. Though the bright colors of dawn still dazzled her senses, she barely noticed them through the dullness of her slow waking. And so ended a short (and poor) night of rest. What with the scuffling of unseen beasts, the night's pitiless nip, her belly's growling and cramping, and the throbbing echo of the day's long walk in her back and legs, sleep had been fitful and shallow.

Her thirst, too, had only worsened during the night. And the aching discomfort in her muscles had blossomed into something significantly more than discomfort.

Trying to ignore the thickness coating her mouth and the protests in her back and limbs, Otter pulled the dented cup from her pack, which she had been using as a poor and lumpy pillow. She set the cup down on the rocky floor. After disconnecting the panels of her tent, she lifted each woven section and lowered one of its corners into the cup and, with the edge of her flattened free hand, painstakingly scraped the dew down the captive leaves and into the tin receptacle. Once she had captured every retrievable drop, she put the cup to her lips, upended it and, tapping the bottom, greedily sucked down all its meager contents. The water was too little, but Otter sighed deeply as it cut through the dryness in her throat.

Otter again pulled out her knife and then, blade and cup clasped firmly, she scrambled down the rock's edge and waded into the grass. On the ground, she found patches of broken reeds, and spots of ground torn bare as if by digging claws. A disconcerting tightness gripped her stomach and the muscles of her neck and shoulders at the thought of what might have prowled so close to her as she slept. But she forced her mind toward more pressing concerns. Dwelling on such disturbing ideas would do her no good.

Just as she had the night before, Otter began the work of separating the long grasses from the earth with her knife. Instead of cutting them in great bunches, this time she grasped each individually, cut it at its base, and then slid her fingers along the reed to scrape its collected dew into her cup. She spent nearly the entire first chill hour of daylight on this task and amassed hardly more than half a cup of water when she was done.

Once again Otter scaled the stone outcropping. She rewrapped her supplies, sparing only a momentary, wistful glance at the shelter she would have to leave behind. She quickly swallowed several bites of cheese and washed them down with the few gulps of water she'd gathered. It was, the girl thought, the most refreshing drink of water she had ever tasted.

Her tiny breakfast done, Otter hitched the pack back onto her belt, this time on the opposite side in the hopes of not aggravating—or at least of distributing more evenly—the throbbing in her back. Her gaze returned uneasily to the bare patches left by whatever animals had lurked about unseen in the night. Forcing her eyes away and up to take in the horizon cutting across the landscape, she stepped forward through the grasses. Exhaling with determination, she returned to her trek along Dirt Road.

As Junkton grew ever farther behind her, Otter again wrestled her thoughts away from any reminder of her hunger, her aches, and her thirst. She recalled her earliest memories, in which she "played" in the Home's drab and musty nursery alongside the other children who were too young to work.

Toys were rare at the Home, even for its youngest residents. Most of what passed for playthings were in fact odd ends of fabric saved from the trash, or worn-out parts from the factory's aging machinery. Small children in threadbare rags stacked spare parts to build rusty castles of scrap. As the children grew, their attendants encouraged them to assemble the spare parts or to cut scraps. These "games," as even the children recognized, were little more than training for the day when they would leave this dingy sanctuary and join their older peers on the factory floor.

As she often did, Otter wondered where she had come from. She had never known her parents, and she did not know how she came to be at the Home. *Why did they leave me there?* she thought. *Why would anyone condemn their own child to the Home? Why didn't they want me?*

That last thought sat suspended alone in her head like an echo in a great cavern. It was an uncomfortable, lonely thought. Not for the first time, she wished the question had not occurred to her.

As she plodded on, Otter began to consider the math of her travel. Grimly she realized she could not withstand many more days like the last one. She stopped walking and looked off to her right. Shielding her eyes from the sun that still hung low in the midmorning sky, she scanned the unending miles of grass and the occasional copse of trees that intermittently punctuated the vast waves of vegetation. Squinting, her eyes settled on the nearest of these.

From this distance, she could tell little about the trees except that they stood high above the tops of the tall grass swaying beneath them, and that their bushy green tops hung gracefully from the heights of tall, slender trunks. Trees, Otter had read, tend to grow near water.

She hesitated for a moment, but she had no other choice. So she turned from Dirt Road and, wading once more into the grass, angled toward the nearest island of trees.

Otter's hands led the way, parting the curtains of grass before her. Once in a while, the thin green blades were so tall she lost track of the trees and had to jump to assure herself that her bearing remained true. Her head would emerge momentarily above the grass, giving her a glimpse of the trees' languidly hanging tops. Having confirmed her course, she would set off on her way once more.

For the first time in two days, Otter hardly noticed her thirst. Even the aches in her muscles seemed to fade beneath her newfound determination to reach the trees. Having an immediate goal within her grasp did more to take her mind from her woes than had all her deliberate efforts at self-distraction. From somewhere deep within her, an ember of comfort glowed at this thought, but she could not say for sure why that should be.

Suddenly, the tall grass thinned to nothing and opened into a spacious clearing. Otter stumbled out from the thicket and found herself only a few paces from one of the gracefully ascending trees. Their foliage, which bore a distant but definitive resemblance to the leaves of grass engulfing the terrain around them, stood between Otter and the sun, washing her in splendidly cool shade. She stood still for a moment, basking briefly in the satisfaction of this minor accomplishment.

*Now*, she thought with renewed determination, *to find water*.

Through squinted lids, her eyes adjusted to the shadows of the tiny, self-contained forest. The trees' long fronds had the feel of warm weather about them, and their tall boles seemed designed to be leaned against while napping. Scanning their upper reaches, she thought she saw red fruits clustered among the greenery. On some of the trunks, vertical marks suggested that clawed animals sometimes made their way into the treetops.

Frowning, Otter recalled the claw marks she'd found around her campsite this morning. She tried not to think too hard about what might have cut these gouges. She instead set her gaze back to the ground and commenced her search for water.

She didn't have to look long.

Near the center of the copse, amid spongy mounds of dense green weeds rising nearly to her knees and adorned all over with tiny, understated flowers, a modest spring bubbled up from a small, rocky bed and babbled pleasantly as it dispersed without particular direction into the surrounding woods. Dappled sunlight worked its way through the shade of the forest's canopy and sparkled off the liquid life before her.

The earth around the spring was rich with vegetation and dark with dampness. Glistening fingers of water disappeared as they crawled away from their stony source. All this Otter noticed in an instant as she broke into a short, limping run and fell to her knees in front of her salvation. The wetness splashed into her eyes and nose as her hands scooped one great draft after another into her mouth. Her fingers and lips grew numb with the water's bracing chill, but nothing slowed her slurping. She thought she might be crying, although she couldn't have said why. But if tears were in her eyes, she could hardly tell them from the wayward splashes of frigid spring water. Crying and drinking, Otter lost track of all time. At moments she forgot herself completely and slurped the cold liquid right off the rocks where it bubbled from. Otter had never tasted sweeter, colder water, even as part of her recognized that the sentiment might only be nothing more than the effect of two days' thirst being quenched.

At some point, Otter found she could not comfortably hold more water, and her frenzied guzzling slowly subsided as she sickened with the water's weight in her stomach. From all fours she heaved hard once or twice, stricken by a fear that she might lose all she'd just drunk in her excessive abandon. Slowly she reined in the urge to evacuate her belly and settled into a slow rocking motion until she felt she could safely move once more. Then, crawling clumsily backward, she scrambled away from the spring on her bottom, hands, and feet, the water sloshing sickeningly in her belly as she went. She stopped a few paces away when she reached the nearest tree and rested her back against its bumpy surface. Wiping tears and spring water from her eyes, Otter sank to the ground beneath the tree and sighed deeply with relief from thirst and nausea alike.

The freedom Otter had felt on her first waking outside the Home paled before the freedom she felt now. The feeling seemed fragile and slippery, as if she might accidentally drop and break it if she weren't perfectly still. So she sat there a while longer, barely daring to move, and listened to the wind murmuring in the fronds high above her.

Otter didn't know how long she sat with her back against that tree. But it wasn't long before the urge to keep moving nudged her, making her restless and impatient. And so she rose to her bare feet and took stock of her situation.

Looking for water near the trees had saved her. Now she knew she would have to hike from one stand of trees to the next if she hoped to survive until she could find some way of carrying water with her. But after her desperate rush into the sea of grass and then the woods around the spring, Otter wasn't sure she could tell which way Dirt Road now lay.

Turning her head, she surveyed the woods around her. One of the trees, unlike its upright brethren, sloped up at a lazy angle, rising gently to its dizzying height. She approached its diagonal trunk, tilting her head slightly in contemplation. She placed her hand on the tree's strange bark, which rose along the trunk sides like a single layer of ridged skin, perforated here and there by networks of the weathered claw marks. After a moment of sizing the tree up, Otter untied her pack from her side and laid it on the ground, where the tree's trunk gradually ended in tiny hills and valleys of roots that plunged with an iron grip into the rocky soil below.

Embracing the tree with her knees and arms, Otter slowly inched herself up its height. Her grasping fingers and toes found extra purchase in the bark's deep notches. The tree's girth was not so great that the climb was difficult, but it certainly wasn't leisurely either. She climbed so that the front of her body faced roughly toward the earth, so she had little fear of falling. But the higher the girl rose above the ground, the less inclined she felt to let her eyes wander to the oasis's rocky floor.

Gradually she worked her way up to the lowest leaves. The front of her body was tingling and raw from scraping against the trunk. From here she could clearly make out the tree's lumpy crimson fruits, and her tiny pack was a mere speck below. The fruits seemed somehow familiar, but she had no desire to climb higher still to examine them more closely. Her view extended from the top of the canopy, and she could see for several miles on all sides from her perch. Most important, from here the dusty trail of Dirt Road was visible as it cut through the grasslands. From this vantage, she could also see the scattered copses of trees dotting the landscape along her way.

Surveying the land gave her an excuse to rest and catch her breath. Focusing on the view also helped her to ignore the stinging scrapes her awkward climb had earned her.

The clusters of trees were more plentiful than Otter had assumed, and the sight of them renewed her hope that the plan of making her way from one oasis to the next could work. Better still, the wooded areas grew more frequent along the way until they merged into a great forest that reached out to the right and eventually met the sky. These woods were every bit as green and dense as Oakwood at its thickest, but *Surviving in the Wilderness* had made no mention of them. Either way, the sight of the woods was a relief. A forest would likely mean water and would certainly mean a place to hide from other travelers. Otter needed both.

To her left, Dirt Road marched relentlessly north. If she continued to follow it, Otter could easily reach the woods at any time along the way.

Her eyes followed the road to a point far distant, where Dirt Road fragmented into three different roads, each at right angles to the next. A small shack sat a lonely watch over the intersection's nearest corner. A listless trail of smoke rose from the squat building's chimney.

West from the intersection, Dirt Road widened into a smartly kept boulevard that ran like an arrow through the heart of a small town. The town looked pleasant enough. But the thought of going among people so close to Junkton tied Otter's empty stomach in knots.

Except that it curved to navigate a smattering of distant hills, the crossroads' northern spur looked very much like the road behind her. It reached far ahead and eventually disappeared beyond the horizon. But in the sky above that unseen distance, gray smoke billowed and dissipated—just as it did from the smokestacks of the libertyslipper factory. Escaping one factory just to find herself in another was not an option.

That left the eastern road. Banked on its near side by the forest and the shack's far wall, that route also shrank away into the distance. What Otter could see of its far side from over the treetops was dotted with occasional signs of civilization. But those sparse pockets were few, and they were farther away than the town to the west. Not so much as a wisp of the belching smoke, so reminiscent of Junkton's humming industry, was visible along that route. To Otter's mind, the eastern road was the clear choice.

Her gaze returned warily to the shack smoking languidly at the junction.

Otter knew her quest would not let her avoid other people forever. But she remained cautious of human contact this close to the place of her former captivity. The tiny shack, still far away, represented a risk she would rather avoid. And the smoke told her the shack was occupied. So she had already determined to steer clear of whoever lived there. *If I can*, she thought.

The woods grew so close to the house's back side that it almost seemed to be growing out of them. Or maybe that the woods were slowly devouring it. She also noted that the forest was too vast to go around. And if she could lose her bearings just walking through tall grass, traveling through the woods seemed foolhardy.

So she would have to take the road. And she could not avoid the shack. All she could do was to stay as hidden as possible on her approach and hopefully pass the house quickly enough that its owner would never know she existed.

Having regained her breath, Otter began her descent. She inched slowly back down the slanting tree's trunk until, after what seemed like an hour of scraping and scooting, her feet once again met the earth. Wincing, she brushed stray splinters from her palms and soles.

Preparing to set off toward the shack she'd seen from above, she began collecting her belongings. But the thought of leaving this place of refuge gave her pause. Here, at least, the trees provided a little additional shelter. More than that, this place had water. The memory of her earlier thirst made a known water source particularly hard to leave. When Otter's skin prickled at the touch of the late-day chill already settling into the air, she looked to the lengthening shadows and made up her mind. She would camp here for the night. With that, she lowered her pack to the ground and began setting up camp.

This was earlier than she ordinarily stopped, so she had a head start on her evening preparations. Her campsite erected, Otter nibbled a light dinner and crawled into her reed lean-to, where she promptly fell asleep before the day had fully dissolved into night.

The next day, she awoke refreshed, despite yet another night of terrifying hidden noises crowded about her makeshift shelter. She ate lightly, then gathered her things once more. Before tucking her cup away, she returned to the spring to guzzle several deep drafts of its cold, clear water. Then, pack fastened to her side once more, Otter set back out for Dirt Road.

Progress was slow—very slow, in fact. Leaving the road during the day to find water, and at night to set up shelter, reduced actual progress to nearly nothing. Seeing her goal from the heights of her perch in the tree, she had thought she could cover the distance in a day or a little more at most. Instead, the journey to the crossroads took nearly three. And all the while, the shack loomed ever larger in Otter's imagination, just as its tireless smoke trail loomed ever larger in her sight. Several times a day, she took cover beside the road as anonymous vehicles coughed and roared by her. But she could not dodge the shack that way. So her quiet dread grew as she gradually approached the inevitable.

Even with her mounting anxiety, Otter's spirits were lighter than they had been since her escape began. Stretching her rations meant her hunger was still always with her, but having water had made all the difference. Her supplies would last another several days, and she stretched them further by foraging in the woods whenever she recognized some wild plant as edible from her reading. The red fruits perched high in the trees tantalized her, but she never found them lying on the ground, and none of the fruit grew any closer to the ground than those she had first encountered. She could not risk expending the energy on another climb for a fruit too far to identify as safe. The closer Otter got to the shack, the closer she kept to the trees beside the road, trying to stay out of sight.

The stands of trees to which she retreated for sleep seldom had the sort of rocky island she had found that first night on Dirt Road. Each night, the girl shivered from within her improvised shelter. Each night, the mysterious scuffling animal sounds returned. But the creatures making those noises never showed themselves, and every morning Otter awoke untouched.

By the time twilight had overtaken the light of the third day, the pockets of trees had already merged into the single deep forest Otter had seen from her treetop vantage. She could spend the night in the woods just this side of the house. That would leave her only enough time to piece together her shelter before night fell completely. But it would also mean trying to skirt the small structure in the following morning's daylight. Or she could make her way around the shack now, in the dusk's failing light. That would leave her shelterless for the night, but it might improve her chances of not being seen.

She decided to risk a night without shelter if it meant avoiding people for just a little longer.

Otter drew close to the shack's nearest outer wall and dropped to her hands and knees.

From this close, the tiny structure itself looked to have once been a charming and smart little cottage. But no longer. It had long since fallen into disrepair. The paint was badly peeling where it wasn't gone altogether. The windows were foggy and laced with spidery cracks. The shutters that remained dangled from their hinges at odd angles. The smoke, which had come to embody her dread, a wispy gray snake rising in silent, sinuous menace from the chimney, had coated the area around the shack in a sharp, unpleasant odor that clung to the wall just as Otter herself now did.

Crawling quietly alongside the shack's grimy wall to stay below the hazy windows' decaying sills, Otter slunk across the shack's meager length. If a car passed at that moment, she would be forced to rise for a hasty retreat, and her sneaking would be in vain.

Having reached the end of the shack's front wall, Otter steeled herself to round the corner of both the house and the intersection. One more wall, and she would be in the clear. Keeping her head low, she poked it furtively around the corner.

On the ground in front of her nose sat a pair of small trail boots, weathered a bit but otherwise in good condition. Otter's dread exploded in her chest and an icy chill gripped her entire body.

Moved against her own will by her fear's firm grasp, Otter craned her neck to lift her head, and her eyes found the boots connected to legs clothed in loose-fitting, coarse brown trousers; the trousers led to a smart, white shirt, with buttons running up the front, like something Otter had sometimes seen important-looking men wear to the factory; the dress shirt led up to a collar from which sprouted a slender neck; and at the top of the neck was a young woman's head, symmetrically framed with two tidy braids that dangled like thick, woven cords from scalp to shoulders. Between the braids resided a dense network of freckles, interrupted by sky-blue eyes, widely set and apparently frozen in a permanent squint, a hookish nose, and beneath them all, a mouth that smiled too broadly, showcasing two generous rows of straight white teeth.

When that mouth opened, the voice that emerged sounded a pitch too high and a touch too eager as it came crashing down on the prostrate trespasser at the speaker's feet. "Hello, little girl!" it said. "What are *you* doing? *I'm* Eliza." The words faded into the encroaching night, and Eliza's mouth resumed its too-broad smile, which seemed to grow broader still now that it had said its piece. Otter's fear grew right along with it.

## ~ CHAPTER 4 ~
# ELIZA

TOO FRIGHTENED TO rise, Otter froze on her hands and knees, as though staying perfectly still might cause this startling stranger, this *Eliza*, to lose interest and go away.

"Are you okay, little girl? Can you talk?" Again, the young woman's voice struck Otter as off somehow, and she flinched a little at its shrillness.

She took in a deep breath and attempted to collect herself after her fright. Rising slowly to her feet, she brushed the dust and leaves from her overalls, never quite taking her eyes from those of the unblinking Eliza. On reaching her full height, Otter found that the stranger stood several inches taller than she, with a willowy, slender frame that looked as likely to blow away in the breeze as to stay firmly planted beside the shack. Yet only Eliza's braids paid the wind any notice, swaying where they hung beside the girl's fair, freckled face.

Otter also noticed for the first time that she and the stranger were not alone. Just behind Eliza's right shoulder stood another girl who seemed slightly younger than Eliza. The girls were dressed in quite similar fashion, but the second girl's clothes looked a little harder worn and seemed to fit her less well than Eliza's did.

Although still gripped with fear, Otter could not help but be momentarily distracted, even fascinated, by this other young woman. Nothing about the girl's physical features invited particular interest. Flat black hair hung limp around a pale face devoid of any colors that might betray the existence of life. Her brown eyes were so lacking in distinguishing features that, although they stood apart from the girl's wan skin, Otter could not imagine anything else they might stand out from.

The girl's mannerisms, on the other hand, begged for notice. A shabby cloth doll that looked once to have been white dangled by its arm from her hands, which twisted and tugged at the worn fabric appendage. Yet she paid no mind to the tireless motion of her hands as they worked over the doll's straining arm.

More captivating still was the girl's odd expression. Slack-jawed, tongue protruding slightly, Eliza's companion stared blankly at Otter with a vague, unwavering grin. Her eyes seemed almost to look right through Otter. But they would periodically blink a few times in rapid succession and refocus for a moment before finding some hidden point in the distance once more. When that gaze did settle on Otter, she couldn't help but feel she was being sized up the way one might evaluate a ripe piece of fruit before taking the first bite. To Otter, that look could only be described as *hungry*.

"She won't answer," Eliza said, turning with a slight smile to address the odd girl. "I don't think she can hear me." Smiling, the other girl looked at Eliza and licked her lips.

Seeing this, Otter shuddered involuntarily. She quickly found her voice. "I can hear," she said. "My name is Otter. I was just . . ." Here, she paused. How could she explain to these strange girls why she had been sneaking around their house in the failing light? Thinking fast, she said the first thing that came to her mind. "I just didn't want to bother anyone?" This sounded more a question than a statement.

As soon as the words were out, she regretted their obvious falseness.

In response, Eliza merely shrugged as if it were unimportant. "It's okay," she said, her smile returning, unfazed. "You won't bother *us*. Do you want to come inside?" The girl behind Eliza nodded vigorously at this, and her tongue lolled outside her mouth in much the way Otter had sometimes observed the tongue of Blotch's squat, scaly beast to do at the Home. The unbidden comparison did nothing to put Otter at ease.

Again, Otter thought fast. "I— I really should keep moving. I'm in kind of a hurry?"

"Really?" Eliza frowned momentarily. "Where are you going?"

Otter's mouth tried to form words, but she had no answer for this.

Eliza nodded as if she'd confirmed a hunch. "Great. Well, just come in for a little while to eat with Desdemona and me. You can rest before you go, can't you?"

Otter could not help feeling from the look in Eliza's eyes that only one answer would suffice.

Just then, Otter's tummy complained with a rumble, reminding Otter just how nice it would be to have a warm meal. She pushed her misgivings aside.

"I guess I could sit down for just a little while. But then I'd really need to be on my way because—" But before Otter could finish, Eliza and Desdemona had flanked her and locked their arms in hers as they marched her gently but irresistibly toward the shack's lone door, with Eliza chatting all the while about snacks and journeys and rests, and Desdemona simply nodding and occasionally emitting an odd, guttural chuckle. The three girls squeezed side by side through the shack's narrow door and into the lamplit room within.

Otter quickly took in her new surroundings. Faded rugs quilted the floor throughout the cabin, including one where she now stood digging her toes into its thick woolen weave. Curtains, although threadbare, were hung with delicate attention, covering the shack's few windows and two interior doorways. Rough-hewn furniture was arranged just so. A long rectangular table with a rickety-looking wooden chair at each side commanded the center of the shack's main room, and a kitchen embedded with an array of cabinets and cupboards stood neatly behind the table. All in all, the interior was surprisingly tidy. It seemed to Otter that much more care had been recently paid to the cottage's aging interior than had ever been spent maintaining its outside. Otter wondered about this for a moment, but her attention splintered as Eliza and Desdemona shuttled her into the middle of the room and sat her down abruptly in the chair at the long table's head.

Desdemona sat down, too, plopping into a chair across from Otter at the table's far end. Her hands held the doll beneath the table, and she looked back and forth between Otter and Eliza as the latter bustled in the nearby kitchen to accommodate their guest. Otter found herself transfixed by Desdemona, whose gaze wandered aimlessly around the room, blithely unaware of the attention of their houseguest.

All the while, Eliza chattered away. Otter could not recall ever hearing someone talk so much. She certainly had not heard so many words convey so little of importance to her. Eliza wondered what kind of oil might silence the cabinet door's squeaking hinge, which had not squeaked until recently. The days had been particularly humid lately, and she speculated that this might have caused the squeak, but she supposed the noise didn't really bother her. She asked whether Otter minded the squeak or the humidity, although she provided no opening for Otter to reply. At some point, the continuous stream of words became little more than background noise.

Otter tore her eyes from Desdemona and turned them to Eliza's frenetic activity and idle chatter.

Otter's host had rolled up her shirtsleeves and now bounced from cabinet to cabinet, opening each, reaching in to extract cracked plates or tarnished silver or assorted packages decorated with pictures of food, and then shutting them again in turn. The images on the food packaging advertised greater varieties of food than Otter had ever known, and most depicted only enticing mysteries. With the cabinets all closed once more, the food packages covered nearly every inch of the counter.

Otter's stomach growled again, louder than before.

Eliza seemed to hear it, and she smiled at Otter knowingly, momentarily interrupting her endless monologue. "Let's get you some dinner!"

In minutes, a stove was flaming and pots were bubbling. Eliza continued to talk. "Isn't it funny how you were crawling by our house like that? I saw a cat chasing a mouse who crawled along next to a wall like that once. You weren't chasing a mouse, were you? It's good that you came around when you did. It's not good to be out at night. It's better to be inside where we have lights and it's warm and cozy. You haven't been out around here at night, have you? You have to be careful." And with this she stopped and turned to Otter with an almost comically serious look. "You never know what you might encounter around here."

Otter gulped involuntarily at the other girl's look. She tried to smile in response, but she knew her nerves had ruined the expression.

With her unsettling, unblinking stare, Eliza smiled back all the same.

Then came the food.

The tabletop's length quickly became crowded with dishes, all steaming temptingly as they arrived. Bowls piled high with mounds of some squishy white substance. Porcelain boats of thick brown liquid. A basket of fluffy bread-like lumps. As the table filled with food, delicious scents filled the air.

Otter had never seen foods like these. During her years at the factory and the Home, she seldom ate anything other than the plainest bread or meat boiled beyond flavor. Some years for her birthday—which was really no more than the anniversary of when she was found at the Home—an attendant would slather sweetened lard over bread and bedeck it with a candle. That was her birthday cake. But besides those rare instances, the food had varied no more than her routine at the factory.

Nonetheless, Otter could just *sense* that the vessels before her held deliciousness to dwarf anything she had tasted.

Even as she stared and her mouth watered, Otter was struck by the room's sudden stillness. Fighting to wrest her gaze from the tantalizing serving dishes, Otter looked up at her hosts.

Eliza wore an expectant, uncertain expression, as if unsure how her guest would regard these offerings.

Desdemona's blank stare held no more emotion than before. But her smile had widened considerably, and the tip of her tongue had begun to absently flick her lips. To Otter's eyes, the other girl's features seemed tighter, as though an invisible hand behind her head were stretching the skin of her face toward the back of her scalp. The effect was almost . . . *reptilian*.

*I'm sure it's just my imagination*, Otter thought. All the same, Desdemona's demeanor put Otter ill at ease, and she looked quickly back to Eliza.

Eliza continued to regard her guest expectantly. Otter, having no experience with eating at another's house and table, reached for the nearest serving spoon, hopeful that this was the proper response. As soon as Otter had dolloped the first spoonful of the white stuff onto her plate, the chatter began again as Eliza took her seat and began heaping generous helpings onto her and Desdemona's plates.

The white mounds, Otter learned, were potatoes that had been boiled and smashed into paste. The brown liquid was gravy, which Otter poured over her potatoes as she had observed the other girls doing. The lumpy bread things were biscuits, which could be dipped into the potatoes and gravy. Dish after dish of these three items, food beyond Otter's most extravagant dreams. After years of only the dullest sustenance, and several days of dwindling travel supplies, Otter could no more stop herself from devouring the food before her than she could remove her mouth from her face. Forkful after forkful disappeared between her teeth, and she savored every bite. Otter had never before experienced what it was like to be *full*. It had never occurred to her that someone could eat so much as to become uncomfortable. But even this discomfort was a strange thrill, and she found herself enjoying it as she had never enjoyed anything before.

Eliza and Desdemona ate, too—Eliza, slowly and daintily, and Desdemona with an abandon like Otter's but without even Otter's untrained manners. While Otter was clumsy with her utensils, Desdemona handled hers like shovels. Every time the odd, pale girl cleared her plate, she licked it clean before refilling it. Otter tried not to stare.

As the meal's pace slowed and the sprawling food had receded, Eliza's incessant monologue changed course. Rising to clear the dishes, she turned to Otter and, as their eyes met, asked, "So, Otter, where are *you* from?"

Otter hesitated. She did not want to seem rude to her host. But she did not want it known that she had come from Junkton. What if Eliza figured out that Otter had escaped? What if she told someone and it got back to Mr. Pickle or someone else who might want Otter returned?

"Not from around here," Otter lied. "From far away."

Eliza smiled quickly and nodded as she had earlier, after asking Otter where she was going. "Well," she announced with finality. "I think we should have some dessert, then. I hope cookies are okay?"

Otter had never had a cookie. But the other foods had been divine, and Otter found herself nodding her assent without thinking.

Turning from the kitchen with a flourish, Eliza marched toward Otter with a stately air, carrying one final platter.

Otter's eyes bulged at the tower of circular objects, golden brown and dotted with dark spots. The smell accompanying the plate—warm and sweet and hinting of subtle spice—made Otter's mouth water despite her full belly.

Eliza placed the platter squarely before Otter and then turned around and proceeded back to the other end of the table.

Confused, Otter asked, "Aren't you two having any?" Certainly it seemed to her from the longing, almost feral look on Desdemona's face that the odd girl wanted some of her own.

"Oh," said Eliza somewhat sharply, drawing Otter's attention back to her. "I couldn't possibly. I'm stuffed. And Desdemona"—both girls turned to Desdemona, who had, to Otter's eyes, come to seem decidedly more reptilian—"Desdemona has had plenty." Her voice carried a slight edge of command. "I'll just start tidying up," she said as she turned nonchalantly away from Otter once more.

Still concerned that ill manners might give her away, Otter took the pile's uppermost cookie and, after the briefest examination, devoured it. She ate it so fast, she barely tasted it. But what she *did* taste was the sweetest, most delectable flavor she had ever dreamed of. A tiny pool began to swell in her eye as she thought of her whole life before these cookies and of the possibility that her life could have gone on till the end without her ever having tasted one.

Otter dug in with gusto, and the pile of cookies slowly diminished. As she ate, she could not help but notice Desdemona's eyes rolling with impatient hunger. "Are you sure you don't want one, Desdemona?" Otter asked, extending a cookie in her hand.

"No!" Eliza said, oddly loud, as she turned momentarily from her labors. "She loves them, but she's allergic to the chocolate chips." Eliza stepped nearer to Desdemona and, with a look of deep affection in her eyes, caressed Desdemona's head and said: "What would she do without me?" Then, turning suddenly back to the tidying and seeming to want a change of subject, her chatter began again. "Does everyone where you're from look like you?"

The cookies were too many for Otter to eat by herself, but she could not bear the thought of them going to waste. And so, while Eliza spoke, Otter decided to slip the cookie she had offered to Desdemona into a pocket of her overalls, looking around furtively for fear she was breaching normal etiquette. No one seemed to notice. But on hearing Eliza's question, Otter's brow furrowed, and she struggled to understand what the other girl meant. "Look like me?" she asked.

"People around here don't look like you," Eliza cheerfully explained. "I see a lot of travelers here. But you're the first *brown* person I've seen."

Otter shook her head slightly to dispel the strange sense that Eliza's voice was coming to her from far away. She suddenly felt as though she had to think hard to make sense of Eliza's statement, and her cheeks flushed warmly as she pieced the words together.

Otter had never really given her appearance much thought, and no one at the Home or the factory had ever commented on how she looked in any meaningful way. She found herself surprised that she had never given any thought to the fact that none of the other people she'd met in Junkton had dark skin like hers.

"I-I'm not sure," she said. Her own voice also sounded strangely distant, and her tongue felt thick and heavy in her mouth.

"You're not sure what people look like where you're from?"

Again Otter found herself having to ponder the faraway voice and the confusing words, trying to make sense of them as Eliza probed her for answers she didn't have. "I—" the girl said, but she never finished.

Alarmed, Otter found that her mouth would not respond. She tried to lift her hands, but her limbs hung heavy and limp. Her eyelids began to sag beneath their own weight, and her vision began to swim. Panic rose in Otter's mind even as unnatural exhaustion stifled it and stuffed it away beneath her sinking consciousness.

"That's okay," Eliza said as she walked over to Otter and pulled back the platter and the cookies that remained. "I guess it will just have to stay a mystery."

The room began to fade in and out. Or maybe it was Otter who faded in and out. But everything Otter saw went from light to dark and slowly back to light again. In the moments of illumination, Eliza's voice floated calmly to Otter's ears, never ceasing, never rising above a tone of casual conversation.

At some point Otter realized she was being carried from the table, with Eliza hoisting her up on one side and Desdemona on the other. Her legs would not move on their own, and her feet dragged along the ground.

"I really am sorry," Eliza said. "But Desdemona is almost completely changed. And when she's changed, regular food is never enough. It's a good thing you came when you did. We always have trouble when nobody comes around in time."

None of these words made sense to Otter, and even in this state Otter didn't think her confusion was all on account of whatever Eliza had done to her. *What does she mean, "eat"? She has so much food. What does any of this have to do with* me?

Otter's senses faded again, and when her consciousness surfaced once more, tiny gasps and grunts punctuated Eliza's speech as she and Desdemona squeezed Otter through one of the interior doorways and into an unlit room. "That's why they don't let me live in the town anymore. They tried to hurt Desdemona when they found out. But she was already changed, and they were afraid of her."

Otter's mind clawed at Eliza's words, struggling to grasp the meaning buried within them. *This is important*, she told herself. *You have to listen.* But the words were slippery, and Otter's confused head and mouth worked them numbly, like fingers exposed too long to frigid temperatures.

As her fluctuating vision grew accustomed to the new room's lack of light, Otter saw she was being dragged toward a squat cage in a dim corner. *That's odd*, Otter thought with drowsy, disconnected concern.

Panting slightly from the exertion, Eliza continued, "They told me I could stay in the town, but only without Desdemona. Even my parents said so. 'She's just a little girl,' they told the other grown-ups. 'She doesn't know any better,' they said. But I knew. It wasn't my fault, but it wasn't Desdemona's fault either.

That's just how she is. She can't help what she has to eat. And I couldn't just *leave* my imaginary."

The flutters of panic in Otter's chest began to creep around the edges of her impaired consciousness as the girls got closer and closer to the cage. During a flash of awareness, Otter realized they intended to put her into the cage. She felt a tear trace a meandering path down her cheek, although she could not muster an audible sob.

"So we had to leave the town and move out to our house. It was already here, empty for years. I've heard older people say it used to belong to a hermit. But no one was here when we came. And now we stay here and wait for travelers for Desdemona." Eliza's voice took on a hurt, almost apologetic tone. "We have always tried to be good when we find someone for Desdemona. We always look for people who are sick or who have no one to miss them. You know—people like *you*. I mean, you don't even have an *imaginary*."

Otter's plight seemed increasingly like a bizarre nightmare from which she couldn't wake. Was Eliza saying what Otter thought she was saying? That Desdemona was no girl but was in fact Eliza's cannibalistic imaginary, whose appetites had forced Eliza into exile, and whose hunger for human flesh Eliza helped nourish. Eliza had given up a family, something Otter could only dream of, to stay with her hideous creation. If Otter could have moved her face, she knew her expression would have betrayed absolute horror.

But before Otter could reflect on her horrific realization, Eliza and Desdemona were carefully but firmly folding her and shoving her into the cramped cell on the floor. Otter was vaguely aware of how tight and uninviting these confines were. Once they had her stuffed awkwardly in place, Eliza knelt by the cage and turned a key in its sturdy metal lock.

"I'm sorry about this," Eliza said again. "I wish we could just finish while you're knocked out by the medicine from the cookies. Poor Desdemona is very sensitive to it, though, so we have to wait. But we'll try to make it easy for you." She paused meaningfully. "If you can, stay asleep in the morning." With that, Eliza's face grew sad and serious. "It will be worse if you're awake," she said.

The last thing Otter remembered was thinking how strange it was to be given advice on how to be eaten by a monster.

When Otter awoke alone in the dark, she did not know where she was. Her limbs and torso were uncomfortably contorted. A sour smell filled her nose, and her face was pressed against a wet, sticky surface. Otter was vaguely aware that she had thrown up while she was unconscious. For one disorienting moment before realizing she was indoors, she wondered at the absence of the feral noises that had haunted her every night since leaving Junkton.

Trying to straighten her neck, she bumped her head severely against an unseen surface. Fear crowded out all other thoughts as she struggled to piece together what had happened. Then Eliza's words came rushing back to her, and she knew. The depth of the darkness suggested that morning was a long way off still. If her gluttony had not overwhelmed and then emptied her stomach, she might not have awakened at all.

Despite the cramped confines, Otter had just enough space in the cage to twist about and shift her weight to find a more comfortable position. A bit better settled, she turned her head away from the wall abutting her cell, and she was startled to see the dim outline of someone staring at her, mere inches from the bars that held her. Desperate, she whispered, "Please, help me!" Then, squinting in the dimness, she realized with dread that the figure outside her cage belonged to Desdemona. Otter would get no help there.

As her mind worked to interpret the shadows around her, Otter was startled anew to find that Desdemona looked much changed. Her face had grown far more angular and, as she had sensed at dinner, reptilian. Desdemona's arms had shrunk, leaving only tiny appendages, one of which still gripped the dingy cloth doll by its neck. She—or *it*—perched on what could have been her knees, but her legs now seemed fused nearly down to the feet—feet which had become far less footlike as well. Her facial features had grown flatter against her head, which had stretched forward into a rounded point. Her eyes shone like amber even in this dimness, divided by narrow black pupils, and her nose had receded to mere slits. Most unnerving of all, her teeth had grown into sharp, sinister points. A long, slender tongue, ending in a delicate fork, flapped back and forth lazily in the air. And the eminently practical clothing now hung limp on Desdemona's greatly transformed frame.

Even as Otter watched, the remaining vestiges of humanity faded from Desdemona's features. With every passing second, Desdemona came to look increasingly like a giant serpent, until her elongated frame could no longer support her clothing, and no limb extended to hold her doll. Both items fell to the floor with a muted rasp like the sound of leaves blown along the ground. An ominous rattling emanated from her fully formed tail end. Otter shuddered with revulsion at what Desdemona had become.

Desdemona's eyes rolled dramatically around in exasperated impatience. Slithering as near to Otter as the bars would allow, the great serpent inhaled deeply from the air about the caged girl and lapped at her with that dry, forked tongue.

Otter shuddered at the contact, and her heart sank into her belly. Her stomach, still unsettled from the evening's feast and the drug she'd been given, wrenched sickeningly.

Through her disgust, Otter couldn't help but wonder, *Why would anyone imagine a friend like Desdemona? Was it a mistake? Or did Eliza mean for Desdemona to be like this? Could other people's imaginaries be equally horrific? Or even worse?* Flinching away from Desdemona's tongue, she was having a hard time imagining what might be worse.

In a moment of desperate inspiration, Otter suddenly recalled the libertyslippers in her pocket. She could put them on and escape the cage, the cabin, and her captors.

But when Otter attempted to reach for the libertyslippers in the front pocket of her overalls, she realized her cramped confines afforded her no room to don them safely. She might be able to retrieve them and maybe even get them onto her feet. But she would have to lie on her back to put them on, and that was out of the question.

Knowing of nothing else she could do, Otter lowered her head and cried.

Life had always been sad, even horrible. But she had always had hope. Hope that she would someday escape. Hope that escaping the factory would bring her someplace better. Hope that she would someday have a magnificent imaginary friend and would play like the other children. So she had seldom cried, despite all that tormented her. But now there was nothing. Now she cried bitterly, knowing it had all been for nothing.

When Otter's tears had run dry, she curled up as comfortably as her cage would allow, trying to keep her face away from the rancid former contents of her stomach, and attempted to do as Eliza had advised and sleep once more.

But sleep would not come. And not just because of what faced her or because of the smell of her vomit. Or even because of Desdemona's expectant panting and the shivery sound her tongue periodically made as it whipped into the world and then back into her mouth. No, something else tingled in the back of her mind, refusing to let her rest. Then Eliza's words came back to her: *You don't even have an imaginary.*

But what if she did?

The idea unleashed a torrent of conflicting emotions in Otter. Of course, the unexpected path to escape buoyed her with dim hope and relief. Yet her heart sank into her belly at the thought of wasting her chance to have the perfect imaginary just to save herself from her cruel predicament. Either way, she was desperate. This might be the only way to save herself. So she came up with a plan. A sad, simple plan that would save her life but end her mission forever.

Gently, carefully, her imagination explored and shaped the kind of friend that could lend her meaningful aid. Imagining for real wasn't like pretending or daydreaming. It was a conscious act, like running. And like running, imagining was not something one was born doing. It required at least some genuine understanding of the gravity of creating an entirely new entity. This was why, Otter understood, that children with head injuries sometimes could not make imaginaries.

With effort she refocused her attention on the task at hand, sculpting in her mind the contours of an imaginary that could set her free for good. Perhaps a giant who could overpower Eliza and her monstrous snake. Or maybe a ferocious beast that could eat her captors. Each new idea pained her as she thought of being bound forever to a monster created only as a tool, as a weapon. She couldn't escape the sense that all this was little better than how Eliza had wasted the precious magic of an imaginary friend.

Yet still her mind worked on her imaginary. And the more she thought, the more creative she became. A tingling sensation, beginning in her toes but working its way ever so slowly up her legs and into the rest of her, began to infiltrate her mind, as if her very thought was a crack between two places, allowing the light of one place to leak into the other. And when her thoughts wandered for a moment to something else, the leaking seemed to recede.

The night wore on, and at last her plan was fully formed. Otter steeled herself to wriggle into a better position to meet Desdemona's gaze once more before summoning an imaginary that would release her from captivity. The earliest hint of the tingling had already begun in her toes when she moved and felt a slight crunching and crumbling from one of her hip pockets. It was then that she remembered the cookie she had stored away for later.

*Maybe there's another way*, she dared to hope.

Thinking fast, she twisted her arm until her hand could reach into her pocket and remove the largest chunk of the cookie, which had broken into a few pieces in her pocket. She then turned to face Desdemona who still sat like a serpentine gargoyle, staring at her presumed prey.

Otter waved the cookie in front of Desdemona's face. "Hey, Desdemona," Otter whispered. "Do you want a cookie?"

The Desdemona-monster-thing's eyes narrowed for a moment then widened in surprise. Otter was startled as Desdemona rushed violently toward the cage, banging her face repeatedly against the bars. After a few strikes, Desdemona realized she could not get through, and she writhed around on the floor, whining in frustration while her snakelike tail whipped about as if with a life of its own.

When Desdemona's antics had calmed, Otter spoke again. "Do you want this cookie, Desdemona? Because I can give it to you."

Desdemona shot upright again like a flash, and she moved close to the cage. Her nose pressed between the bars as far as it would go, and her tongue strained to probe at Otter and the cookie. But her eyes shifted to meet the captive girl's, and Otter knew Desdemona was listening.

"Do you know where the key is, Desdemona? The key to the cage?"

Desdemona did not—perhaps *could not*, Otter realized—respond in words. But after a momentary pause, her stare became more intense, and Otter thought she detected a slight nod from the giant snake's head.

"If you bring me the key, I could unlock this cage and give you the cookie. I just"—she breathed deep, trying to appear calm and confident even as she bargained with a monster for her life—"I just need the key. Can you get it?"

Desdemona's eyes narrowed again. Otter held her breath, wondering whether Desdemona was intelligent enough to forgo the treat out of loyalty to her master. But after only a few seconds, the snake's giant form swung around and glided off into the dark adjacent room.

Otter listened close but could hear nothing from the other room. As the minutes passed, she began to worry that her scheme had failed. Just when she was sure she would need to give up and return to her prior plan, Desdemona came slithering quietly back, the key clasped firmly in her fanged, lipless mouth.

Otter sighed with relief. "That's it, Desdemona," she whispered. "Now bring it over to me so I can give you the cookie."

Desdemona approached, her sinuous body making a soft slithering sound as it moved across the floor. Otter tried to draw back as Desdemona's face pressed against the cage, her nose protruding slightly between the bars. Holding out her hand, Otter fought the urge to snatch the key from the jaws of her terrifying and unexpected accomplice. Just as Otter's patience began to wilt, Desdemona's fanged mouth parted, and the key fell to the floor of the cage.

The monstrous maw closed, but the head did not withdraw. Desdemona eyed Otter expectantly, awaiting the promised reward.

Like a flash Otter grabbed the key and tossed the cookie away from the cage.

Desdemona rushed to where the cookie had landed, and she fell on it with abandon. In seconds the cookie had vanished, and Desdemona returned to her previous perch beside Otter's cage, as if nothing else had passed between girl and snake.

Otter withdrew as far from Desdemona as her tiny cell would allow. Then she watched and waited.

She didn't have to wait long.

In only minutes, Desdemona's eyes seemed to lose focus, her tongue slowed in its incessant flickering, and her head began to sway and droop closer to the ground. Finally, with a dull thud, her great scaly head fell the last few inches to the floor. Otter knew from experience that Desdemona was helpless.

Otter waited a few moments more to be sure Desdemona was indeed unconscious. And that the beast's graceless descent to the ground had not disturbed its slumbering real. Once satisfied on both counts, Otter scooted quietly toward the cage's door and reached through the bars with the key in hand. She bent her wrist awkwardly but carefully into the proper position and delicately inserted the key into the hole.

Her exaggerated caution reminded her of when she had first donned the libertyslippers back in the bunk room of the Home. Both instances presented an unforgiving need for precision and no opportunity for second chances.

Turning the key gently, Otter felt the lock engage, and the door popped ajar with a click.

With alarm, Otter realized that Desdemona's fallen form had partially blocked the door's path. Holding her breath, she pushed gently but firmly against the door, slowly nudging the sleeping monster's limp body out of the way, hoping her cautious shoves would not wake it. When she thought she had opened the door just enough, she twisted and turned to squeeze her body out through the opening and then lay on the ground, panting as quietly as she could.

Regaining her breath, Otter stood. Looking down, she was struck by the smell of what she'd thrown up, having been too distracted by her predicament earlier to register her disgust. She began swiping at the front of her clothes to remove the offending odor but found her effort fruitless. Giving up on it, she silently scanned the room for her belongings and eventually found them spread out on a small table as though someone had been going through them.

*Someone* has *been going through them*, she thought. This intrusion, this indignity somehow compounded the terribleness of the fate she'd nearly met.

While quietly reassembling her few possessions, Otter looked around for her makeshift bag. She saw it on top of a pile of other empty bags beside the table. A mound of assorted clothing lay next to the bags. In a moment of horrid realization, it occurred to Otter that the bags and clothes must belong to other travelers whose journeys had ended in Eliza's horrid shack.

Otter pushed her own improvised bag aside to reveal a sturdy-looking backpack. The backpack could carry far more than her cloth, and it would not weigh her down unevenly or bang against her hip. Swallowing an awful pang of guilt, she removed the bag from the pile and placed her meager possessions one by one inside, until only her knife was left.

She reached again into the pile of belongings of Eliza's other victims, this time searching for clothing. She removed a sturdy pair of pants and a comfortable-looking shirt. The toes of a rugged old pair of canvas shoes poked out of the pile, and Otter took these as well. For a moment she held the shoes reverently. She had never worn anything on her feet besides the libertyslippers, she realized before adding them to the other clothes she'd pilfered. She'd worked and lived barefoot back in Junkton.

Glancing self-consciously over at Desdemona's motionless coils, Otter quickly stripped out of her threadbare overalls, which were damp and rank from her sickness. Before putting the overalls aside, she used one unsoiled pant leg to wipe away any regurgitated remnants from her face, and then removed the libertyslippers from the pocket and stowed them, gently folded, in a pocket of her new pants. Otter tossed the old overalls in a ball toward the pile of ownerless clothes and pulled on the pants, shirt, and shoes in silence.

She reached now for the last item on the table, her knife, and held it tight as she closed her bag and heaved it onto her shoulders.

Otter looked once more to the cage and the monster sleeping beside it. Anger and hurt and slowly fading terror warred within her mind, threatening to overwhelm her. For a moment she thought of what she might do to this sleeping beast that would have devoured her, just as it had done to others, with neither remembrance nor remorse. Her grip on the knife tightened as she approached the drugged brute's body. For a long moment she stood there, staring down at Desdemona.

In the end, she could not bring herself to do any more than that.

Instead, she walked to the cage, swung its door shut with a click, and pulled the key from the lock. Placing it in her pocket, she permitted herself a moment of satisfaction in thinking that, with the key gone, at least the cage had held its last prisoner. Otter had a hazy recollection of Eliza suggesting that her imaginary needed fresh victims to survive. But Otter could spare no compassion for the creature's evil compulsion, and she evicted the recollection from her mind without a second thought.

Knife still in hand, she crept into the other room. Eliza lay sleeping on a smallish cot, her legs a little too long for it and her feet extending over the end. Once again, Otter was overcome with conflicting emotions. Once again, she contemplated her knife and what her captor had planned for her. Once again, she could go no further than contemplation.

Careful not to make a sound, Otter turned to the kitchen and looked for supplies she could carry with her. She unslung her backpack and filled it with a half dozen biscuits and a few of the picture-adorned boxes, although she was unsure how to turn their shaky-sounding contents into the lavish dishes displayed on the packaging. Rummaging through the cupboards, Otter found a rusty old canteen. Ignoring the canteen's battered exterior, she added it to her supplies. If her journey thus far had taught her one thing, it was the necessity of water. And that strangers were not to be trusted.

Her supplies fully stocked, Otter reached into the pocket of her new pants and unfolded the libertyslippers. She leaned over and pulled them onto her feet, careful not to lean on anything nearby. She stood up to her full height and looked over once more at the slumbering figure of Eliza. Anger and sadness and pity and terror fluttered and collided in Otter's head and belly until she thought she might throw up again.

Otter made her way to the sleeping girl's bedside and looked down on her. Otter thought she might wake Eliza and tell her that she and Desdemona had failed. That they had been unable to hold Otter. That they would never again lock an unwitting traveler in that cage. That she had taken what she needed and would escape, never to be caught. That she didn't deserve to be treated like cattle. That Eliza was bad for what she did to travelers.

In the end, though, Otter said nothing. She looked around the room and got her bearings, recalling which way the road led away from this shack, its residents, and the town that had made and spurned her. Then she walked away from them all, passing through girl and cot as if they were nothing but mist.

~ CHAPTER 5 ~
# A FELLOW TRAVELER

THE SUN WAS already peeking out from under the world by the time Otter stopped for a moment's rest. She had removed the libertyslippers soon after escaping Eliza's shack because she dared not wear them through the uneven wooded terrain, especially given the scant offering of light from the stars and moon. But she stopped no longer than that in the dark hours that followed. She doubted Eliza or Desdemona would have roused any earlier, but even the thought of being caught and recaptured by the girl and her creature motivated Otter to put as much distance between herself and the shack as she could.

Otter went on like that through dawn and then until sunset without sleep. She paused only twice to pull some of her original food from her new pack, but she resumed walking at once, eating as she moved ever farther from her former prison.

Somewhere off to her left, Otter sensed the new road—no longer Dirt Road—through the rumbling sounds of traffic and bolder rays of sunlight. That sense was her only directional guide as she wended between trees and through the woods in the days that followed.

Those days were anything but easy. Otter slept little and poorly. Dark memories of Eliza's shack made sleep an elusive quarry, and they haunted her dreams, jolting her awake only a few minutes after she closed her eyes.

The noises, too, continued to stalk the night. Just as before her night in captivity, the darkness seemed to mask creatures she heard but could not see.

But with the passing of days as she roamed through the trees, always keeping the road's vague presence to her left, her fear slowly ebbed. The noises never materialized further. Her pace slackened a little each day, and her periods of rest expanded with her distance from the nightmare she had escaped.

By the time Otter's pace had settled to mere hiking, she had lost track of how many days had passed, and her biscuits were nearly depleted. The packages of unprepared food, which seemed such a boon when Otter had packed them, now struck her more as an impractical burden. The girl was ill equipped to transform their contents into the meals depicted on the boxes, and her back quickly learned the cost of carrying them.

Emboldened by time, distance, and hunger, Otter began to feel a gentle tug from the road. *North*, she thought to herself. During the first full day after her escape, she determined that she was traveling east, just as she had hoped to do before her encounter with Eliza. That meant the road lay to the north. Now she found her path angling ever closer to that invisibly felt northern border, running parallel to her as she walked.

At night, she rested as she had before, on bedding collected from her surroundings, or on the ground if her environs were stingy. If she found or collected enough water, she could turn her boxed food into cold, thick mush, allowing her to save the shrinking pieces of biscuit for when water was scarce. But anything more substantial or appetizing, she realized, would require fire, and Otter had none.

One morning, the road's tug had pulled her north until the road was in sight. The road went from something Otter caught in glimpses where the trees gave way to a scene interrupted only occasionally by the trunks and limbs of crisscrossing trees. Its smooth flatness stretched lazily in an unending line of tidy, passive gray. Traffic, on the other hand, was varied and lively. Vehicles of all sizes—some even sporting sleek openings from which words and laughter chaotically issued like the random ringing of bells—cruised back and forth throughout the day, thinning only slightly as night approached and settled in. Otter thought of Dirt Road and its apparent disrepair, its sparse traffic of trucks carrying goods to and from the factory in Junkton. This road was different. Bland as the road was, she could tell that someone tended it, that people used it with many destinations in mind beyond Junkton.

The next morning, Otter woke as usual and renewed her daily trek. Her mind wandered as it had in the days before Eliza, but she now afforded herself the regular distraction of watching the people zooming by in their vehicles. Sometimes the passengers stopped briefly on the road, and Otter would stop, too, eyeing them warily and waiting until they had sped away before resuming her hike. Her mind thus occupied, the days passed quickly, and the gradually approaching threat of short supplies only rarely gnawed at the edges of her mind. Set back a safe distance from the road, Otter slept more soundly that night than she had since her journey began.

Rising with the sun, Otter gathered her few possessions and set off once more. Immediately she cut over toward the road, her daylight walking companion. But as the smooth, calming surface came into sight between the trees, Otter froze in midstep.

Someone was there.

Creeping along the ground, Otter peeked out at the stranger. He was a young man, but from his face Otter guessed he was older than most people Otter had met, and a bit older than Eliza as well. But where Eliza's clothing had been threadbare shadows of once-fine clothing, the stranger's garments were casual and nondescript, suitable for a long walk, but looked new and well kept. He wore a light sweater tucked into plain blue trousers, rugged brown shoes, and a cap that shaded his face from the sun. Despite his mature appearance, the man seemed somewhat small of stature to Otter, and his trim build seemed out of place beside his square jaw and a rather serious expression.

The traveler stood hunched over, bending to tie the shoelaces of his boots, which looked smart and new. Beside him, a tall and neat backpack, stuffed full with supplies, leaned against a rock. Otter guessed he had stopped only momentarily. He seemed to be alone. Even his imaginary was nowhere to be seen.

Holding her low crouch, Otter craned her neck awkwardly to look up and down the road. *His imaginary must be hiding somewhere*, she thought anxiously as Desdemona's cruel, vapid face flashed unbidden in her mind.

In planning her escape from Junkton, she had hoped to avoid people for a while after leaving. Her experience with Eliza and Desdemona had only reinforced this desire. Still crouching, she backed slowly away from the road to let the traveler pass before going on. Too late to stop, Otter felt her foot coming slowly down on a twig. A sharp crack echoed through the morning air. Crouching lower still, she froze. Otter had moved only a few steps back from where she had initially spied the man, and she was sure he would see her from here. She held her breath and steeled herself to bolt at the slightest move in her direction.

The man's head shot to attention at the noise, and he squinted, peering hard into the woods to search for its source. For a moment his eyes seemed to rest vaguely near Otter, and the girl felt every muscle in her body tense for escape. But after a moment that seemed an eternity, the man heaved his large pack onto his back with a grunt and began ambling eastward.

Otter could not say how much time passed before she moved again, but the sun had risen noticeably higher in the sky. Her heart still pounded in her chest, and she glanced around nervously, afraid the man's imaginary might emerge to follow him even now. *It must have gone ahead of him*, she thought. *Or perhaps it keeps pace with him in the woods and out of sight.* A chill shook Otter at the disconcerting thought that the traveler's imaginary may have seen her without her seeing it in return.

Once her nerves had settled, Otter set off again in the same direction the man had gone. But her feet kept a slower pace now. She was none too eager to encounter the traveler again.

The sun peaked in the sky at the same time as the growling in Otter's stomach. Pausing in her march, she fished her hand into her pack to pull out half a biscuit. The thing had grown harder and brittle, and it no longer inspired her appetite as it had when it steamed atop Eliza's table. But it padded her hollow belly, and she knew it was safe to eat. Swinging her bag to her back, she resumed her march and nibbled at the biscuit's hard edges as she walked.

It didn't last long. Otter wiped crumbs of the vanished biscuit from her mouth with the backs of her hands. Taking in the path ahead, she saw in the distance a blurred dab of color against the road's monochrome backdrop.

The young man from that morning had taken a seat on a stump near the road, and he appeared to be having his own lunch while he rested.

Otter stooped low and advanced slightly toward the seated traveler to get a better look. She wondered how long he would follow the road, and it suddenly occurred to her that this road's vast length had not yet encountered any intersecting roads or spawned any branches. Apparently the one thing it had in common with the stretch of Dirt Road she had walked was its isolation from others of its kin cutting through the landscape. Otter despaired for a moment to realize that, if the road continued in this solitary way for long, she would keep seeing the traveler along her way indefinitely.

She eyed him suspiciously from her hidden vantage in the woods. The stranger ate intently, as though deep in thought. Once, she was sure he must have heard her, despite her furtive movements, for he looked about again as though expecting someone to emerge from the forest. Perhaps he expected his imaginary, which was still out of sight.

Time slowed to a crawl, but Otter was determined to let the man go before continuing, lest she alert him to her presence with another misstep in the uneven terrain. Eventually, he stood, brushed off his hands and lap, and set off once more down the road.

Still Otter waited, both to allow the distance between herself and the stranger to grow, and so she could watch for signs that his imaginary might appear and follow. But the only movement she saw was from an occasional passing car and from the wind agitating the nearby grass and trees.

Satisfied that the stranger and his hidden imaginary were long gone, Otter rose to her full height and stood thinking in place.

She hatched a plan.

Otter would remain at a safe distance behind the traveler for the remainder of the day and then continue traveling through the night to pass him as he slept and put that safe distance behind her. If she stayed far enough ahead of him, she reasoned, their paths would never have to meet. That was the only way to be sure she could avoid him altogether.

But as she resumed walking, Otter noticed something had been left on the stump where the stranger had sat. Curious, but cautious, she approached.

A small square package, neatly wrapped, sat alone in the center of the stump. *He must have dropped this*, she thought, wondering whether it might be useful. Craning her neck to scan for hidden eyes, Otter snatched the object and ran with it back into the woods until she was far enough from the road not to be seen if anyone else passed that way.

She looked down at the thing in her hands and slowly unwrapped it. Inside was a square of colorful layers: the top and bottom were soft squares of spongy white, reminiscent of her nearly depleted biscuits; between them were crisp, fresh plant leaves, a slice of some watery red fruit, and still more slices of what Otter assumed was meat, although fresher and more tender than any meat she'd ever had. And some of the layers were coated in a viscous yellow paste. She put the thing to her nose and inhaled slightly. Fresh, wonderful smells filled her nostrils, and her mouth began to water. Surprised, she realized it was food.

Her mind went back to the last time she had taken food from a stranger, and her arm jerked involuntarily as if to throw the thing away from her.

She never completed the motion. Her imagination was working over the memory of the food's subtly delicious scents, contemplating how they would translate into taste. Slowly, her arm relaxed.

She looked back to where she'd retreated from. No other sign of the stranger remained. Surely he had left it by mistake.

And if it was a mistake, he would have no reason to do anything nefarious with it.

After another scant minute's thought, she took a single bite. The flavors exploded in her mouth, crisp and fresh, slightly sharp and tangy, and Otter was again stunned by how delicious food outside the factory could be. Still, she now knew that bad food could taste good. Sitting in place for nearly half an hour, she waited for the poison's effects to kick in. Yet at the end of it, she was still alert and in no pain—except for her stomach's impatient complaints. Finding this to be proof enough of the food's safety, she ate the rest of the deliciously layered square.

Moments later, a few crumbs remained scattered about her, the only evidence that anyone had ever eaten there. She leaned back gently on her pack and relished her satisfaction, her eyes closing gently in an unfamiliar state of relaxation.

Try as she might to savor the moment, her stillness gradually dissolved into restlessness and unease, and she rose slowly to her feet, knowing she still had to travel quite a distance if she hoped to put the stranger safely behind her.

And so she began walking again.

The day grew long, and Otter grew tired. She kept a watchful eye on the forest around her and on the road, which peeked out at her here and there from between the trees. Occasionally a strange noise stirred unseen in the woods, and she froze, waiting to see what danger might appear. Yet none did. She was still afraid, but she was mildly surprised to find her long walk on a full stomach in the dappled sunlight and gentle breeze to be quite pleasant, which was an unusual sensation. She could recall no time when she'd had fun, but she knew that *fun* was the word for what the children frolicking outside her factory window experienced, and she wondered whether the way her spirits seemed to rise with her feet might not be something like fun, in spite of her fear.

The effect was temporary. Otter's pleasure gradually melted into fatigue, and fatigue into exhaustion. The day's light softened from its harsh midday strength to the warm glow of late afternoon and then dusk. From the edge of the forest where she could see far ahead of her on the road, Otter picked her way through grass and gravel as she nibbled a tough biscuit crust. With night approaching, the traveler would set up camp soon, and Otter would close the gap between them once more. But he had yet to reappear.

The sun set, and the shadows grew long, groping along the forest floor until darkness shrouded everything in sight. The stars blinked alive one by one in the clear night sky, and a sliver of moon shone bright where sky and road collided in the distance. As the light receded without a sign of the traveler, anxiety rose to a simmer in Otter's chest. *Where could he be?*

"Did you like the sandwich?"

Otter jumped, as if the question had been a thunderclap, and her feet reacted before her mind could. Without so much as another breath, she bolted back toward the safety of the woods, cursing her foolishness for trusting the road, as if she could ever be safe so close to the goings-on of other people.

Her flight ended as abruptly as it began. Her weight slammed into something solid that had not been there when she'd approached the road. She fell backward, unbalanced by the backpack, and landed with a thud.

She heard the new voice again, this time with a grunt from the impact. "Oof!"

Otter looked up in terror and saw in the failing light the dim outline of the traveler she had thought she was following. *But he was following me*, she realized with horror.

The traveler hunched over and panted from the collision. He struggled to straighten himself. "That kind of hurt," he said. "Are you okay?" The traveler's voice was deep but soft, and the words came with surprising speed, as though only pausing from a pressing task. Its tone was unfamiliar to Otter's ear, a kind of softness and warmth she might otherwise attribute to concern.

But Otter would not be fooled. From her position on the ground, she kicked at the traveler's legs while she squirmed to escape the backpack that held her down. Her fingers dug reflexively into the earth, which she flung haphazardly in her assailant's direction.

The stranger jumped backward with alarm, even as he doubled over to cradle his freshly bruised shin. "Hey! Cut that out!" Confusion had replaced concern on his face, and he eyed the girl warily as she struggled against her pack.

The backpack's straps would not relent, and Otter's efforts slowed as she realized she could not untangle herself, rise, and flee without being caught by this stranger. She had been careless and let him sneak up on her unawares. With a silent snarl, she gave in to exhaustion and grew still.

Defiantly, she glared at her assailant, tears welling in the corners of her eyes. "You can't trick me," she said, her voice icy.

"Trick you?" The traveler's eyebrows raised to their utmost, and he looked around as though expecting to see someone else behind him. "What are you talking about?" His round baritone rose slightly in pitch as if with surprise.

"Go ahead and hurt me or kill me or whatever, but just do it." A calm had settled over her mind, and her voice came flat and distant, as if someone else spoke with her mouth while Otter only observed. "If you're going to hurt me, I can't stop you. But you can't trick me. I already know, and I won't be tricked."

"Um, I'm confused," he said apologetically, his hands before him where she could see them. The words rushed in deep tones from his mouth. "And maybe I'm not the only one. Look, I don't want to hurt you. I just thought you might be alone and need help. If you'd prefer, I can leave you alone. But I'm alone too. And I just thought the company might be nice. I'm sorry I scared you. I'll go." And with that, he turned.

"Why did you sneak up on me?" she asked to his back.

He turned again to face her. "I'm sorry?"

"I was following you, and you knew it. I was watching for you on the road, but you hid in the woods and snuck up on me."

"That's what you think?" His tone matched the wounded look on his face. "You're right that I knew you were following me. But I didn't hide. And I didn't sneak. I always make camp in the woods because it's safer than by the road. I didn't know whether you would keep following me, and it certainly seemed you hadn't been since this morning. I also didn't know you would catch up with me." He paused, his eyes searching hers. "But when I saw you, I assumed you'd caught up for the company. My mistake." He turned again to leave.

"Wait!" The word surprised Otter even as it burst from her mouth.

The traveler hesitated and then turned again, expectant.

"You don't want to hurt me?" she asked, trembling.

The traveler put his hands on his hips and furrowed his brow. "I don't want to hurt you."

"And you don't want to trick me?" A tear rolled down the pinned girl's cheek.

"I don't want to trick you." His eyes were large and round, and they seemed to see more than they should as they bored into hers. He again seemed to be waiting for something from her.

Otter locked eyes with him and chewed her lower lip, as she sometimes did when trying to figure out a tricky malfunction on her conveyor belt at the factory.

The girl's voice was barely a whisper, and the man leaned closer to hear. "Do you have to go, then? I'm sorry for . . ." She looked down, unable to finish her thought or to meet his gaze.

"It's okay. I'm sorry I scared you," he said again, smiling gently. "My name's Melvin. What's yours?"

Otter raised her eyes and tried to return the smile, overcome by the wave of emotions crashing without name or distinction against her mind. "I'm Otter."

The traveler—*Melvin*, Otter reminded herself—was true to his word. He didn't want to hurt or trick her and, as she came to understand, his help may well have saved her. This she realized even on her first evening with Melvin while they discussed what lay ahead.

"I'd say we have another five days in this direction before we get somewhere with more supplies. *If* you have the money." His large, round eyes searched hers for a moment, but Otter said nothing to confirm his suspicions. It was enough that he expected she had no money—and that Otter knew he was right.

Even if she did have money, five days meant a long way to stretch her meager rations. Her belly was full now, after Melvin had shared another sandwich. But images of the hungry road that could have been played across her mind. She saw those miles stretching into the distance even as her eyes stared into the crackling fire, which flung short-lived sparks into the air between the two travelers. Its flames flushed her cheeks, but she welcomed its warmth against the cold night air.

She raised her head to see Melvin's face just above the flames. He looked back at her with a quizzical expression.

"I . . ." his low voice began before losing its steam. "Where are you going?" he blurted out instead.

Otter didn't know how to answer. *Where* am *I going?* she wondered.

"You don't have to tell me," Melvin said in his rushed manner of speaking. "I just thought we might be going to the same place. You know, since we're both so . . ."

"So . . . ?" Otter echoed back.

"So, well"—his round eyes probed hers, clearly expecting her to volunteer an end to his sentence—"so alone," he finally finished, with the wind that drove the sails of his speech seeming to subside for the first time since they'd met.

The word *alone* echoed in Otter's skull. She suddenly recalled that she had yet to see Melvin's imaginary, and fear gripped her chest as she tried to look in every direction at once.

Alarmed by Otter's sudden alertness, Melvin stood and looked around. "Did you hear something?"

"Where is your imaginary?" she responded, her eyes narrow with suspicion.

Melvin recoiled, looking hurt. "I could ask you the same question," he half shouted at the girl.

A missing piece fell into place in Otter's mind. "You're a loner, aren't you?"

"I am," he said, pulling himself up to his full height. Diminutive though Melvin was for a full-grown man, Otter thought he cast an impressive figure, his defiant pride evident on his face. "And it seems you are, too, unless your imaginary has been hiding in the woods all this time." His stare was a challenge to Otter, and she blinked at its intensity.

She struggled to find a response. "I don't . . ." *Was* she a loner? Could she even say if she weren't? If she were a loner, she would have even less idea of where she was going than she thought. "I don't *think* I'm a loner," she said quietly. "I feel as though . . ." She paused, her brow furrowed. "I think I'd know," she finished meekly.

Melvin's glare softened and his demeanor became curious once more. "What do you mean you don't know?"

"I mean I've never tried to imagine one." It was now Otter's turn to look defiant. She had suffered the taunts of others for as long as she could remember for deciding—*supposedly* deciding, everyone else might have said—not to conjure for herself the sort of sad, gray husks the other children in the factory called imaginary friends. Even Mr. Pickle's imaginary, who hung on his real's every word, seemed a poor effort at a true friend in Otter's estimate.

Melvin's eyes widened further with shock and, Otter thought, a hint of disbelief. "But—why?" was all he said.

"I don't know anything about imaginaries. Or much about anything else," she conceded, the heat rising in her cheeks at the admission. "I've seen next to nothing of Imbria, and I don't want to be stuck with just any old imaginary. When I'm ready," she concluded, "I will."

Melvin, visibly shaken by Otter's answer, sat back down with a thump. Silence grew in the space between them, and even the noises of the forest and fire seemed muted following Otter's revelation.

"I don't think there's anything wrong with being a loner," Otter offered, trying to revive the conversation she'd inadvertently derailed. She wasn't sure she had ever even considered what she thought of loners. But she'd heard all her life how pitiful they were and about the shame they bore. She'd also heard all her life how useless and expendable *she* was. She had long ago learned to ignore such talk. Ignoring what she'd heard about loners was but a small step further.

Melvin smiled, the kindness returning to his eyes. "That's nice of you to say." He grabbed a stick from the ground and poked at the fire. "Maybe I wish I thought the same."

Silence settled again as Otter searched for an appropriate response. She changed the subject instead.

"You said you thought we might be going to the same place. Where did you mean?"

The young man's eyes brightened, and he leaned forward as if eager for this new topic. His incongruously deep voice returned to its naturally enthusiastic meter.

"That's right. Before, when I thought, well, you know." Melvin paused for an uncomfortable instant, his cheeks pink with embarrassment. He shook it off and resumed his normal pace, the words rolling quickly out in his distinctively resonant staccato. "I assumed you were also going to the Farm." His eyes searched hers for comprehension. Finding none, he sighed and reached into his bag and withdrew a rectangle of paper folded many times over. He rose and walked around the fire to Otter while unfolding the paper and extending his arms outward in the process. It was a map.

Spreading the map on the ground beside her, he poked a dent in its surface with his forefinger. "This is all of Industriopa." A great continent commanded the map's center, surrounded on each side by ocean. "We"—his finger hovered over the continent before landing with a jab on a point of the map roughly in the middle of the great landmass—"are right about here."

Otter peered down at the map. She found Junkton and its eggshell perimeter of Oakwood Forest a few inches southwest of Melvin's fingertip. *That's how far I've come*, Otter thought as she tried to comprehend the real-world distance depicted in those few inches.

Sliding his finger a few inches farther to the east, Melvin said, "And right about here is the Farm. We are about ten days away from there now."

Otter peered at the spot for a moment before looking back up at Melvin's face. She had a question but didn't want to offend her new companion. "But why do lone—um, people without—well, I mean." She stopped and composed herself. "Why are you going to a farm?" she finally sputtered out.

The subject of loners was generally taboo, especially when in the company of one. Not that anyone in Junkton seemed to care much about such niceties. But the prohibition was taught even where it wasn't observed.

Melvin's gentle smile eased Otter's embarrassment for discussing the forbidden topic. "It's okay," he assured her. "And it's not *a* farm. It's *the* Farm," he explained. "Everyone in my family on my mother's side is a loner. For as far back as anyone can remember, my mother's relatives have traveled to the Farm once they came of age and were ready to undertake the journey. A powerful poly lives on the Farm, and she helps loners get imaginaries." He paused at Otter's confused expression.

"Who's Polly?" she asked.

"No, her name isn't Polly," he said. "You know, a *poly*." He searched her face for recognition, but none came.

"Wow!" he exclaimed. "You really don't know?"

Embarrassed, she shook her head meekly.

His shook, too, but in surprise and mild disbelief at her ignorance of the commonplace. "Well, let's start with the basics. Almost everyone in the world, all over Imbria, can imagine a single imaginary, and *only* a single imaginary, right?"

Otter nodded patiently, although even she knew this much.

"But some people, like me, can't imagine even one, no matter how hard we try."

She nodded again, and he continued.

"Well, a poly is like the opposite of a loner. A poly can summon multiple imaginaries. Usually, that means two or three in a lifetime, or sometimes even several across a lifetime, with several years between. But in rare instances, a poly can just imagine and imagine and never have to stop. A poly like that lives on the Farm. And she helps loners like me."

Otter's head tilted as she considered Melvin's words. "But you said your mother's family has gone to the Farm for as long as anyone can remember. Has the poly there lived so long?"

"I don't think so, but I don't know for sure," Melvin admitted. "I think maybe her family is like mine in that way. So just as I come from a long line of loners, maybe she comes from a long line of polys. But that's just a guess. Anyway," he continued, "I'm of age, and I felt ready for the journey, so here I am. I'm going to the Farm for an imaginary of my own, just as my mother did, and all her family before her." His explanation concluded, he looked at Otter with his chin held high.

Otter rubbed her jaw as she sat contemplating Melvin's words. It had never occurred to her that some people could have multiple imaginaries. She'd certainly never read anything about that in *Surviving in the Wilderness*. Questions flooded her mind, but she lacked the words to give them voice. She settled for: "I hope she gives you the perfect friend." And she smiled.

Melvin returned the smile and stood. "Me too."

The fire had grown dim and red between them. Melvin brushed his hands free of crumbs on the thighs of his pants as he stood. "We should probably settle in for the night."

Otter rose too. She turned to regard the tent Melvin had erected. She had been amazed to learn that such a thing could be made to fit into the tall supply pack he wore on his back. And his offer to share its floor space with the girl had nearly overcome her. Digging a spare blanket out from among his other supplies, he had said, "It's not much, but it will beat sleeping on the ground."

Thoughts of sleep brought to her mind the invisible animals that stalked her nights.

"Melvin?"

Melvin stopped tidying the camp and turned to her, his face shrouded in shadow where the night's darkness pushed back the flames' faltering glow. "Yes, Otter?"

"You've been camping in the woods for a while now, right?"

"That's right. Early on I stayed at inns, but that was when there were more people around. I haven't seen an inn for some time, so I've been staying in the woods since. Why?"

"Do you ever . . ." Otter paused, not wanting to seem childish. ". . . hear things?"

"'Hear things'?"

"Yeah. You know. At night?"

He studied her a moment. Otter wondered what he thought of her young age, of her being alone in the woods, of her fright at their meeting. If he was curious about her, he had not pushed for more information. His expression certainly suggested the questions he might like to ask. But all he said was "I hear normal things. Insects. Small animals. Birds. Is that what you mean?"

"So you don't ever hear larger animals?" she pressed. "Larger animals that don't come around in the daylight?"

"I'm sorry, Otter. I've never heard anything larger in these woods. We're too near the road for most animals to venture, even at night. Have *you* been hearing those kinds of noises?"

"I don't know. Maybe. It was probably nothing." Her tone invited no further questions, and Otter returned to tidying her things. Their remaining tasks around the campsite proceeded in silence.

By the time the pair had settled in for the evening, Otter's head was still reeling from the day's events. For the first time ever perhaps, but certainly for the first time on her journey, she was sleeping in relative peace and safety. Her mind tested this strange but comforting thought for a long time as she lay awake. It was her last conscious thought when sleep finally came.

Well, nearly the last. At precisely the moment she surrendered to her sinking eyelids, Otter realized that the nightly noises had for once stayed away.

The next morning, Otter woke refreshed. She rose with the songs of the dawn's first birds and began shuffling around the camp in search of work to be done. She did not want to go through Melvin's things, and her own supplies were too meager to provide a proper breakfast. So she restarted the fire, using skills she'd only read about but never until then had a chance to employ.

Melvin emerged from the tent and smacked his lips lazily as he stretched. His smart-looking clothes were rumpled from sleeping in them. "I see you found the matches," he said.

Otter's head turned quizzically. "'Matches'?"

"Don't tell me you built the fire without matches," he said, his eyes wider than usual with surprise.

"It took a little while because this was my first time. I was too afraid to start a fire before . . ." She shook off the thought, unable or unwilling to give it substance outside her own mind. "But it wasn't as hard as I thought," she continued. "It just required patience. I'm quite patient," she said, a touch of pride lifting her voice and her chin.

Again he regarded her, but now as though seeing something he'd previously missed. "Yeah. I guess you are," he said with a laugh. He walked toward the edge of camp, his hand giving her head a brief but affectionate pat as he passed her.

Otter couldn't recall being touched with anything resembling affection before. She flinched slightly at the unfamiliar gesture but tried to sit firmly so as not to offend Melvin. If he noticed, he did not mention it.

He returned presently and sat beside Otter before the fire. "If you're up early again, you can help yourself to supplies for breakfast. Do you not have food of your own?"

Otter perked up at this and flashed a sheepish grin. Moments later, the small array of her provisions adorned the ground at their feet. Food from the Home was now exhausted. The biscuits from Eliza's shack were reduced to crumbs. Only the boxes remained.

Melvin examined the narrow side of a box, the image on its front facing Otter at his side. "Say, these will actually come in handy. I have a pan and some other supplies we can use to prepare them." He looked down at the girl. "Why did you bring these if you didn't have a way to cook them?"

"If you show me how to make them, I'll help," she said, avoiding his question.

His face told her he saw through the deflection. Yet he only said, "I'd be happy to. In fact, the box tells you how. You just need to have the right things."

Breakfast was dried fish, fresh apples, and wedges of one large biscuit Melvin grew over the fire in a single black metal skillet. His voice rumbled and raced throughout the meal, making small talk of every kind. He talked about the birds winging past, the clouds floating over, the trees that ringed the campsite. He talked of everything they saw and heard. But he asked no questions.

Otter listened, saying nothing.

Eventually, their appetites sated, Melvin's monologue wound down, and stillness settled between them.

In silence they rose and packed their things. Soon the camp had vanished. The tent folded impossibly into Melvin's pack, and the fire steamed angrily at being doused by a cup of water. The travelers found themselves looking once more at each other, their belongings mounted on their respective backs.

They both broke the silence at once, each speaking awkwardly into the void that separated them.

"Is it okay if I go with you?"

"Do you want to come with me?"

Each surprised by the other's question, they both laughed.

Melvin spoke again first. "I don't know where you were heading before, but I'd be happy to have you come with me. If you'd like," he hastily added, a grin of uncharacteristic bashfulness parting his lips.

She lost no time answering. "I'd like that very much."

Melvin's smile widened further, and Otter wondered whether it could reach his ears if he were happy enough. His hand extended down to her.

Unsure of his expectation, Otter looked at the hand from both sides before reaching tentatively toward it and grasping it with her own. His hand locked with hers, Melvin gave her arm a few vigorous pumps before releasing her again, laughing. "It will be good to have a friend for the rest of the journey," he said.

*Friend.* Otter's brain rolled the word around, playing with it, testing it. She had no idea how far her quest for the perfect imaginary friend would take her. But smiling up at her new companion, Otter saw the first glimmer of what she thought she was looking for.

~ CHAPTER 6 ~

# THE FARM

THERE WAS NO question about it: traveling with Melvin was better than traveling alone.

The pair's young friendship thrived on the road. Out of habit, Otter spoke little. Melvin, on the other hand, craved conversation, and he was happy to speak for them both. His quick, eager manner of speaking made his words seem like dogs pulling hard against their leashes to rush ahead. In rapid succession, he told Otter at length about a great many things, and Otter listened with equal enthusiasm.

She heard all about Melvin's family of loners, generations of whom had lived and worked as accountants in Bankton, a town deep in Industriopa's western region. He spoke of the many wondrous imaginaries each of his family members had brought back from the Farm. "And each one was perfect," Melvin sighed, his words weighted with envy and wonder. Otter's ears perked up at these words, but they settled again on hearing what kinds of friends accountants found "perfect." Not that they didn't sound nice. But they certainly didn't sound perfect for her.

Upon discovering how little Otter knew of Imbria, Melvin spent a great deal of time telling her all about their world as well. He spoke of Chimerica, Fidelia, and Pragmatica, the continents of Imbria beyond Industriopa.

He described the life of a loner in a world of happily paired reals and imaginaries. In telling Otter more about the Farm, he also spoke in somewhat hushed tones about polys generally. "Some people think polys are indecent, even unnatural," he explained, as though he were sharing an embarrassing secret. "But," he hastened to add, blushing, "I don't think there's anything wrong with it!" Otter imagined he might be more sensitive than most to imaginary-based prejudices.

As they walked, he also pointed to trees and animals, naming all he knew, and he was surprised to learn that Otter also knew many of these names. "From reading," she explained succinctly.

Many people borrowed from nature's endless variety in choosing their imaginaries, Melvin explained excitedly. "I know a girl back home with a bird just like that one over there. Except that hers is big enough to ride. By tradition, every imaginary in our neighbor's family is a wolf!"

This topic piqued Otter's interest. "Does anyone ever imagine a person?"

Melvin gasped, horrified. "No, Otter. No. No one can do that. I've heard of people trying, but it just doesn't work. I heard a story once of a boy back in Bankton who tried imagining a person and it *did* work. But his imaginary had no thoughts of its own to communicate. It was like an empty shell. It didn't even need to eat or drink. It only breathed. So the boy's family left it to sit on the porch, rain or shine, where it stared into nothing, while the boy went around with no imaginary. He was basically a loner with an imaginary." Horror widened Melvin's eyes but did not slow the pace of his narration. "The story goes that a storm came along one day and knocked the imaginary off the porch in the middle of the night. By the time the family found it the next morning, the imaginary had drowned in a puddle where it had fallen."

Otter didn't care for that story at all. Neither did Melvin, apparently, and the two of them walked for a time in rare thoughtful silence.

Melvin's knowledge of the life around them was typically much less grim. As the small party passed a copse of tall trees like the one she had climbed early in her trek along Dirt Road, Melvin even put a name to the tree and its brightly colored fruits.

"Those are specterines," he announced, pointing toward the mass of fronds at the tree's towering top. "They grow all over this region. And they're delicious," he said with a smile. Otter recalled her reluctance to climb for the fruits despite her hunger, and she felt a fleeting pang of regret. She had read in *Surviving in the Wilderness* that specterines were plentiful in these parts, and edible besides, but she had been unable to identify them earlier. The realization left her wondering whether climbing for the fruits might have spared her a night of anguish at Eliza's shack. She chased the pointless and unpleasant thought away and returned her attention to Melvin's eager dissertation.

Otter absorbed it all. And for the first time, listening to her companion name the flora and fauna along their way, she was sure she was happy.

Then, on their third day of travel, Melvin asked Otter where she was from.

She mumbled something about being from far away, the same answer she had given Eliza. But Melvin wasn't satisfied. "How far?" he persisted.

Otter bristled at her companion's prying. Why would he push her about this? What could he really want by asking? "Why do you want to know?"

The hurt look from their first encounter had returned. "Because we're traveling companions? And friends? Because I've told you everything about myself? Because I'd like to know you better?"

His words stung. Melvin had not earned her distrust. Quite the opposite.

"I'm from Junkton," she said simply.

Deep channels furrowed Melvin's brow, chasing away his wounded expression. "Really?" he asked. "I've known some Junktonians, but they look just like everyone else around here."

"'Just like everyone else'?" Otter guardedly asked.

If the girl's tone had reopened the wound that her suspicion had cut in him, Melvin's face didn't show it. "Haven't you ever noticed that pretty much everyone has light skin, but you . . ."

Otter stopped in her tracks and looked at Melvin, waiting. "But I?" she finally asked.

"Well." The prominent knot in his throat bobbed with a nervous swallow. "But you don't," he replied.

Her curiosity about her own unknown origins brought down her guard as no prodding could have. Looking down at herself, she slowly rotated her hand to examine its chestnut back and the paler palm in turn. "Is it true that no one else has dark skin like mine?"

"Not *no one*," Melvin said. "But no one from Industriopa." Otter looked away from her hand to meet Melvin's eyes, and pink rose in his cheeks as he blurted, "No one I know of, anyway."

Otter wasn't sure why, but Melvin's words left her feeling alone in a way she never had, even during seemingly endless hours of desperation in Junkton.

Melvin seemed to sense Otter's withdrawal. He approached her and placed his hand gently on her shoulder. "It's not *bad* to look different," he said.

Hearing this declaration, Otter recalled what she had said to Melvin about being a loner. She wondered whether she believed either statement now.

"You know," Melvin continued, "I've heard that people outside of Industriopa look different from Industriopans. I haven't traveled much, and we don't see so many foreign travelers in Bankton. But I've known people who have left Industriopa for a time. They bring back stories of the different peoples of Imbria. A family friend once told me people in Chimerica have darker skin. I didn't think much about it at the time, but maybe you're from there." He paused, waiting.

"I'm from Junkton," she repeated.

The furrows returned to Melvin's brow.

"I've never known anywhere else," she added in barely a whisper.

Melvin's eyebrows raised slowly as realization set in. "Otter?" he asked softly. "Did you *work* in Junkton?"

Junkton's use of young workers was no secret. Otter had witnessed tours of visitors being led around the libertyslipper factory by Mr. Pickle, and she'd heard him boasting of Junkton's efficiency in putting the orphans to work and of the virtues such industriousness would instill in them. Otter did not personally know of a child working in the factory who had grown up to take advantage of these learned virtues.

Her silence was answer enough. Melvin bent to one knee, where his short stature put him level with the young girl, and looked at her downcast eyes for a long moment. Then he embraced her.

Otter's body became rigid, as if she'd been turned to stone. She had never been hugged before—not that she could remember anyway—and she didn't know how to respond. Gradually, the stone in her spine melted. Sensing it was the right thing to do, she lifted her arms to return the gesture.

When she finally released him, her face was wet with tears, she had no recollection of shedding. She stepped back, self-consciously rubbing the wetness from her cheeks with the meat of her palms. She stifled a sniffle.

"We don't have to talk about it anymore," Melvin said. "I'm sorry."

"It's okay," Otter replied. "I don't know why I'm upset. I'm out now. Most never will be." Her voice shrank to almost a whisper, but she continued. "I don't know anywhere other than Junkton," she repeated. "My first memories are of the nursery in the Home. I can't even say for sure what the memory was, or when it was, because it was so much like every day until I left the nursery and started working. They wait till we can read and know enough to do our jobs. Some kids have trouble learning to read and get sent to the factory early. Others learn to read quickly. They get sent to the factory early too." She paused, peering directly into Melvin's eyes. "I learned to read quickly."

Melvin listened in silence as she continued. His face was a mask of studious control. But his eyes betrayed his horror and sympathy as the young girl's soft litany of injustices buffeted him.

A tightness released in Otter's chest as she put her past into words, as though they were washing away her heartache as they flowed from her. She told Melvin of the factory and the Home, of the libertyslippers she made every day, and of the final pair she'd worked on piecemeal for years. She told him of her escape into Oakwood Forest and her flight down Dirt Road. She choked on a sob as she told him of her capture by Eliza, of Eliza's ravenous imaginary, and of Otter's escape from the vicious duo. She told Melvin of her fear upon seeing him walking along her way, and of her decision to pass him in the night. And she told him about her reason for all of it, her mission to imagine the perfect friend.

Other than to raise his eyebrows in surprise at the revelation that his traveling companion possessed her own pair of libertyslippers, Melvin was motionless throughout.

When Otter had finished, the two of them looked out into nothing without speaking. Somewhere during Otter's narrative, Melvin had taken hold of her hand, and they continued to sit with their hands clasped as dusk and silence enveloped them. Otter was surprised to find comfort in holding the young man's hand, and she wondered whether fathers consoled their children in the same way. She wondered whether her own father would have comforted her and whether he was a kind man like Melvin.

With darkness overtaking their campsite, the two quietly rose, exchanged looks laden with unspoken meaning, and set to readying themselves for sleep.


The rustling sounds of Melvin breaking camp mingled musically in Otter's ears with the songs of the day's early birds. Lying there, Otter squinted at the light invading the tent and then rubbed the sleep from her eyes. The dull, lumpy hardness of the stones beneath the tent had grown more pronounced during the night, and she rolled to one side to relieve her back from their remorseless prodding.

The two of them ate in warm silence, both deep in thought about what had passed between them the day prior. The quiet continued as the girl and the young man broke camp, and it persisted until they reached the road again.

"Where will you go after the Farm?" Melvin asked. His usually quick manner seemed subdued and his voice husky.

Otter thought about the question, repeating it in her mind. "I don't know," she finally admitted.

"I just want you to know that you can leave *with* me," he said, before quickly adding, "That is, if you want to." His gaze was fixed on the road ahead, and it seemed to Otter that he avoided looking anywhere else.

The silence had stretched until Melvin began to think she might not answer at all when she finally replied. "I don't think I can," she whispered. Otter looked up at him, and the fear of Melvin's response to her statement was plain on her face.

Melvin smiled. "It's okay," he reassured her, placing a hand on her shoulder. "I thought you might say that. But I wanted you to know you had the option all the same. You *still* have the option," he added as he cast a meaningful look at the girl beside him.

She smiled in response, and he gave her shoulder an appreciative squeeze before they continued in silence once more.

The prior energetic meter of their conversation—or more accurately, of Melvin's monologue—returned later that day. Otter had not realized until then that she'd missed Melvin's informative chattering. Hearing him tell her about their world, Imbria, felt a lot like reading her book, except that this was effortless and unrushed, unlike the scant paragraph or page she'd snuck in the moments between her workday's end and the failing of daylight.

His unending speech also made the time pass more quickly. Before Otter knew it, the sun had risen and set several more times, and the few-inch span Melvin had shown her on the map had disappeared beneath their feet. The road where they'd met was long gone, having withered into unpaved and unnamed tributaries cutting through the countryside. The pair now stood staring at an ivy-shrouded gate where their path met its verdant end.

Otter, for once, spoke first. "Shouldn't we go in?" Her tone was less decisive than her words.

"I suppose so. I just—"

Otter waited for him to finish until it became apparent he would not. She reached toward her friend and gently grasped his hand in imitation of his comforting gesture, giving it a squeeze.

Melvin looked down at her and his cheeks grew flushed. An awkward but warm smile chased the chagrin from his face, and he returned the squeeze. "Otter, I'm not sure I really knew what bravery was before I met you. When I first saw you fall to the ground, trapped by your own pack, I thought I was rescuing you. But you didn't really need rescuing, and I'm grateful you came along with me."

A warm glow enveloped Otter at her friend's kind words, and the two walked hand in hand toward the gate.

A metallic clang ripped through the forest's stillness, startling the approaching pair. Something had struck the top of the gate. Looking at each other, each saw confusion and apprehension on the other's face, while muffled grunts and thumps slowly rose up the opposite side of the gate. Something was climbing. Otter and Melvin returned their attention to the noise, and their eyes followed it upward, growing wider as the noise increased in elevation.

*It was a ladder*, Otter realized. *That loud noise came from a ladder striking the top.* And whatever had propped the ladder there was using it to scale the gate. A gulp stuck in her throat.

Just as it seemed that whatever was climbing could rise no farther without coming right over the gate and falling upon the nervous visitors, a great, furry head extended from behind the gate and peered down at them with giant orbs of eyes that protruded from the top of the head as a frog's eyes do. Hooded in thick, furry lids, the bulging eyes gazed down on the pair in wordless expectation.

With his back arched and his head tilted all the way back, Melvin put his hand over his eyes to shade them from the sun as he looked up at the odd new face. Clearing his throat, he offered greetings in his characteristically crisp baritone. "Hi," he announced.

"Hello," came the creature's high, raspy response. The unusual voice reminded Otter of the sound her conveyor belt had once made when debris had infiltrated its gears and caused them to seize.

The visitors exchanged another perplexed look and turned back to the odd greeter hovering over them. The greeter, in turn, looked placidly back.

Melvin tried again. "We're here to see . . ." He stopped, searching for the words.

Again the rasp responded with a lone syllable. "Yes?"

Melvin thrust his shoulders back in a dignified manner and visibly straightened to his full height, such as it was. "I'm here for an imaginary."

Otter detected the same defiant pride in Melvin's voice as she heard when he first told her so many nights ago now that he was a loner.

The strange doorman nodded slightly but seemed otherwise unaffected by the young man's pronouncement. Then its head turned fluidly to regard Otter, gently squinting as it scanned her, from the canvas shoes she'd obtained at Eliza's shack up to the top of her tightly bound, jet-black curls. "And you?"

Otter clamped down on her urge to run. She didn't trust anyone except Melvin, but he seemed to trust in this complete stranger. She knew him to be no fool, but . . .

Melvin gave her hand a gentle squeeze of encouragement.

Grateful, she squeezed back. "I'm with him," she said, trying to sound braver than she felt.

The creature's fuzzy orbs blinked momentarily before the head at their bases nodded again. Then head and eyes disappeared beneath the gate's edge, accompanied once again by the creature's invisible shuffling on the concealed ladder.

Just as the visitors had begun to wonder whether the creature had abandoned them, they heard the jingling of keys and the sound of hands fumbling with lock and latch. A decisive click liberated the gate, which began to swing slowly outward so that Melvin and Otter had to move out of its way or be struck by it. Forgetting all trepidation for the moment, both peeked curiously inside to get a better glimpse of what had greeted them.

They were surprised to find an elderly man with a long white mustache and a shock of white hair standing beside what appeared to be a massive, furry caterpillar, with rather long, thin arms protruding at regular intervals along its body. That was what had stuck its head over the gate to greet them.

"Well," the old man started in a slow wheeze, "you're here." Reaching gnarled fingers into a rumpled breast pocket, he retrieved a brightly wrapped candy, which he unwrapped and then popped into his mouth with a flick before stuffing the wrapper back into his pocket and returning his impassive attention to the pair of strangers before him.

Melvin looked first at Otter, who saw his throat bob with a hard swallow, and then back to the man. "Um, yes, we are. What do we . . ." At a loss, he paused. "What do we do now?"

Gently tugging one end of his mustache, the old man exchanged a look with the long, undulating beast by his side, and when he turned back to Melvin and Otter, the barest hint of a mischievous grin peeked out through the hairy veil that framed the old man's wrinkled chin. "What do you *want* to do now?" he asked, his long mustache rising and falling in a way that reminded Otter distinctly of the man's long, hairy companion.

"Stop teasing them, Fortescue," scolded the high-pitched rasp of the caterpillar, who also wore a smile. "He thinks he's hilarious, but he's not." Despite the creature's harsh words, one of its many arms ruffled the man's hair with obvious affection. "I suppose you're here to see Luna."

Melvin exhaled visibly, as if remembering the need to breathe. "Is Luna the, um . . ." His light baritone again seemed at a loss for words.

"This is *Luna's* Farm," the caterpillar patiently offered. "And if you're here for an imaginary," it added, "you're probably here for her."

Melvin nodded, while Otter remained silent by his side.

The old man and the caterpillar—his imaginary, Otter surmised—silently returned the nod, and then the old man pivoted around into a brisk walk away from the visitors as though expecting to be followed. The caterpillar turned in the opposite direction and returned to the gate, where it retrieved a book it must have set aside upon hearing the arrival of strangers. Realizing they'd been left with the half of this odd couple still on sentry duty, Melvin and Otter sprinted to catch up with the surprisingly quick old man.

"So," Melvin began, panting slightly, "your name's Fortescue, right?"

Without pausing his quick stride, the old man shot Melvin a suspicious sideways look and grumbled, "No. The name's Whipley," before setting his mustachioed visage back to the path ahead of them.

Melvin shared a confused look with Otter, who only shrugged in silent response.

"Oh! Apologies, Whipley. I thought your, um, friend called you Fortescue. I must have misheard."

This time Whipley didn't even turn his head, so Otter and Melvin had to lean in to understand his grumbling. "Fortescue Whipley. But only Bridget"—he jerked his thumb back over his shoulder toward the creature they'd left behind—"only she calls me by my first name." Despite Whipley's gruff words and demeanor, a small smile escaped from beneath his mustache, making clear that this grumpy fellow was happy to indulge his long, furry friend with this mild indignity.

Naturally, Melvin wasn't finished talking, despite their guide's taciturn demeanor. "Did Luna, er, introduce you to Bridget?"

Whipley replied with only a grunt and a slight nod. Melvin needed no more encouragement than that, and his chatter was unleashed from there. "Well, I think she's just marvelous. Is she perfect for you?"

Whipley seemed a bit taller as he walked, and Otter thought the man almost glowed with pride and affection. "She is," he said, beaming.

Melvin pressed on. "What's Luna like?"

Whipley glanced at Melvin from the corner of his eye and said only, "You'll meet her soon enough, then *you* can tell *me*." After that, even Melvin made no small talk as they made their way across the Farm's grassy expanse. Whipley made no further noise beyond the shuffle of his feet and the occasional click of the candy against his teeth.

The conversation's halt allowed Otter to focus on her surroundings. Their feet were beating down the besieged weeds of a casual path, neither trod enough to be bare nor let alone enough to grow wild. Ahead, a large farmhouse grew as they drew nearer to it, and Otter was sure she could make out the moving silhouettes of people and creatures scurrying about their various tasks in the vast field standing between her small troupe from the house.

As the three approached, the silhouettes solidified into real living beings, and their vividness and variety took Otter's breath away. She was reminded of her view from the factory window and the children who played with their menagerie of imaginaries. But while the children all seemed to have imaginaries suited only to playtime, these imaginaries seemed much . . .

*Deeper*, Otter thought. Yes, that was the word. When Otter observed the children in Junkton interacting with their imaginaries, they seemed to treat their imaginaries like mere *things*, as elaborate toys they owned. Yet seeing *these* reals talking and working and playing and living with their imaginaries, she saw a bond as between family members or dear friends. And the imaginaries themselves seemed to possess a similar devotion to their reals, but not in any submissive way. It was as if each imaginary had come into being with the whole of its real in mind. If the real limped along on a bad leg, the imaginary was large enough to ride. A woman deftly worked wood on an outdoor workbench, and her multiarmed imaginary seemed equally skilled in carpentry, anticipating its real's every need. These were no mere playmates; they were companions in the truest sense.

The sights astounded Otter even as they sowed doubt in her mind. *If everyone who comes to the Farm can get such perfect imaginaries*, she wondered with unease, *why shouldn't my journey end here? Why should I even keep going?* A darker thought flitted across her mind. *And what if I really am a loner? If I leave without an imaginary, will I have missed my only chance?*

The many reals and imaginaries along the way barely noticed the approaching group, looking up only briefly at the sight of the newcomers Whipley was leading toward the house. Otter realized that these people must see countless unfamiliar faces make this same trek from the gate, loners who had all come here with the same purpose and expectation.

Otter brought her attention back to the path ahead and noticed the figure of a woman standing on the house's broad, whitewashed porch. Unlike the many people and exotic creatures that paid the three of them no heed, the woman watched them intently as they approached. A mass of writhing blackness weaved around the woman's lower legs. With a start, Otter realized that the undulating mass was alive, a creature as attached to the woman as her own clothing. Unlike Otter, the woman seemed utterly unalarmed by the creature's contortions.

Otter shook off her astonishment and lifted her eyes to better see the woman who stood so plainly in command of that porch. Coal-black hair was pulled back from her face in a ponytail, into which flecks of gray seemed to have crept at odd intervals. She was dressed for work: a blue flannel shirt was tucked smartly into her rugged canvas trousers, which were themselves tucked into the high tops of black rubber boots, as though she had just come from cleaning a stable. A pretty blue gem, uncut but polished, dangled from a hoop in the woman's left ear, the only adornment on her person seeming to serve no practical function. Her sun-darkened face bore a kindly expression beneath knitted brows, and her gently angled eyes conveyed curious intensity, as though she was looking not merely *at* the newcomers but *into* them.

Whipley strode up to the woman, who bent down slightly to hear his whispered news. But she never took her eyes off Otter and Melvin.

Being accustomed to bad things following from undue attention, Otter grew anxious under the woman's gaze, despite its warmth. She suppressed the urge to run—to where she had no idea—and did her best to return the intense gaze.

When they were close enough to the porch to be heard without shouting, the woman's unfathomable expression parted to reveal a broad, welcoming smile that had been waiting behind it, as white clouds will reveal the sun's glow when a summer wind pushes them aside. "Welcome," she said, her voice soft and clear. "I'm Luna." At these words, the mass at her feet untangled itself from her and raised its glittering black reptilian form around her body to join in regarding the company from her shoulders. As the creature displayed itself in this manner and stretched out its thin but expansive wings with a yawn, Otter realized it was a small dragon. In her surprise, a small, nearly inaudible squeak escaped unbidden from her mouth.

Whipley spoke next. "If you don't need anything else, Luna, I'll head back to the gate." Their guide then spared a final suspicious glance for his two wards before turning to leave.

Luna smiled warmly at Whipley's retreating form. "Give Bridget my best."

Pausing to look back at the woman on the porch, Whipley returned her smile with a blushing, mustachioed grin before turning to depart once more.

Otter and Melvin were left alone with this stranger. *Well,* Otter silently mused, with one wary eye firmly on Luna's creature, *as alone as you can be on a farm surrounded by a small army of people and their imaginaries.*

Luna turned her attention from Whipley back to her two new guests. "We don't often see visitors in groups unless they're family." She cast a glance at Melvin so slight that Otter was unsure whether she'd imagined it. "Spending life ostracized as *loners* may be the reason. But you two don't look much like family." This sounded more a question than a statement. "What brings you here together?"

Luna's comment reminded Otter of how different she looked from most other people she met, and she thought how this had rarely occurred to her before leaving the factory. Life outside those confines had left her more self-conscious and reticent than usual. Luckily, Melvin was eager to step in.

"I'm here to see *you*. And Otter here is a friend I met along the way." He looked down at Otter, and the girl saw in his expression that he had not missed the comment or its significance. A gentle squeeze from his hand to hers seemed to transfer some of his vigor to her, restoring her confidence. She returned her eyes to Luna, straightening her back and squaring her shoulders.

Nodding as Melvin spoke, Luna arched one eyebrow on hearing they'd met along the way. When he had finished, she squinted at Otter and seemed to examine her more closely, as though discovering within the girl something new and unexpected. "And you are here to see me too?" Doubt colored the question.

Otter did as many children do when strangers speak to them and silently drew nearer the one person present whom she knew. Melvin placed his arm around Otter's shoulders and gently pulled her closer to his side. "She's with me," he said stiffly.

Luna squinted, frowning slightly while she probed the two of them with her eyes as if working through a difficult problem. The creature at her side had lost interest in the newcomers and wrapped itself sleepily around Luna's shoulders like a shawl even as the woman's gaze intensified. Then, shaking the stern expression from her face, Luna smiled again, the clouds once more parting before the sun. "Yes," she murmured. "So I've heard." And with a sudden clap that startled both Otter and Melvin but had no effect whatsoever on the sleeping dragon, she said: "Well, let's not lose the whole day. Shall we go in?" Her feet liberated from the dragon's coils, she turned and went through the house's front door, leaving the visitors only a moment to decide between following and waiting outside by themselves.

They hesitated for only a few heartbeats, exchanging bemused looks, before shrugging and then jogging to catch up to their host.

The house had looked large from the outside; inside, it was enormous. High ceilings soared above wide chambers and long passages that interconnected so that everywhere in the house seemed to lead to everywhere else. Steep stairways spiraled to unseen heights and depths.

Wide-eyed, Otter and Melvin followed the fading sound of Luna's voice as she led them haphazardly through the corridors. At one point, they thought they'd lost her after she ascended a towering flight of stairs, but they found her again by peeking down another long hallway lined in doors. She stood there smiling, a ring of keys jingling from her delicate fingers.

"This will be your room, Melvin." Luna looked at the young man and then down at the girl beside him, still clutching his hand. "Ordinarily our guests have rooms to themselves." She raised an inquiring eyebrow. "But we can make an exception if you'd both like to stay together."

"Together," they replied in unison, Otter for once finding words just as quickly as Melvin. "Please," she meekly added.

Again, the woman's smile came, and Otter felt her anxiety crack beneath such vivid happiness. "Of course," Luna said. "Someone will be by soon to set up a second bed. Otter," she said, squatting so that her eyes were level with the girl's, "I was hoping for a few minutes of your time. Alone, if that's okay with both of you."

A squeeze from Melvin's hand awakened Otter to the viselike grip with which her own fingers clutched her companion—although if Otter was hurting him, Melvin gave no indication. She returned the woman's gaze, looking intently into eyes that seemed to twinkle with obvious and genuine kindness. The dragon languidly raised its head for a moment, flicking Luna's earring with its tongue before returning to its torpid repose and hiding its head beneath one wing.

Slowly Otter peeled her hand from Melvin's and looked up at him with a nervous smile. "I'll be okay," she said, and stepped closer to Luna, who departed, strolling down the long hallway as if expecting to be followed. Otter did so, and Melvin stood in the doorway to their room, following Luna and Otter with a concerned look as they slowly departed in the company of Luna's sleeping dragon.


Passage after passage, the pair walked. Their stroll took them past occasional entryways to vaulted rooms eclectically decorated. Woman and child said nothing for several minutes, and Otter was just beginning to wonder whether something was wrong when Luna broke the silence.

"Many people come here for a friend. You may be the first to already have that friend on arrival." She looked down intently but kindly at her young walking companion, as though wishing to gauge the girl's response.

Otter made none.

Luna continued without notice. "Like anyone else, you are welcome to stay as long as you care to. But I would prefer to know whether you want my . . ." She paused, and the moment swelled with unspoken meaning. ". . . my *services*," she concluded.

Otter didn't know what to say. What would happen if she declined Luna's services? Why did Luna want to know?

Luna's look of concern melted again into her radiant smile. "I can see that trust is going to be a challenge," she said under her breath, as though to the dragon draped like a boa across her shoulders, but just loud enough for Otter to hear. "Let me tell you a little about me and what I do. Maybe you'll feel safer confiding in me once you know me a bit better." She looked to the girl for a response and, upon seeing the slightest affirmative nod, began.

"My family has lived on this farm for as long as anyone remembers. I do not know when we first settled this land, but my parents and grandparents told me we came when Oakwood Forest still covered nearly everything in this region, providing us a place to live without the fear of persecution for our differences."

Again Luna paused. Otter's eyebrows raised at the last words, prompting Luna to continue.

"Polys have not always been welcome in Industriopa, even though many of us are born here, and always have been, to my knowledge. Before Industriopa became obsessed with the business of production, polys—like loners—were ostracized as unnatural or even evil. But we're just people like you or Melvin, despite our differences.

"And so our family fled to the forest, where the commerce and people of Industriopa seldom intruded until recent years. With the help of our many imaginaries, we built a sanctuary. But that's not to say we never saw outsiders, or that those we saw were all bad. Travelers came this way from time to time, and we have always welcomed those who meant us no harm. Word spread of a safe place where all were admitted in peace, and the numbers of curious travelers increased. Inevitably, some were loners."

Otter chewed her lip thoughtfully as their conversation took them around the house's wide halls. Although large, the manor was not as enormous as Otter had originally thought, and she soon realized she was seeing some spaces again as she and Luna meandered through the maze of hallways weaving in and out of one another throughout the house's second floor.

Looking up at the walls that banked them, she noticed for the first time the framed images of smiling people paired with what Otter assumed were their imaginaries. People of all shapes and sizes beamed from the frames. Their smiling imaginaries possessed even more shapes and sizes still. Otter was fascinated by their intense variety. She noted with curiosity that, whatever their variety, none of the humans had skin that looked like hers. *I wonder why*, she thought as she leaned in to more closely examine one of the images.

Luna noticed the girl's attention on the pictures. "Each of these is a picture of someone, a loner, who came here and found a friend. From every walk of life, from every corner of Industriopa, they have come. Once the Farm's reputation spread, the only visitors who came were loners looking for help. And," she added through a mouth that had taken a sour turn, "those who came to stamp out what they saw as our unnatural activities. That sort is looking for trouble, and they invariably find it. We are peaceful, but we are also well protected."

After a moment's pause, Otter spoke up for the first time. "So no one ever comes here for anything else."

Luna's smile returned undiminished. "Well, not in a long while, anyway. At least, that is, until today."

Heat rose in Otter's cheeks. "Why do you say that? How would you know why I'm here?"

"I guess I don't know for sure. But having done what I do for so long, I have a pretty good sense of who is looking for my services. And"—she arched one eyebrow slyly—"when asked, you told us you were here for your traveling companion."

Otter smiled despite herself. "That's right, although that doesn't mean I'm not also looking for my imaginary." The statement sounded small as Otter's soft voice tinkled like chimes off the corridor's broad walls.

"I suppose that's true," Luna answered, and the pause grew pregnant with what she left unspoken.

The flush grew on Otter's cheeks. "Do you think you could really give me the perfect imaginary?"

Luna stopped and turned to look hard at the young girl, who felt as though the young woman's gaze pierced her soul. "I suppose I could," she finally said, slowly articulating each word. "If that's what you really want."

Otter responded with equal deliberation, "I don't know that I can get what I'm looking for from someone else."

Luna nodded as though her suspicions were confirmed, sighing deeply. "Neither do I," she answered with a sense of candid finality.

They walked again in silence, the pictures of Luna's satisfied visitors passing by in succession. One portrait in particular caught Otter's eye, its subject's beady eyes staring down in near ecstasy over a familiar bulbous nose. Beside the owner of the domineering proboscis, a tall insectile form smiled in equal elation, its countenance coordinating precisely with that of its mate. Otter stopped in her tracks to further inspect the perfectly matched pair, the loud, matching bow ties beneath their chins captivating her attention.

Luna noticed. "Do you know them?"

Otter hesitated a moment before responding, "Yes, I know them," she said, still staring at the surprisingly happy visage of her longtime tormentor, Mr. Pickle, beside his imaginary, Greeble. "They, um, worked with me in Junkton."

"Yes," Luna said thoughtfully. "I remember them too. Years ago, Pickle came here, as many loners do. Alone and insecure, his dream was for an imaginary who would make him feel important. Unfortunately, he left before I could ensure the fit of his imaginary. I hope it was a good one. But sometimes it takes a while to get every piece into place with a new pair."

Otter looked at her host in mild astonishment.

Luna laughed. "Do you think I'd force them to stay?" Her gaze remained kind but was also piercing, and it disconcerted the girl. Unfazed, Luna continued, "People come and go pretty much as they please here. We lack the manpower to hold the uninterested against their will *and* secure our perimeter, all while trying to make and sustain a happy community. Pickle came to us alone; he left with Greeble. And life went on. But . . ." She paused. "I thought we were discussing *you*."

Otter hadn't exactly been thinking of keeping anyone against their will. But remembering the steady stream of abuse she'd suffered at that pair's hands, she struggled to understand how someone like Luna could have been responsible for the likes of Greeble.

She changed the subject. "When you give someone an imaginary, does it stay connected to you?"

A small frown turned the corner of Luna's mouth as she absently caressed the dragon head resting on her shoulder. "Yes, for a time. But imaginaries need presence to remain connected to our existence. Over time, healthy bonding creates a new connection. This happens fastest when the imaginary and its new real leave the Farm. But it happens regardless. One day, I wake up, and the bond is gone. I feel its absence, but the imaginaries don't seem to notice. After the bond breaks, they actually seem more at peace and satisfied, as though liberated. Some have stayed here long after their pairing, and I have had to bury many reals and imaginaries I brought together. With the bond gone between me and the imaginaries, their lives are no longer tethered to mine, so they expire when their adopted reals die . . ." Luna's voice cracked faintly as her explanation trailed off.

Otter looked at Luna from the corner of her eyes. Otter could not guess the woman's age from her smooth face. She did not seem young, exactly. But hers didn't seem a face that had seen enough years to talk now of burying so many friends. It was a sad thought, nonetheless, and Otter was keen to change the subject.

"Is this one"—she gestured toward the creature cloaking Luna's shoulders—"your own imaginary, then?"

The vibrant smile returned. "That's right. Midnight is the only imaginary on the Farm who truly belongs with *me*. We've been together since I was quite young, and I've never felt the need for another."

The older woman's feet began to move again, and Otter spared one final glance at Pickle's smiling portrait before following. As she pulled even with Luna, Otter asked, "But why do you need to know whether I also want your, um, services?"

"What I do for the Farm's visitors comes naturally," Luna replied. "But it doesn't come easily. Neither in the act of creating another imaginary nor in reaching a point with a prospective real that I can properly tailor the imaginary. Each act of imagining takes a toll on me—mentally, spiritually, and physically. When I was younger, it was easier, and I could imagine three or four times a week. Now I'm lucky if I can imagine once in that span. Luckily, that's usually more than the actual demand for what I do. Even so, each imagining requires me to rest and recover, so scheduling newcomers is important."

She searched Otter for comprehension, and she continued upon finding it in the girl's eyes.

"That's not the only reason. Creating an imaginary that will properly bond with a surrogate real requires me to spend significant time with the surrogate. I get to know each one through observation, working and living side by side for a time, and by creating a bond between us, not unlike the bond

I create to a new imaginary that I will eventually pass on to the surrogate. The process takes time, and it requires effort. Before you, no one came to me for a friend they already had, so every new arrival has had to be accounted for in time and effort, to ensure that everyone—including me—is properly taken care of. You are a new arrival. I need to take account. And that is why," she said, exhaling heavily and earning an annoyed look from Midnight slumbering on her shoulder, "I need to know what you came here expecting from me." A shadow of sternness flitted across her voice as she concluded, but an apologetic smile followed her final words, softening their impact.

Otter nibbled at her lower lip as she looked within herself for a proper response. She found it more quickly than she'd expected.

"Thank you, Luna," she said, drawing her shoulders back and straightening her spine, much as Melvin had done when he announced his intentions to Whipley at the gate. "I'm here for Melvin. If you'll let me, I'd like to stay for a little while. But then I'll have to keep going."

A muted echo of Otter's pronouncement bounced back at the two of them, and Luna looked at Otter for a long time after silence had resettled between them. Finally, she nodded slightly and spoke. "I suspected as much, Otter." Then her smile returned, warming the girl and brightening the hallway. "As I said, you are welcome to stay as long as you wish. When you are ready to leave, you can do so with our blessings."

Looking up at Luna, Otter smiled in spite of her natural suspicion. She had found a true friend in Melvin. She was trying to trust that she could find another in Luna.

Luna's eyes twinkled with patient understanding. She slowly raised her arm toward Otter and extended her hand, palm upward, to the girl, who looked repeatedly between Luna's hand and face before her own hand rose to lace her fingers between those of her host. Then, without saying another word, they turned and began walking the hall again toward the room where they'd left Melvin, while Midnight snored gently from her perch.

When they arrived, Otter quietly thanked Luna for letting her stay and told her that she'd be happy to help with work around the Farm if Luna liked.

Luna laughed. "We aren't accustomed to having children work here, but I won't stop you if you feel compelled. We seldom have young children visit us, but when we do, they spend most of their time wandering around and playing. As long as you aren't in the way as we work, you can enjoy free rein of the Farm. We have plenty here, and you're welcome to what we have. And we are friendly folk, so I suspect many of us would like to meet such a strong young woman as you."

Otter suppressed her shock at the suggestion that she was a "young woman," but Luna's words warmed the girl's insides, and she smiled again.

"Such a pretty smile," Luna cooed as she extracted her long pale fingers from Otter's shorter brown digits. "I'm going now to check on the kitchen. We normally dine together, so I hope we'll see you and Melvin in the dining hall this evening. In the meantime, you might enjoy exploring what we have here. Wild berry thickets hedge the Farm on all sides. You can also join some of the younger imaginaries who like to play in the field behind the house when their work is done. And, of course, there's the library on the third floor."

Otter's eyes grew wide at Luna's words. She thought back to her cherished *Surviving in the Wilderness* and the pitiful "library" lying largely unused in her quarters at the Home. Luna did not seem the kind who would keep a library of that sad sort.

"Did you say 'the library'?"

~ CHAPTER 7 ~

# A CARELESS STEP

STRANDS OF BLOOMING grass swayed defiantly in an unrepentant summer breeze and tickled Otter's feet as she lay panting on the ground where she'd collapsed. Otter had found the field in one of the Farm's seldom-visited outlying stretches. From her vantage on the ground, the unshorn grass carpeted and curtained the field, framing the sapphire-blue sky and the occasional wisp of cloud above her in the waves of the field's green sea.

Beside her, a bellowing yawn erupted, and Otter giggled in response. "Tired?" she asked, even as she allowed her eyelids to slowly close against the vivid sky. She wasn't tired, she told herself; she just wanted to rest her eyes.

Melvin smacked his lips lazily, and his baritone voice, slower than usual, answered, "Little kids always have too much energy."

Otter smiled at his good-natured teasing, and she reached over to take Melvin's hand in her own. The two of them lay there without speaking for several minutes until Otter overcame gravity and lifted her head out of the grass so she could see her friend.

"Melvin," she began, a worried quaver betraying her voice even to her own ears.

Melvin heard it too. He lifted his head to meet his young friend's gaze. "What is it, Otter?"

"I have to go soon." Nearly three months on the Farm had filled the hollowness of her chestnut cheeks and erased some of the strain from around her eyes. She had spent weeks on end roaming the Farm's expansive grounds with Melvin, or cloistered in Luna's library, poring over everything from fantastic tales and whimsical poems to great, thick novels and tomes on every subject ever deemed worthy of print in Industriopa, and on every continent of Imbria besides. In a few short months, she had chartered a worldwide voyage, with the printed page as her ship, taking her from the mysterious land of Chimerica with its secretive and dark-skinned spiritualists, through Fidelia where people worshipped imaginaries like gods, and all the way to the austere hermit continent of Pragmatica, where it was said imaginaries endured in bondage, created only to serve, never to be free. And eating—Otter had fed her belly almost as much as her mind, and her culinary horizons had greatly expanded in the process.

Otter now felt better—in every way—than she ever had. Yet she also felt the pull of her quest grow stronger and more persistent with each day that passed, even as she spoke of it less and less. The longer she stayed, she knew, the harder it would be to finally leave again. The last few days had tested her resolve, and she lay awake at nights weighing the memory of her mission against her newfound friends and comfort. She knew she must depart soon or forever lose the will to do so.

"Already?" He sat upright and spread his arms as if to present her with the entire Farm as a reason to wait. "But we've only just gotten here. Maybe another week or two to prepare?" Despite the question in his voice, his eyes confessed to knowing the futility of his words.

"I *am* prepared, Melvin," she softly said, retracting her hand, her eyes more serious than any Melvin had ever before seen in a child. Any child besides Otter, that is. "I have been for weeks. You know that," she finished in barely a whisper.

Melvin exhaled with a sigh, knowing the girl was right. He turned his eyes away from her and toward the horizon. Just as Otter began to wonder whether he would speak again, the question came, soft and low: "Where will you go?"

"I've talked to Luna, and she thinks I should go north and east. I'll have to cut through a long stretch of forest to stay off the road a bit longer. But she says I'll find a newer road beyond the woods that will lead to a port city. The city is far enough from Junkton that Luna thinks I won't have to worry about being seen. I figure I'll stay there for a time to see what imaginaries in the city are like. After that . . ."

"After that—*what*?" Melvin pried.

"After that, I don't know. I've thought about crossing the sea. But I haven't decided yet."

Melvin said nothing. When Otter looked to see whether his face betrayed his thoughts, she found only her friend's concern.

"Otter," he finally said with a sigh of resignation. "I won't try to stop you. But you need to be careful. You are so mature, and you've seen so much, that I sometimes forget you're still a child. I think *you* forget too," he added, raising his hand firmly to cut off her protest before it could interrupt him. "So all I ask is that you be careful." He stared at her for another moment as though daring her to argue. Then he lowered his hand, his piece now said.

Feeling her eyes begin to sting, Otter wiped the wetness from them with the back of her hand. She tried to speak, but the tightness in her throat choked her voice. She closed her eyes and inhaled deeply to regain control, and when she had done so, she said, "Thank you for everything, Melvin. I left Junkton so I could have the perfect friend." She paused for a moment, the choking sensation nearly rising again as though it had merely been waiting for the girl's guard to lower. "You are the first friend I've ever had. And you will be very hard to top." She surged forward and embraced her friend tightly, catching him off guard and nearly knocking him over. When she released him, his eyes were wet as well.

Luna was awaiting them when they returned. The flagging sun's dim red glow stretched their softened shadows into the distance, and the crickets had taken up their chirping call-and-response all around them.

As Otter and Melvin neared the porch where Luna leaned with her languid imaginary dragon, Midnight, taking its usual position about her shoulders, the older woman smiled at them and waved. Even in the failing light, that smile seemed to brighten the world around it, as though adding another moon to the dusky sky.

"You missed dinner," she chided with a playful wink.

"We took food with us," Melvin responded. A patch of dried stickiness on his cheek strained against the movement of his mouth as he spoke, alerting him to its presence. "And, um, we got a snack from the orchard and berry patches," he mumbled sheepishly as his hand worked to wipe the evidence from his face.

Luna's smile grew wider and brighter still at Melvin's confession. The smile turned to bear on Otter and wavered a little as the woman regarded the girl before her. "I suppose you have said what you needed to?"

Otter nodded, tight-lipped.

"Are you still determined to leave tomorrow?"

Another nod.

Luna's chest heaved with a resigned sigh. "I suspected you would be, although we will be sad to see you go." The draped dragon briefly raised her head to scan the group of them before flopping back into place, silently announcing its apathy. Luna tapped its nose with a finger in mock scorn. "Even you will miss her and the late-night snacks she sneaks you, Midnight." Midnight snorted almost imperceptibly and retreated beneath the cowl of its wings. Otter felt an invisible flush rise in the skin of her chestnut nose.

"So you knew her plan?" The hurt was plain in Melvin's voice.

Luna met his look squarely but apologetically. "It wasn't for me to tell you."

Luna and Melvin stared at each other in silence for a moment. Melvin chewed the inside of his cheek as though physically holding back words in his mouth, but he said nothing, and the tension between them grew.

Otter cleared her throat, severing the taut silence and drawing the adults' attention back to her. "I have a lot to plan before tomorrow." She was embarrassed for having upset Melvin, and her toe scribbled in the dust, betraying her unease, even as her gaze remained steady. "I could use your help." She looked up at Melvin pointedly and took his hand again. "*Both* of you."

Melvin blinked as though remembering where he was, and he seemed to release his ire with a sigh. "Of course, Otter." The sad tone in Melvin's rich baritone was unmistakable, but he smiled for her sake.

Once Otter and Melvin had changed and cleaned up from their day outdoors, they all reconvened in Luna's parlor. From mugs of hot cocoa, steam rose toward the room's vaulted ceiling and the ornate scenes of exotic creatures and plants that long-forgotten hands carved. A fire crackled on the hearth, casting a flickering glow onto the bookshelves lining the walls and the map spread before the three humans. Midnight had undertaken the unusual step of extricating herself from Luna's shoulders to lay sprawled in front of the fireplace, her scaled legs splayed in the air, her tongue lolling from her mouth, and her belly turned toward the heat of the flame. If the words exchanged over the map reached her warm repose, Midnight gave no indication.

"How many days until I'm out of the forest again?"

"Of course, it will depend on your pace," Luna cautioned. "But I would expect you to take no more than a week to reach Harborton." Her fingertip came down over a point on the map to the north and east of the Farm. "We can provision you for longer than that, and . . ." Luna paused, uncertainty flitting across her face before retreating from her familiar vibrant smile. The woman reached into the pocket of her overalls and deposited a small canvas pouch on the table. It jingled with the impact. "And you will be able to replenish for a while, at least, with this."

Otter's eyes widened at the sound of coins. "Luna, thank you, but I don't—"

Luna's raised hand cut the girl off. "It's a loan only. I expect you to repay me in full when you return, whenever that may be." Her tone was firm, but her radiant smile tempered the curt pronouncement, making its generosity plain.

"Thank you, Luna." Otter lifted the small purse to pull it closer, and its compact weight surprised her. She knew Luna assumed it to be a gift, despite her host's words. Otter did not know how, but she *would* find a way to pay Luna back. *Someday,* she thought.

But in the present, she needed to plan.

Following a red line on the map north through the network of forest footpaths, Otter would cross east over a small river where she could replenish her water after only a few days. She would finally reach Harborton a week or so later. Once there, Luna's scribbled list of names would guide her to people who would help her settle in for as long as she needed to. After Otter had thoroughly explored life in the city and its environs—*I'll deal with that when it happens*, she decided, pushing those thoughts aside for the time being.

"Remember, the forest is full of danger." The stern tone had not left Luna's voice. "You were lucky when you traveled on your own before. This time you need to be smart and careful too."

Otter's eyes rolled a little as her mouth opened to protest.

Luna would have none of it. "Yes, yes, I know about your outdated book and your obvious ingenuity. And you've done very well with little more than those. But listen, Otter. You have been free in the world for only a few months, and you spent most of them within my walls. I have spent almost my entire life in these woods, and the dangers can *swallow you whole. Literally.*" The steady tap of Luna's index finger thrusting into the heart of the map's flat forest emphasized the last of her words.

Otter gulped. "I understand." Her tone was sober, and Luna eventually relented in her grave glare with a nod.

"Good. Now, you've spent all day running about, and you'll need solid rest before you go. You head off to bed, and Melvin and I will go over your provisions one last time." Luna smiled, but her tone invited no discussion.

Otter had been through her supplies repeatedly, often with Melvin and Luna supervising. Leaning against the wall nearest to the door and farthest from the map, the pack stood nearly as tall as the girl and almost overflowed with hard bread, dried meat, cheese, and other trail-safe nourishment, to say nothing of her other hiking and camping supplies. Still, Otter understood how uneasy Luna and Melvin were with her decision, and they displayed their concern by looking over her shoulder and helping as much as they could. They were, Otter realized, the closest thing she'd ever had to parents. "Thank you," she said, as she embraced them each in turn. "And good night. Luna's right. I'd better get some rest."

The three of them exchanged warm smiles, and Otter made her exit, her tired feet shuffling as though to foreclose any denial of her exhaustion. The hushed tones of her friends' worried whispers followed her down the hall before fading to inaudible nothings.

A hazy red glow illuminated the Farm, glittering from the spires of the entry gate and onto a small army of people and assorted imaginary creatures that had gathered at dawn to see their young friend off. The crowd formed a rough semicircle around Otter, whose new pack, mounted on her back, reached above her head and occasionally threatened to topple her with its heft. The awkwardness of her burden only increased as she made her rounds of thanks and farewell, with every other hand containing some small token of friendship needing to be tucked into her overstuffed belongings. She tried to remind herself that her pack would get lighter along the way, and that she should be grateful for her bulging supplies—and for the friendships contributing to that bulge. She was largely successful.

After the procession of handshakes and hugs stood Luna. "It will have been a lot to go through if you say yes, but I want to remind you one last time that you are welcome to stay here." Luna's smile put the sunrise to shame, but her eyes carried a sadness uncommon for them.

"I know, Luna. And thank you. Thank you for everything."

Luna nodded in resignation and spread her arms wide. When Otter finally withdrew from the woman's embrace, both of them wiped wetness from their faces. Luna's lip trembled and Otter sniffled loudly as they shared a lingering final look.

"You're always welcome here, Otter. If you change your mind in fifteen minutes or just decide you miss us in fifteen years, you'll still be welcome. Don't ever forget that."

A grateful smile was her answer, and it was enough.

Now only Melvin remained. For a moment, he and the small friend he'd met by accident along his way stood silent, exchanging looks laden with unsaid and unsayable things. Then Otter lunged forward to embrace the young man, nearly bowling him over and eliciting a sharp "Oof!" from the impact, echoing how Otter first crashed into Melvin's life only a few months earlier.

"It's not too late to change your mind," he whispered.

"Thank you for being my friend," she replied. She stepped back and exchanged a sad smile with the young man, both of their cheeks streaked with tears.

The sound of a pragmatic throat clearing interrupted the moment, delivering Otter back to the present and the journey ahead. "If you hope to stay on schedule and arrive at your first campsite by nightfall, you probably need to get moving." Luna's tone dropped. "Unless you'd like to reconsider your schedule," she finished wryly.

Delay was no longer an option. A day would become a week, and a week a month, until eventually Otter's quest became only a memory, a story of what could have been for her to tell in her old age. That image in her mind, she set her jaw and turned to the audience of friends assembled to see her off. "Goodbye," she said, waving. "I'll miss you all." The gate swung slowly open, and Otter departed, not daring to look back until after she heard the creak and clang of the gate shutting her out of the Farm.

And with that, Otter was out in the wilderness again.

When she escaped the factory, Otter had kept a swift pace, her negligible belongings adding almost nothing to her load, and her bright spirits counteracting her empty belly. Leaving the Farm, her belly and supplies were once more balanced, now because both were full. But the weight of her supplies also matched that of her spirits, and the beginning of this new chapter of her journey found Otter plodding painstakingly along, her feet slowed by the heaviness on her back and in her heart.

Many of the doubts she'd had on entering the Farm's gate seemed to have been waiting for her there. Now they returned uninvited to haunt her with what she had just left behind. These ghostly memories were a poor substitute for the traveling companion she'd left behind on the Farm.

A slight pang gnawed her heart at the thought of leaving Melvin behind. Although she rarely thought of it, Otter was suddenly quite aware of how small and young she was to be out in the world alone. When she'd first gone out on her own, the factory stood behind her, its grim menace making small deterrents of her youth and the journey's perils. Now she was leaving a comfortable home, dozens of kind reals and imaginaries, and Melvin. Traveling with Melvin was the first time she'd ever felt safe. Yet here she was, by herself again.

Making camp the first night was nothing like the other nights she'd spent traveling alone. Shelter, fire, and food were all simple matters with her heavy pack providing everything she needed, although she would need more water before long. The sun had not fully disappeared by the time Otter had assembled a tiny camp at the site she'd planned with Luna, and she was holding her hands toward the flame crackling discreetly in front of her tent. She alternated absent nibbles between a wedge of bread and the supple cheese from the cows Otter had sometimes milked alongside her friends at the Farm.

That night she slept uneasily as she tried to tune out the sounds of the forest. The animal noises she had heard early in her voyage had returned, although nothing disturbed her tent.

She woke poorly rested in the morning to the singing of birds frisking in the branches above her. She ate in silence and then broke her camp, dousing the last embers of her breakfast fire under the same birds, now silently swooping flecks in the sky. Her things squeezed once more into her pack, Otter thought of the animal sounds and the lonely road ahead and sighed. She lowered her pack and removed her tiny knife, which she placed into the pocket of her new breeches.

The tall trees that had crowded her path since she'd entered the woods still occupied much of her vision as she picked her way dutifully along the route she'd plotted with Luna and Melvin. Rare was the trunk so short or inclined that she could shimmy up and harvest the lumpy bounty of specterines on its branches. But with summer wearing away during her time on the Farm, the specterines, which had ripened along with the season, grew more susceptible to gravity. With the seasons advancing, she now found the occasional fruit freshly fallen, and she made a point of collecting the windfall and eating it as she walked. Wiping sweet specterine juice before it dribbled from her chin, Otter recalled with embarrassment how she had thought specterines to be some common, familiar fruit when she first saw them clustered at the top of the tree she'd climbed to survey the terrain ahead on Dirt Road. She was sure she'd never had them before her journey began, but she'd had them many times since.

Within five days of resuming her journey, Otter had settled into a routine. Each day she rose, ate, broke camp, and walked, stopping only as necessary to fetch an item tucked deep in the mass of her pack, to eat when she grew hungry, or to rest.

Then one day, the path forked.

Straddling the fork, Otter squinted through the morning haze down each of the divergent paths. The map in her hand crinkled gently in the breeze. *This isn't supposed to be here*, she thought.

The two paths ran roughly north, making her map useless from ground level. But even from her view, Otter could see that the forest quickly grew into a wall between the paths, necessitating a choice between them.

Her pack struck the earth with a thud. She squatted and took a seat on the pack. The map, unfolded to its full unwieldy expanse, quivered in the breeze as Otter examined its details and contemplated her choice. No matter how hard she stared at the map, or how long she stared down the mist hovering above two routes where one should have been, Otter could not discern which one she and her friends had intended her to take.

Dull dread began to creep up her spine, reminiscent of the fear that had marked much of her prior travels alone.

Steeling herself, she stood and heaved her pack back onto her shoulders. She approached the fork for a closer inspection, map still in hand.

The left-hand path bore signs of neglect. Tufts of fluff-topped seeding weeds and islands of tall grasses dotted its uneven floor, with potholes interrupting what little of the bare surface remained. Daylight barely penetrated the thick boughs overhanging the path, leaving the irregular surface poorly lit. It was, to Otter's eyes, uninviting. And although she was now heading north, she knew from Luna that she would have to cross a river eastward, and the left path was the more western route, even if not by much.

The other way could not have been more different. Squinting down the long, straight path, Otter found a hard-packed surface, clear of vegetation save for a thin layer of leaves and occasional fallen branches. The trees seemed to recede from the path as though trimmed or trained away from it. Sunlight bathed it in warmth. And it was nearer the east, where she needed to go eventually, although she had no way of knowing whether it was better to head eastward now or later.

She studied the map again, hoping an answer would reveal itself to her. It did not. But the map *did* tell her that another day's travel should lead her to the river crossing. And so assuming that the wrong path would eventually either converge with the correct one or veer into a wrong direction, and that either eventuality would prove the virtue of her choice with only a day or so lost, she chose the path to the right, with its more hospitable conditions, and tried to bury her misgivings at this unexpected dilemma.

Her choice gave her reason to be confident. The late afternoon sun shined down on her, warming her as she walked. The forest lining her way danced half-heartedly in the shifting breeze, tickling her nose with the scents of an autumn that was soon to be. Not even a bird interrupted Otter's view of the clear blue sky.

In fact, Otter realized, this was the first time in her travels she'd heard no birdsongs accompanying the soft but steady cadence of her gait. She had perhaps never in her life encountered a place so serene and free of distraction, and she took full advantage of the moment to become lost in thought.

Her thoughts led wistfully to the friends she had left behind. To her surprise, although she missed Melvin most, it was Luna's face that occupied her mind. Luna's offer to provide her with home, family, and an imaginary came again and again to the girl as she walked. The thought that she had been foolish to decline such generosity rose and receded in her like an internal tide. She built dams in her heart against that tide, yet it always returned. *Can I really hope to find better than the Farm, Luna, and Melvin?* she wondered sadly.

She also thought of the factory. Otter seldom thought of her old home—if one could call it that—in Junkton. When she did, it was with great relief for her escape from her wicked antagonists, the ceaseless work, and the trauma of constant vigilance against the mortal dangers of toiling in the factory. But this time was different. Now her thoughts turned to the children she had left behind, and how their torment and terror continued even as she had gone on to adventure and something akin to fulfillment. Otter wondered who had taken her place on the factory floor and whether her replacement was savvy and experienced enough to last for a while. These thoughts fed a desperate, growing hollowness inside her, and she could imagine nothing sufficient to fill it as long as children toiled in the prison she'd escaped. Someday, she vowed to herself, she would return to the factory to end its evil industry and set its young captives free. *Someday*, she thought sadly, *but not today.*

The setting sun signaled an end to the day's journey, interrupting her melancholy musings. The forest beside the path was too dense for her to hide her tent, so she set her pack down upon the hard-packed ground and reluctantly began to pitch her camp on the path's right margin.

She ate enough to make her belly comfortably full, but not too full, before entering her tent for the night. Sparing a final wary glance from the tent's entrance, she shut out the sinking red sun and sealed herself within the tiny structure's thin walls. Her compact sleeping bag offered more comfort than anything she'd improvised before meeting Melvin, and she snuggled down into its warmth, shutting her eyes against the day's dying light.

Yet even before night had snuffed the final rays of day, her eyes flashed open in terror as a familiar noise invaded the tent. The savage animal sounds that had haunted her early in her journey returned, louder and closer than ever, seeming at times to come from right outside her tent and from everywhere around it. At times, the fabric walls seemed to pulse with the invisible monsters' hot snuffling breaths.

Otter huddled inside her warm tent and sleeping bag, shivering with fear. She wondered whether the path she had chosen was the noisy beasts' home. She thought of the neatly cleared path, preternaturally silent, and the way the trees receded from it on all sides. And she imagined how giant clawed feet tramping up and down the way might have packed the surface down. Sobs racked her small body as she imagined what those claws could do to her too.

The small tent that had seemed cozy until now felt claustrophobic, reminding her of the cramped prison where Eliza had stuffed her to await being devoured by Desdemona. Panic rose in her throat, acrid and burning. As she had done from Eliza's cage, she worked to tamp her terror with the only method she knew: she formed a plan.

It was a dreadful plan, and as familiar to her at this point as the sounds outside. Lying awake, she again readied on the tip of her mind the most fearsome companion she could picture. That tingling she recalled from the nightmare of Eliza's cage began welling up in her again, and her toes wiggled with the odd sensation. Her mind suppressed it, holding it in balance between thought and flesh, as she prepared to bring her imaginary into being the instant anything from outside dared to try her tent.

But nothing did.

How long she'd lain there shivering and crying and tingling when the snarling, the scratching, and the pounding of feet began to wane, she couldn't say. At first, she didn't allow herself to believe it. When she was unable to deny her good fortune any longer, the sounds had fallen silent, and the filtered light of dawn began to imbue the tent's interior with a pale glow.

Otter lay for many minutes without moving, save for her subsiding sobs. Finally she found the courage to rise slowly from her bedding and peek her head through the flap. Squinting against the dawn's crisp rays, she inhaled a great draft of the silent morning air.

The path and forest outside were just as she'd left them, the disruption of the leafy carpet providing the only evidence that the prowling pack of nocturnal animals had ever been there.

Otter broke her camp in haste. Her belongings once more on her back, she left without eating even a bite. Breakfast could wait. Eating and walking was better than spending even an extra minute in this wretched place, she thought.

But which way to go? She had already come quite far down this path, and her map told her she could expect to find water in only a few more hours of walking, even at her normal speed. But Otter felt sure her lingering fears from the night would motivate a faster pace despite her exhaustion.

She decided to continue along the same path. She would forge ahead, refill her water, and backtrack to the other path all before nightfall. She would not spend another night on this one, in any event.

The nighttime noises had unveiled Otter's eyes. With her newfound clarity, she now saw signs of the ferocious creatures—whatever they were—everywhere. The tree limbs she had at first thought trimmed she now saw had been torn from the trees, their severed ends splintered and frayed. The hard-packed earth beneath her feet bore occasional gouges she now saw for claw marks. The forest's unnatural silence was now the loudest of warnings. Otter thought back to Luna's admonition and wondered how she had missed the obvious signs of danger all around her.

Shaking off these thoughts, she determined never to let hubris and carelessness lead her again into such danger.

By midmorning she had reached the river, right on schedule. It was wider than she'd expected. She had not known what to expect, though, having never seen a river herself, despite reading of them in her book. But reading had not prepared her for this mass of living, flowing water. The current was fast, rushing the edges of its confines as though testing them for somewhere to stage an escape. Swirling cataracts frothed opaquely at odd intervals beside the banks, but the water was otherwise clear enough to see the pebbles lying beneath it. Every thought since Otter had vacated her camp that morning had been a goad to greater speed, but the river held her captive in her tracks as her factory-raised mind worked to comprehend a thing of such power and beauty. Even her months on the Farm had not presented her with such raw natural majesty.

Recovering from her amazement, memories of her sleepless night and its cause urged her on, releasing her feet from awe's tight grip. Looking around, she squinted to examine the river and her environs with purpose.

The signs were the first things she noticed. Bright red paint slashed across planks affixed to the trees overhanging the river's far bank. At this distance, their message was little more than a blur. She considered crossing the river to get a closer look. And while she would gladly put the water between herself and last night's monsters, her survey of the shores revealed no way across the mighty stream. So she ignored the signs and focused on the task at hand. She had no time for messages addressed to the side of the river she could not reach. Perhaps she would find similar signs if she ever made her way across. But that would not happen here. The lack of a crossing here confirmed her fears: she had picked the wrong path, even aside from whatever monsters prowled here.

She wasted no more time. Laying her pack down, she gave her canteen a shake and heard its dwindling contents slosh hollowly within. She scurried to the riverbank, where she began delicately picking her way over smooth, slick rocks, careful not to slip or to douse her only shoes. She thought momentarily of the libertyslippers, whose magic would allow her to pass through water as well as any wall. But the precarious footing here made that prospect especially frightening, and she focused all the harder on choosing her steps with care.

The rocky shore quickly became an archipelago of tiny islands, increasingly isolated from one another, but connected by a loose network of roots radiating out from the trees that clung to the shore. Her strides grew long as she made her way in. By the time the river was deep enough to dip her canteen in, she dared go no farther. The wide river lapped with lazy hunger at her rocky perch.

Squatting, she placed the lip of her canteen below the crystalline surface. Startling coldness splashed over her hand and created tiny whirlpools of protest at being diverted from the river's ordinary course. She barely noticed. Her eyes scanned her surroundings with constant vigilance. Stooping on a rock surrounded by flowing water, she was exposed and vulnerable to whoever—or *whatever*—came her way. She looked impatiently at her canteen and wished its small mouth would admit the water faster.

The passing seconds and her swiveling gaze gave her occasion to observe her own reflection beside the canteen. She thought of her factory window and the dim reflection she had occasionally seen there. The Farm's many comforts included the occasional mirror, but habit kept her from looking too often at herself even there. The river flowing at her feet, with the sun's rays directly upon it, now presented Otter with the first chance to do so while she was traveling.

The face that looked back at her seemed almost unfamiliar now. Her hair, no longer pulled back in a severe ponytail, hung in tight curls around her head. Happy days and warm meals on the Farm had filled in the hollowness of her cheeks, which hours of leisure in the sun had darkened past their prior chestnut hue. Her clothes were still practical and plain like her former overalls, but they were newer and better fitting. And her eyes no longer bore the sadness she had not quite noticed before, despite the tight anxiety that now ringed their edges.

With a smile, Otter realized she looked almost like a new girl.

She shook off this satisfying distraction and returned her attention to the chore at hand. Her fear stretched the process to what felt like an hour, but the canteen was full in less than a minute, and Otter exhaled breath she had not realized she held as she capped the vessel tight. Slowly she stood to rotate and return to her things on the near bank. Having safely made her way in, she placed her first step back with more confidence, landing it upon one of the larger stone island steps, which was crisscrossed by arteries of thick roots.

Her confidence was misplaced. So was her step.

The thick roots promised purchase that the rock's slick surface belied. On planting her foot, it slid across the stone and twisted painfully beneath a thick root, where it stuck, pinning her foot at an awkward angle.

Otter's arms flailed in a vain effort to regain her lost balance, sending the canteen splashing into the river, which quickly carried it away. A moment of panic for her lost water fled as she attended to a more immediate concern. She had barely avoided falling into the current herself. Her foot was tightly wedged. The near fall had twisted her ankle painfully. Teetering on her regained footing, she stood as much as the rigid wet root would allow, wincing at the pain that throbbed in her contorted joint.

Concentrating, Otter closed her eyes and calmed herself with several deep breaths. Upon opening her eyes, she confirmed her foot's captivity and examined the woody bonds for a weakness that could allow her escape. Her focus faltered as her fear began to swell. Being stuck on the river was bad enough; being stuck out in the open where anything might come prowling was almost unbearable.

It didn't matter. Her examination revealed nothing useful about her foot's bindings. Bitterly she tried to blink away the moisture welling up in her eyes, but even that seemed futile.

Through her tears, she looked around her in the desperate hope that some means of extraction lay close at hand. She found nothing.

She did, however, notice that she was now within reading distance of the signs on the river's far side, a fact she had not recognized when filling her water.

Otter wished the signs were still too distant to read, because their messages carried a chill that dwarfed the water's cold bite:

DANGER!

GO BACK!

DO NOT CROSS!

By then, of course, it was too late.

# CHAPTER 8

# UNEXPECTED HELP

OF ALL THE places to be stuck, this seemed the worst: surrounded by water, on a path menaced by vicious creatures, and a stone's throw away from ominous warning signs.

Otter tried not to panic. She failed.

Frantically she twisted and yanked her foot, trying to pull it free from its living confines. Her foot was wedged too tight to wriggle it out of her shoe. Her eyes widened with momentary hope as she recalled the knife in her pocket. Sawing vigorously with her dearest traveling tool, she tried to cut the root away. But her hope imploded on contact with the thick living cord's unexpected durability. A sickening snap interrupted her desperate prying as the thin blade broke and arced majestically into the air before diving almost noiselessly into the current. Her mouth agape with voiceless despair, she stared after the broken blade, wondering why she had targeted the stout root instead of the thin canvas shoe. *Too late now*, she thought, as the blade and its many useful applications vanished beneath the water forever. Her failure to anticipate had come at a steep price.

Running her mind through the contents of her pockets and whatever options they provided, hopelessness engulfed her just as the river had engulfed the knife. Finding no effective options, she cried—equally without effect.

Hours passed this way, with Otter alternating from fruitless despair to reciting yet again the short litany of her available resources and futile options. She wondered how she could have allowed this to happen. How could she have been so careless?

Lunchtime came and went, and her stomach began to complain noisily. Her food was safe on shore. If only she could have said the same for herself. The angle of her bind prevented her from even sitting, and her leg, cramping from the strain of the constant contortion, ached in sympathy with the cramps in her hungry belly.

Otter looked anxiously to the sky and saw the sun in the latter half of its passage, announcing that night was now nearer than morning. And the night would bring dangers more pressing than hunger.

She tackled her bound foot with fresh resolve, and all her effort now fueled only that task and the angry muttering beneath her breath. Anger at her carelessness. Anger at her foolishness. Anger at her inability to escape the consequences of her misstep.

Her foot protested her work by throbbing painfully. The water's relentless splashing seemed to mock her: its untiring coolness relieved the growing heat in her foot even as it drew the canvas of her shoe tighter.

"What are you doing?"

The voice seemed to come from behind her. Otter froze. For an instant she thought she'd imagined the sound, a girl's voice, not her own, a trick her ears had played with the sound of her own low, frustrated vocalizations.

"Are you okay?"

This time Otter looked up, turning her torso around with difficulty to better see the source of the voice. What she saw surprised her.

Standing on the opposite shore was a girl, close to Otter in age, and with an eye-catching head of red curls. This new girl, this stranger, looked at Otter with wide-eyed horror, her complexion pale with fright. The new girl spoke again as Otter watched frozen and mute, her eyes confirming the source of the voice. "You shouldn't be here."

Otter straightened from her work to stand upright, twisting to face the new girl as best she could with her foot still bound between rock and root. She tried to ignore the water's taunts as it lapped at her captive extremity.

A moment of indecisive silence stretched between the girls and then passed, before Otter answered simply, "I'm stuck."

The new girl responded quickly, "But you shouldn't be here. Didn't you see the signs?" Her voice held an urgency that chilled Otter beyond anything the river's frigid water could.

Otter felt her cheeks flush, and she didn't know how to respond. Had this girl posted the signs? What was this girl doing in precisely the place the signs warned travelers to avoid? More worrisome still, what were her intentions now that Otter was stuck here? Knowing the answer to none of these questions, Otter reverted to her prior answer. "I'm stuck."

The new girl seemed no surer of how to respond to Otter's presence than Otter felt. She glanced at the sky with an exasperated sigh, her eyes narrowing with worry at what she observed there. Otter took no comfort in realizing that the two of them likely shared the same concern for the late hour. Although the afternoon sun still shone brightly on them both, it would soon take cover behind the treetops and cast girls, river, and path in shadow that would lengthen before sliding into twilight and then night.

The girl returned her gaze to Otter. "You have to turn around and go back. Now. You don't have much time."

"Until what?" Otter asked, fearing she already knew the answer. She saw no need to wait for it. "I can't go back. I'm stuck," she said again.

The new girl stared at her a moment longer and then set her jaw in a manner Otter was sure Melvin or Luna would readily have recognized on her own face. Without another word, the girl turned to her right and ran.

Puzzled and exasperated, Otter watched her go. Thinking the new girl had abandoned her as quickly as she'd appeared, Otter was surprised to see her stop a few meters down the shore, reach down into the layer of leaves that carpeted the forest floor, and seize a long wooden plank, which she dragged back to where she had first stood questioning Otter. Clearly the girl knew to find the board there, and it dawned on Otter that she must have hidden it in that spot.

Turning her back to Otter, the girl pulled the rough board out onto the river, picking her way expertly across the stones as though she'd memorized each one and bounded from shore to shore a million times over. Then she set the board down to create a narrow bridge from the riverbank to a large rock whose flat surface protruded from the water like a pedestal.

Looking at that flat stone, Otter saw that it occupied the farthest point a person could reach from the far side of the river. The farthest without swimming, she realized.

The girl squinted at her work and gave the plank a probing push with her foot before running back across the board to shore, where she repeated the process, this time dragging another board across the wooden path she'd already laid down. As her feet neared the end of the plank resting on the flat rock, she squatted and edged the second board out in front of her until it bridged from the first board to another sizable rock near the river's center. Twice more she produced boards from beneath the leaves and dragged them into place until the bridge extended to the rock where Otter's foot had caught.

Seconds later, the girl was squatting before Otter and staring hard at the root that held Otter's foot fast. The girl's fingers probed the root's length in search of any gap or weak spot. "How did you even do this?" Her tone was hushed with quiet exasperation.

Otter felt the flush return to her cheeks. "It was an accident," she mumbled, embarrassed.

The girl at her feet lifted her head and looked at Otter. The girl's brown eyes, so light they seemed almost amber in the afternoon sun, were pinched with anxiety, but she managed a reassuring smile and gave the captive foot a comforting pat. "It's a *bad* accident. And badly timed. We have to hurry." And with a swift pat to the ensnared foot, the new girl raced back across her bridge. "I'll be right back," she shouted over her shoulder with a reassuring smile. "Don't go anywhere."

Otter laughed despite herself. If only she *could* go somewhere!

Once back on shore, the girl bolted deeper into the woods at full tilt, leaving Otter alone again.

Otter grew nervous waiting, and worrisome questions flooded in as if carried to her mind by the current sweeping tirelessly past her. Why had the girl been so concerned with the time? Was it the monsters from the previous night? Where had the girl come from? Otter pondered the hidden boards and the girl's sudden departure into the woods. Surely the girl lived nearby. But where were her adults? Her imaginary? And, perhaps most important, *would* she actually return?

But these thoughts had little time to stretch their dark wings, for her wait was brief. Mere minutes after leaving, the girl was already bounding back to the river, a small cloth bundle in her hand. She picked her way quickly across the makeshift bridge back to Otter and squatted once more by the trapped foot.

Curious despite her predicament, Otter looked down at the red curls pulled loosely back from the young girl's head. Otter had thought the girl was her own age, but on closer inspection thought she was perhaps a couple of years older, though not more than that. "Thank you for helping me. I'm Otter. What's your name?" she asked.

The cloth lay spread out on the rock's surface to reveal a knife inside. It was large, dwarfing Otter's own tiny broken blade. Barely looking up from Otter's foot, the girl took the knife in hand and began to saw at the root, far enough from the foot to avoid injuring Otter. "Cherry," she said between the low grunts that punctuated her efforts.

Otter repeated the name. "'Cherry'?"

"That's right," Cherry responded.

The root was thick and tough. That and the river's constant splashing made for slow work. Otter's foot ached with the awkward angle, made worse by her straining to watch the other girl's progress. The sawing tugged rhythmically at the root, chafing more with each pass of the blade.

Searching for distraction, Otter scanned her environs. "Do you live out here?"

"Yes."

"Are you . . ." Otter paused, not wanting to pry. But her curiosity was piqued. "Are you alone?"

Cherry kept at her work without answering for several seconds. Just when Otter thought she would receive no response, the other girl spoke. "Are *you*?"

This was not the answer Otter had expected, and it made her stop and think. Perhaps Cherry was as nervous about strangers as Otter was. But Cherry was trying to help her and seemed genuinely concerned, so Otter decided to trust. "Yes. I am."

For a few moments, the river's babbling and Cherry's determined sawing were the only sounds between them. Never stopping or even looking away from her work, Cherry responded, her voice so low that Otter nearly missed it, "Me too."

They fell silent again. But Otter, usually reticent, craved both company and information. After a few minutes' hesitation, she asked, "Do you know what the monsters are?"

For the first time since her work began, Cherry stopped sawing and looked up at Otter, squinting quizzically. "'Monsters'? What monsters?"

It was Otter's turn to be puzzled. "I heard monsters on the path last night. Aren't they why we're hurrying?"

"You stayed on the path last night?" Cherry's eyebrow arched skeptically.

"Yes, I—"

"*This* path?" The doubt remained, unmistakable.

Again Otter attempted to answer. "Yes, I—"

A light snort escaped as Cherry resumed her work. "I don't know what you heard, but that's not why we're hurrying. I've lived here most of my life, and I've never seen monsters. In this forest"—she looked hard at Otter—"there is only *one* monster."

It was Otter's turn to be skeptical. "I heard them all night. There can't have been only one."

"Like I said, I don't know what you heard. Because if he—the only monster you need to worry about right now—had been there, you wouldn't have heard him. And you wouldn't be here now." Cherry held Otter's gaze without blinking until Otter grew uneasy. Otter saw dark circles under the other girl's eyes, something she hadn't seen on a child since leaving the factory. Then they both blinked, and Cherry returned to her task without another word.

Minutes passed and the shadows grew long. The river babbled by, accompanied by the steady rhythm of the knife against the stubborn root. Cherry periodically looked to the sky as she raced against the daylight. The race would end soon, one way or another.

The repetition of Cherry's sawing arm stopped abruptly with a muted click, and Otter stumbled, sputtering and flailing into the water with a splash. Cherry's hand found Otter's, and a moment later, shivering and dripping, Otter found her feet back on the rock. She hissed in pain as she tried to make the recently liberated foot support her weight.

"Thank you," Otter gasped through gritted teeth.

"We have to go. *Now*."

Cherry's face was gray with anxiety as she squinted down the path where Otter's pack still lay. Otter felt her heart racing, and it was no longer from her former predicament or the fall. "Okay," she said. "Let me just get my things."

Otter turned limping toward the bank where she'd started, but a firm grip on her arm held her back. Otter looked and saw Cherry's hand.

"You don't have time for your things right now. We have to go. *You* have to go. And you can't go back the way you came."

Before Otter had formulated a response, she felt herself pulled firmly in the opposite direction from her pack, despite her futile resistance. She stumbled on her throbbing ankle and protested her rough handling, but Cherry was unmoved. Even as they struggled, Otter saw the sun's last rays blinking out, blocked in their weakened state by the forest's green canopy. The light around the girls faded from life, slowly cloaking the world in darkness. Otter's resistance died with the light.

Once it was clear that Otter would cooperate, Cherry's arm went under Otter's shoulders to help support the hobbling girl's weight. They picked their way back across Cherry's makeshift bridge, the smooth planks slick with moisture, making the journey just that much more difficult. With Cherry's help, Otter led the way, choosing her steps with care. Each time they reached the end of one board and stepped onto the next, Cherry kicked the prior board into the flowing current. The discarded boards traveled in turbulent fits down the river as they alternately snagged on protruding rocks along the shore and then surged free toward the next obstacle.

Otter gasped with the pain of her ankle and the demands of the pace Cherry set. "Is that so it can't cross?" Otter panted as Cherry kicked another board into the water.

Cherry choked out a bitter chuckle. "No, nothing can keep *him* from crossing. I'm losing my bridge boards to keep anyone else from following once he's here. I don't see many strangers on this path. But"—she turned her head to look meaningfully at Otter—"it does happen from time to time."

Heat rose in Otter's cheeks. She wondered why she *had* come this way, with so many warning signs counseling that she turn back. She also still wondered what Cherry was doing alone out here in such danger—and why she was now helping Otter limp to safety, since the extra weight could only slow Cherry down.

Distant, feral rumblings behind them left no time for these thoughts, and Otter looked over her shoulder with unease. "Is that him?" She heard the panic in her voice as though it were someone else's. Her pain, too, seemed remote, as if it didn't belong to her. Otter realized with alarm that the combination of her injury and a day without food was loosening her grip on consciousness, even as she struggled to contribute to her own escape. Her head swam, and for a moment she nearly laughed as Cherry's red curls tickled her nose. *Keep it together, Otter. This is no time to lose your head.* She tried to focus on just planting her good foot in front of her again and again as they fled.

Cherry shook her head, exacerbating the nose-tickling effect. "I don't know what that is, but it's not him. If you could hear *him*, it would be too late."

A shudder worked through Otter's body, and fear sliced into the curtain descending over her consciousness to allow the fading light back in. Looking around, she took in her new surroundings for the first time.

No path was evident in the thin gaggle of trees they were hobbling through, but the way was clear enough without one. Wooden signs nailed to the occasional trunk shouted out to dissuade any travelers determined to continue this far past the many other warnings dotting the sylvan landscape. Ahead lay a small cottage, mildly dilapidated, with a tidy wood-tiled roof and wooden shutters smartly whitewashed. Innocuous-looking weeds sought to encroach on all sides.

Otter thought briefly of another small house inhabited by a girl with no adults around. But this charming little house could not have been farther from Eliza's dismal shack. Somehow it just felt—*different*.

Cherry was guiding them toward the homey house. Without slowing, she shot a wary glance over her shoulder, and she squinted into the distance behind them. The sounds following them from the deepening night grew in ferocity, but their source remained out of sight. Despite her assurance that those noises were not the source of her worry, Cherry's pace quickened as their volume rose.

Panting with exertion, they crossed the cottage's wooden porch and reached the door just as pale evening stars began to appear in the disappearing sky. Cherry seized the door and threw it open, banging it loudly against the clapboard outer wall. The tired hinge protested the rough treatment with a shriek, and the door bounced back to where the girls had been only a split second earlier. Cherry stopped for the first time since their run had begun and slid the door's three separate iron bolts into place. The dusk that had shrouded the world outside was deeper still inside, where no lamp had yet been lit, and the cottage's single room was visible in only the grossest detail.

Turning again, Cherry helped Otter shuffle to the middle of the room, where she reached down to the smooth floor-boards that ran beneath a well-trod rug. She seized a handhold she found there and raised a hatch the rug had concealed. The open hatch revealed a ladder into a hidden cellar, darker even than the dim interior above.

Cherry gestured toward the lower chamber and looked at Otter expectantly. "You have to get in. I'll follow you, but we can't both use the ladder. It isn't made for two people. Can you climb down yourself?"

Otter balked, remembering the cage in Eliza's back room. "But you bolted the door—"

Cherry grabbed both of Otter's shoulders firmly and looked her squarely in the eyes. Cherry's slender face was pale, and her round eyes were pinched with fear as she spoke—fear and something else, Otter thought. Perhaps it was determination. "You aren't listening. The bolts will not hold him. Nothing will keep him out for long. He will come inside, and he will find whoever is not hidden inside *there*." Her finger jabbed toward the blackness yawning below. "You don't have time to be afraid or to talk this out. You only have time to live or to die. And you have to decide right now which you will do."

Otter had never seen such a serious look in another child's eyes, nor heard such an urgent tone. She searched her soul only a moment longer before crouching gingerly and lowering herself into the dark space beneath them. As she climbed, she absently noted that the animal sounds seemed to have stopped. *Probably can't hear them from inside the house*, she thought. *Or maybe whatever was making them doesn't want to be heard anymore.* She found herself hurrying despite the pain throbbing in her ankle with each step.

Cherry did not wait for Otter to reach the bottom of the ladder before following. Her feet moved quickly to whichever rung Otter's hand had just evacuated. When she had descended enough, Cherry quietly lowered the hatch, making the darkness around them nearly complete.

Solid floor once more beneath her feet, Otter reached out and found the cellar's cool wall only a few inches from the ladder. The wall gave her somewhere to lean and take the weight off her injured foot. It was also her only landmark in these dark environs. Slowly, though, her eyes adjusted, and a pale light seemed to emanate from the walls, casting a faint, ghostly glow.

Otter felt a silent tap on her shoulder and turned her attention back to Cherry. The other girl had come close enough to be seen despite the poor light. Squinting, Otter saw Cherry place a finger against her lips, and she understood she was being commanded to silence. Otter began to whisper a question but was cut off when Cherry's finger moved to Otter's own lips with a firm shake of her head. It seemed there could be no exceptions.

Removing her finger, Cherry put her arm around Otter's shoulders once more and guided the girl to a corner of the cellar away from the ladder. The illumination from the walls was wan but, in the absence of all other light, was far better than nothing. Still, Otter was relieved the floor was clear of obstacles hidden in the darkness. A stumble now would hurt her ankle—to say nothing of the noise it would make.

When they'd reached the opposite wall, both girls leaned against it, panting. Seeing Cherry slide to a sitting position on the floor, Otter followed her example. She stretched out her leg to give her foot some relief. The darkness behind her closed eyelids seemed to pulsate to the rhythm of her ankle's throbbing. The only sound she could hear in the silence was her heart thumping in her ears and the muted panting as both girls caught their breath. Gradually their breathing returned to normal.

In the corner of that dismal cellar, two slender necks craned upward as each crouched child slowly raised her gaze to the ceiling. Otter was painfully aware that the earth overhead was also the floor to the cottage above them. Her eyes probed the ceiling's shadowed surface for signs of movement as she waited for something—*Him,* whatever *"he" is,* thought Otter—to arrive and put his weight upon it.

The minutes dragged endlessly on as they waited. Even a loud breath invited a sharp silencing gesture from Cherry. Just when Otter thought the danger must surely have passed, the silence came to an end with an abrupt thump.

The warped timbers of the porch groaned under some great weight, squeaking with the slow beat of stalking footsteps. The creaking ceased for a moment, then was replaced by a series of fast, pounding beats followed by an enormous crash and a bang that shook the cabin even down to the girls' hiding place. The sudden commotion startled Otter, who had to bite her lip hard to stifle a cry as her tiny body shook in terror. Tears streamed down her cheeks. She realized with horror that whatever was hunting them had found the door locked and simply come through anyway. For the first time since escaping from Eliza and Desdemona, Otter began to doubt whether she would see another day, whether her journey would end in tragedy, terror, and tears.

After its dramatic entry, the unseen beast seemed to lose its sense of urgency. The procession of heavy feet lightly placed made the floorboards above the girls' heads strain and moan as the mysterious beast made its way across the tiny cabin's darkened interior. The creature planted each silent step with the measured care of a predator stalking prey, even as the dust continued settling from the crash of the battered, fallen door. The only sounds betraying its motion now were the periodic hisses of its breathing and the creaks of the floorboards struggling to stay strong beneath its feet. *Many feet*, Otter judged by the long pattern of falling dust.

Otter sat trembling in the musty cellar, terrified. She realized she'd been holding her breath since the door had come crashing down, and she forced herself to inhale once more. The inward rush of air steadied her. Choking back a sob, she wiped the tears from her face with the back of her hand. Flashes of the silent path full of warnings and her misplaced step flitted across her terrified mind, taunting her with the memory of how her own actions had brought her here. Silently she cursed her bad luck and carelessness. *This is regret*, she realized. The thought of having survived so much just to have her journey end in a dark basement knotted her stomach in agony. Her eyes fluttered as she blinked hard to keep the stream from renewing their course down her cheeks.

The only good thing about these thoughts warring within her was the small distraction they afforded from her peril. Her torment was a cold and cutting mercy, effective despite its unpleasantness.

So complete was her distraction, in fact, that she nearly jumped—and had to cover her own mouth to stifle the startled shout that had attempted escape—when she felt an unexpected touch on her hand. Relief washed away the momentary panic as she realized it was Cherry, who had gently but firmly taken Otter's hand into her own. Otter inhaled deeply and smiled in the darkness at this small act of kindness and comfort. Somewhat surprised, she noticed that Cherry shook too. It occurred to Otter that this young stranger—by all appearances brave, pragmatic, and self-possessed—was nearly as frightened as she was. Otter gently returned a squeeze to Cherry's hand, hoping it conveyed her appreciation to this stranger, who had risked great danger in taking her in.

Time passed without much indication of its motion, and Otter could not tell how long they'd been huddled in the dark darkness when the sounds of movement above them subsided. She could tell little more than that the sun had not yet risen to illuminate the cabin. She and Cherry sat, hand in hand, still not daring to move.

Otter was exhausted, despite her terror. Sitting in the darkness, focused on the silence above, she noticed her eyelids growing heavy. The world went dark for seconds at a time, each lapse ending with a sudden start, and the next enduring just a few moments longer than the previous.

And then everything was extinguished in a frenzy of terrified dreams, where an unseen and unheard menace chased her through the woods. From all around her among the trees echoed the rumbling and roaring that had haunted her nightly campsites. The farther she ran from whatever hunted her, the deeper into the forest and the beastly cacophony she stumbled. Dreaming Otter felt certain that both threats would end in her doom. But she had decided to face the one that announced itself rather than the one that did not. And so she ran and ran and got little rest from her sleep.

Otter's eyes fluttered open, and her mouth stretched with a yawn as she arched her back, disoriented, taking in her surroundings. Motes of dust floated lazily in the variegated beams of sunlight that sliced between the boards of the cabin floor above her. The tiny subterranean room was tidy, its hard-packed floor free of loose dirt and debris. A ladder stood at attention in one corner, opposite from where Otter lay, and terminated at the ceiling.

From the other corner of the opposite wall, a low, narrow tunnel gaped, its depths receding into darkness. Otter took all of this in before her yawn had released her jaws. Then the events of last night flooded back to her, and it dawned on her that she was alone in Cherry's basement. Unbidden, a single, disjointed thought ricocheted off the recesses of her mind: *Trapped again.*

Panic surged, and Otter rose to her feet in a single movement before her eyes could even blink again. She looked up suspiciously at the entrance through which they'd come last night. Even if the trapdoor had no lock, there was no telling what awaited on the other side. She padded quietly to the hole in the wall. Ever so cautiously she poked her head into the dark tunnel's mouth, wondering whether it might offer escape.

With a bang, unseen hands flung open the trapdoor in the cellar's ceiling, startling Otter so badly she jumped, thumping her head painfully on the tunnel's earthen roof. Roughly she fell onto her bottom with a grunt and a thud. Blindly she scrambled from her awkward sitting position and backed into the corner to face whatever came through from above.

"Are you okay?" The voice overhead was tight with genuine concern. Through her panic, Otter recognized the voice as Cherry's. The girl's head hung upside down through the floor, her freckled cheeks flushed and her red curls dangling into the cellar.

Inhaling deeply, Otter tried to compose herself. "I'm—I'm fine. Where did that . . . thing . . ."

For a moment, Cherry said nothing. The girl's taut expression was the only visible evidence of an internal war waging silently across her face, making her torment plain despite the odd angle of her head. Otter resisted the temptation to turn her own head to compensate for Cherry's inversion and confirm her observation in a more familiar frame of reference. Her effort was stopped short by Cherry's shift to a decisive smile and a brief announcement. "You should come up for breakfast." And then her upside-down head vanished into the ceiling, leaving only the open hatch in its place.

Otter rose slowly. A haze of dust jumped from her pants as she brushed herself off before walking to the ladder. Standing at its base, she stared up the rough rungs and into the sunlit cabin above. With a resolute sigh, she began her ascent, pulling herself up rung by rung. She flinched at putting weight on her throbbing ankle, but much of the swelling had mercifully receded in the night. By favoring the tender side, she could climb with only the occasional grunt to betray the lingering discomfort. Reaching the top, she peeked cautiously over the hatch's wooden lip and scanned the room for signs of danger.

None were present. In fact, Otter noted with curiosity, even the evidence of past danger had been erased, leaving the cabin more or less unharmed, albeit slightly more run-down than Otter had realized in the failing light and the rush of escape. Yet the cabin had charm and was clearly cared after. Turning her head, she looked to the door she had heard had come crashing down and—

"The door . . ." Otter's eyes widened in astonishment. The door still stood, flush in its frame.

Seated at a humble wooden table with knobby legs worn smooth by age, Cherry shot a casual glance over her shoulder to the door. A morsel of fork-skewered food was suspended in her hand between the table's round top and her mouth. Turning back to Otter, she smiled wryly. "That wasn't the first time the door has come down, and it probably won't be the last. After the first time, I realized it didn't make much sense to spend a lot of time and effort putting it back up. The hinges come off pretty easily now, but at least the door—um—slows things down." Cherry's eyes turned downward as her last words faded to a whisper. Redness again rose faintly in her freckled cheeks.

Otter was confused.

She gathered that Cherry, a girl little older than Otter herself, lived alone in this cabin and was accustomed to having her door battered down by whatever it was that had chased them here. These details alone were enough to confound Otter. But what really puzzled her was Cherry's demeanor. The girl seemed friendly enough, having brought Otter to her home to hide, and now offering her breakfast. And she seemed quite capable, having survived in proximity to a terrifying beast for goodness knew how long. Yet the contrast between her calm now and her near panic the evening prior was difficult to reconcile. And her apparent embarrassment when discussing her predicament was doubly so. Friendliness aside, Cherry was a mystery. And Otter was in the habit of treating mystery with caution.

"Are you going to sit?" The words jolted Otter from her ruminations. "I made enough breakfast for both of us. I don't know whether your pack had food—or even that it's still there this morning—but I thought you'd be hungry after missing dinner last night."

At the word *dinner*, Otter's stomach demanded to be heard, issuing a litany of complaints. She had missed more than just dinner, having been stranded by the root for nearly all of the day before. And she was ravenous.

"Thank you," she said. A fleeting memory of Eliza and Desdemona flitted across her mind, giving her pause. But the momentary wariness it brought was soon pushed aside by hunger. Her feet did not wait for her brain to decide, and she found they had carried her to the table of their own volition. Having arrived there, she obliged them by pulling out the other chair, sitting down, and digging in.

A large bowl of fleshy, red fruits sat at the table's center. Otter now recognized them as specterines, and she piled them onto her plate. The table was adorned with various other simple dishes: a rough loaf of bread and a jar of chunky fruit jam, a wooden bowl of raw leafy greens, and slices of dried meat and hard cheese, all arrayed with care. Otter knew many of these foods from the Farm, and she helped herself with what restraint she could muster. It wasn't much. Her dark cheeks bulged as she chewed and took in more of her surroundings.

Cherry kept her tiny cabin neat. Nothing about it disclosed its strange circumstance of being occupied by a single child and, apparently, being regularly besieged by a giant monster. Not wanting to offend her host, Otter held back her questions for now.

Cherry, meanwhile, served herself from the table's offerings, although with more measured enthusiasm than her guest. Smiling, she said, "I'm glad you like specterines. They're not just for libertylions, after all."

Otter paused in her chewing for a moment and tried to speak around a prodigious mouthful of food. "Whu?" she asked, as best she could.

"You know, specterines? Libertylions eat them. Before the wild populations were hunted and captured, libertylions roamed all the forests in this region because specterines grow almost everywhere. My dad told me that specterines are what allow libertylions to move through solid objects." Then Cherry blushed again and looked down at her food.

Otter wondered whether the reaction had to do with the mention of Cherry's father, who was quite evidently not around. Not wanting to pry, she returned to the topic of fruit, letting the comment flow by her as if unnoticed, like one of the many anonymous leaves that had glided past at the river where Cherry had rescued her. "I didn't know that," she said, swallowing. "I only had them for the first time recently." A vague memory of the fruit teased at Otter's mind as she thought again of eating specterines on the Farm, and of failing to recognize them in the tall trees when her journey began. Not for the last time, she wondered how much easier and safer her trek would have been had she only known of the bounty growing all along her way.

Cherry nodded. "Is that because they don't grow where you're from?"

It was Otter's turn to stop with a forkful of food in midair. Did Cherry suspect that Otter was a refugee from Junkton? What did Otter really know about this strange girl, anyway? Otter glanced furtively around Cherry, eyeing her path to the door should she need to escape. Eliza's face seemed to wink at Otter from her memories, and Otter felt a small shudder scurry up her spine.

Cherry must have detected the change in her guest's mood because a concerned frown and furrowed brow replaced her open smile. "I'm sorry if I've said something wrong," she said, setting her utensils down and raising her hands as if to prove their emptiness. She continued quickly, like a child trying to preempt a parent's scolding: "I don't get to talk to people very often. I'm by myself except when I hike somewhere to trade and buy supplies, and I can't do that often. I have never had a guest before, so I didn't know if it's rude to ask where you're from. I'm sorry for assuming you aren't from Industriopa."

Momentarily disoriented, Otter blinked. She realized she had misunderstood the thrust of Cherry's comments and stumbled to regain her place in the conversation. "No, it's fine. I—I don't know where I'm from originally. I don't remember ever being anywhere but Jun—er, Industriopa." She shrugged, her footing returning with the odd comfort of a conversation she'd had many times now. "Some people think my parents must have been from Chimerica, but I never knew them, so I can't say."

Cherry nodded again, and her brow wrinkled further on hearing of Otter's never having known her parents. Reaching across the table, she filled Otter's cup from a teapot wrapped in a web of gossamer cracks. "I'm sorry about your parents. I haven't seen my parents in a very long time, but I like to think of them sometimes when I'm sad or lonely. I can't imagine what it would be like not to have those memories." Steam now rose from both girls' cups, and Cherry set the teapot down with a sympathetic smile.

The smile lent comfort Otter hadn't realized she'd needed. With that, Otter found herself bathed in an overwhelming sense of kinship for this strange girl, and she felt certain she had made another friend.

Which was why she hated to ask the question foremost on her mind.

"Cherry?"

Wiping her mouth daintily, Cherry seemed to smile with her eyes when she answered. "Yes, Otter?"

"What was that thing that was up here last night?"

The smile vanished, as Otter had feared it might. Silently, Cherry placed her napkin on the table beside her chipped plate and stared for a moment at the slightly tarnished fork resting upon it amid the remains of her morning meal. The silence stretched until Otter wondered whether Cherry intended to answer. Then the other girl lifted her head to meet Otter's gaze, her chin jutting forward as if in defiance, despite the faint trembling of her lip.

"That's Mister," she said, her voice thick with emotion. "He's my imaginary."

# CHAPTER 9

# MISTER

"HE'S YOUR *WHAT*?" Panic had returned in force. The warm camaraderie Otter had felt only seconds earlier had shrunk back as if burned. Her gaze drifted back toward her escape route.

"He's my imaginary," Cherry repeated. "I wish he weren't, but he is. And I can't do anything about it."

Measuring her path to the door, Otter stole a glance at her host's face and saw red eyes welling up, then a single droplet rolling down her cheek. This was not the face Otter would expect from someone who would imagine a monstrosity. Otter saw nothing like loyalty and affection Eliza had displayed for the horror she'd animated. Cherry's face told a different story altogether, and Otter found the mystery of that story arresting. The tension that had coiled in her legs as they had prepared to spring her forward subsided ever so slightly, and she found herself lowering back into her chair without recalling she had ever risen from it.

"Why would you imagine a monster?" she whispered. "Why would *anyone* do that?"

Cherry sat a little straighter at the question, as though offended. "Where is *your* imaginary?" she demanded.

Otter blinked, whipsawed by Cherry's unexpected question. "Wh-what?"

Warming to her umbrage and interrogation, Cherry straightened further in her seat. Her words shot at Otter in rapid progression, each syllable rising in volume and intensity just enough to be noticed. "I don't see an imaginary with you. Where is it? Are you a loner? Do you even know what it's like to summon an imaginary? Do you even understand what *happens* when you do? How something you only *think*, even by accident, even against your will, can come crashing and roaring into the world? How it would have a mind of its own? How it could ruin everything in your life?" Cherry was standing upright now, the crescendo having reached the point of shouting through her tears, while Otter sat frozen, stunned in her seat. "How it could take *everything* from you so that all you have left is that *thing* that *you* created? That *thing* that is worse than having nothing at all? Can *you* even *imagine*? *Can you?*" The barrage at an end, Cherry stood looking defiantly at Otter, who could respond with only wide-eyed silence. "I didn't think so," she murmured, and then collapsed back into her chair and buried her face in her hands as shuddering sobs racked her body.

Otter was at a loss. Her horror at learning that the beast—that *Mister*—was Cherry's imaginary, had been replaced by horror of another kind. The onslaught and inquisition had caused her to question everything she thought she knew about imagining a friend—the very thing she had escaped Junkton to achieve. She was horrified not only by the implication of Cherry's diatribe but by the effect of her own words on the girl now crying across the small table from her. Timidly she reached over the plates and placed her tiny brown hand on Cherry's arm, afraid the other girl might reject the gesture. "Cherry, I'm sorry. I didn't mean anything. You're right, I don't know what it's like. I didn't mean anything," she repeated.

Cherry lifted her head to reveal bloodshot eyes and cheeks streaked with tears. She looked at Otter as if searching for something in her guest's face. She sniffled slightly and then wiped the wetness from her face with the back of her hand as she looked away, withdrawing her arm from Otter's touch. "Anyway, you can stay until about midday, or a little earlier if you want to see whether your supplies are still there. Any later than that and you'd likely need to spend the night in the basement again. Mister comes back every night, and he *will* hurt anyone who isn't me." Cherry's voice had lost its earlier heat, but it had also lost some of its warmth, and her words carried the tired tones of resignation. "We can go after breakfast."

"Why doesn't he hurt you?" Otter pressed.

Cherry snorted a bitter laugh. "He would if he could," she said. "But our bond means he can't hurt me much without risking himself."

Otter recalled what Luna had told her about the link that bound an imaginary to its real, and how imaginaries die when their reals do. "Is there no way to stop him?"

Cherry focused intently on the table where she scratched at an invisible spot with her nail. She squinted, as if seeing something through the invisible spot that refused to be scratched away. "I used to live here with my parents when I was little. Before Mister. My dad and mom would sit at this very table and talk to me."

Otter scanned the table. Its wooden grain had long since worn smooth, with an occasional nick or gouge marring its surface, betraying some long-past carelessness. She closed her eyes for a moment and found herself thinking of what it must have been like to live in a nice little cottage like this, to sit and share meals with parents who loved her. As her imagination briefly transported her to that life she'd never had, an odd sensation descended on her, as though her mind were peeking behind a curtain within her own soul, a curtain that had always been there but that she had never before noticed. Her imagination had taken hold of the curtain's edge and, just as she longed for a home and a family and a life like Cherry's, her mind longed to lift that curtain, to reveal the thing hidden behind it, the thing that had also somehow always been there but that she had never known. Fear and anticipation tickled her mind as she felt the curtain's—*fabric* was not the right word—*substance*, yes, its substance, as though it were a physical thing she held between her fingers. For a brief moment, all that existed for Otter was the image of Cherry's life with a family and the desire—no, the *need* to pull back that invisible curtain.

And then the cottage and the table and the sound of Cherry's voice pulled her back, and she was in the real world once more. She shook her head as if to clear a drop of water from her ears, startled by the vivid strangeness of where her mind has just been. *Exhausted, hurt, and hungry*, she thought. *I had better eat.* She unobtrusively reached to serve herself more fruit while trying to focus on Cherry's words.

Cherry continued, unaware of Otter's brief sense of absence. "I remember being afraid of the dark. We didn't see many other people out this way, but when we did, their imaginaries were strange and frightening. Not like my parents' imaginaries. Mom and Dad had small, cute imaginaries that liked to play or cuddle. Not at all like the strange creatures we encountered when we went into town. I was sitting here at breakfast one day . . ." Cherry's voice and gaze were distant, as if she had wandered too far into memory to be heard at a kitchen table so thoroughly anchored to the present.

Otter waited patiently, chewing, and eventually Cherry picked up where she'd left off.

"We were at breakfast, and I asked my dad whether my imaginary would be scary too. He laughed and patted my head. 'I don't think so,' he said. 'You're not scary, so why would your imaginary be scary?' But he didn't really know. He was just guessing."

Otter passed a gentle squeeze to Cherry's arm, trying to convey support even as she waited in dreadful anticipation of where the story was headed.

"At night, I would lie in bed, terrified and trying not to think of what might be hidden in the shadows of the room." She pointed to a corner of the cottage containing two beds, one small and one large, and Otter realized that Cherry was indicating the birthplace of the memories now recounted. "I thought of all the frightening imaginaries I had seen, and my childish mind just knew that they could be anywhere. So I tried to imagine a friend who would protect me and comfort me. I tried to imagine a nice friend before I could accidentally imagine a mean one."

"And that—*that* was *Mister*?" Otter was shocked at the thought.

Cherry smiled sadly. "No. It never worked. I tried and tried, but I just wasn't ready to summon an imaginary. My mind was too young, I suppose. Then, one day, it wasn't. And that was too late.

"I can never forget that night. Rain battered the house, and the shutters kept slamming against the wall outside. Every time the thunder crashed, I imagined the other noises it could be hiding. Every flash of lightning caused the shadows to jump across the floor and up the wall, turning the familiar things

I knew into strange and hideous distortions. At one point, I remember thinking that the house would surely come down, and feeling a wave of dread and expectation so strong and high that it seemed to transport me away from here, as if I had ripped through our world and into another. And when the wave subsided and I returned to my bed, I brought something back with me."

Cherry fell silent, trailing off as she stared deep into a faraway point in time.

Perched on the edge of her seat, Otter resisted with difficulty the urge to prod Cherry for further detail. She had so many questions, and her anticipation for the rest of the tale had pulled her physically toward her host. But she could see the painful toll the narration was taking on Cherry, so she clenched the words in her jaws and waited for Cherry to resume on her own.

"I lay without sleeping until the storm passed. When the sun's first rays began to light the cabin, I found an egg."

Otter tilted her head in surprise. "An *egg*?"

"Seems harmless even for an imaginary, right?" Cherry smiled, but the expression was devoid of warmth. "It was as big as my head and speckled with different colors. My dad joked that it was freckled just like me. I remember thinking how pretty it was. At the time, I doted on it. I polished its shell every day. I sat up with it when it seemed agitated."

"The *egg* seemed agitated?" Otter couldn't resist the amazed question.

"I know how it sounds. But it shook whenever anyone came near it, and my presence and attention seemed to soothe it. So that's what I tried to do. Still, the shaking got worse as time wore on, and I just knew it would hatch any day.

"I named it Mister without even meaning to. I was so little, and I kept calling it Mister Egg to my parents. They had to remind me that it probably wouldn't stay an egg forever since eggs tend to hatch. So Mister it was. But it stayed an egg longer than I expected, and it spent more of each day rattling around. It worried me to see it quake like that, and sometimes it shook so violently, it frightened me. But still I would stay with it, gritting my teeth"—Cherry bared her teeth in illustration—"and, it seemed to me, in those moments when I was most afraid of what might be revealed when its shell finally cracked, that's when the egg was most at peace."

The eating had long since ceased, and the girls sat surrounded by stillness, their eyes studiously averted, as if each of the room's opposite corners contained an object of intense interest to each child.

Otter tried to imagine Cherry's thoughts, then and now. She squirmed in discomfort at the effort. The entirety of her remembered life had been bound up in her singular desire to be joined by the perfect imaginary. The idea that desire might not be enough unsettled her deeply. What made those children on the playground outside her factory window more deserving of kind and happy imaginaries than one sad and frightened girl in the woods? Otter could not imagine.

"Not many people lived in these woods even then," Cherry continued. "One day my parents said we were moving to the city because they couldn't make a living here anymore. My father was a carpenter. Maybe he still is. . . ." Once more, her voice trailed her thoughts around a corner where her audience could not follow before finally finding its way back to her tale. "My mother sold pies. Rows of them used to line this table after cooling on the windowsill over there." She nodded to one of the windows beside the door without looking. "But nobody came this way much anymore, and things were slow. My dad worked in the city, and my parents said we'd have better luck if we moved there."

Otter looked again at the table, its smooth lines and skilled craftsmanship, now eroded by time's slow and loving march across its surface, and she realized that much of the cabin's charm was likely the work of Cherry's father. She found her finger etching its grooves as though following a path back to happier times in the tiny cottage's history.

Cherry continued. "So we loaded our things into the car and left. I packed Mister into a box padded with feathers and straw. I even put one of my stuffed toys in with him so he'd have something to play with if he hatched along the way." Cherry chuckled wryly and shook her head. "I was beginning to think he would never hatch and that I'd be stuck with an egg as an imaginary forever. But all the same, I gently tucked his box into a snug space among our other things packed in the trailer behind our car. And I practically danced at the promise of the adventure ahead."

Cherry paused and looked at Otter as if searching for something in the other girl's face without being sure what that might be. Otter shifted nervously in her seat. She wasn't sure how her face was reacting to the history unfolding before her, but she hoped it made the telling no worse for Cherry.

Her tone suddenly flat, she carried on: "We arrived in Harborton and I ran into our new house. I don't know what I was expecting. But after spending my whole life until then out here, I can tell you I didn't expect a cramped, bare cube. But that's what I found. It was only one of many like it where other families lived in our building. It felt like a single cell in the comb of a great beehive. So I shuffled back to the car to get my things. But my disappointment transformed when I saw Mister's box jiggling violently in the back seat. I knew the wait was over, that my life was about to change forever."

Otter could see the great effort on Cherry's face as it contorted to contain another flood of tears. Yet even as the story horrified Otter to her core, she could not help but be fascinated by the horror. Rapt she sat, nearly coming off the edge of her seat. Even as she pained for all Cherry had suffered, she could not help but fixate on every detail of the other girl's tragedy and its relevance to her own quest.

A moment of silent tension grew to fill the air between them, swelling near to bursting with anticipation of the tale's next dreadful scene. Cherry deflated it simply. "I was right." She smiled sadly, dabbing the corner of her eye with her wrist before continuing. "Mister had already hatched. I opened his box and I—I screamed. I had never seen anything like it. I felt bad, as if maybe my reaction hurt its feelings. I had been afraid of so many imaginaries before—I thought maybe it only looked like a little monster but that it was nice, the way people always said their frightening imaginaries were actually nice. But then, I noticed. I noticed, and I knew."

Recoiling as though she herself had just opened the box for the first time only to find a monster where her imaginary should be, Otter felt her hands climbing toward her neck. "Noticed what?" The question was intended to sound strong and comforting, but it snuck out as a hoarse whisper instead.

"The stuffed toy I had packed with Mister to cushion the egg and to keep him company if he hatched on the way. Gone. Just gone. Mister had torn every bit of it to shreds, and pieces still hung from his—" Cherry gestured vaguely toward her own mouth, as if not wanting to speak of Mister's. "My parents said it was nothing to worry about. My dad told me a story of a puppy he'd had as a child. The puppy did the same to my dad's favorite stuffed toy, and more besides in his bedroom. Still, I saw it in their eyes, the worry exchanged in a silent glance. And they were right to be worried, it turned out.

"Every night, Mister did something new and terrible. He'd tear up the curtains or destroy a flower bed outside. We quickly learned that no one could even approach him except me, and he would attack or destroy anything that got near him if he wasn't kept on a leash or in a cage. And the way he grew . . ." A brief shudder interrupted Cherry's recollection.

Otter was as fascinated as she was horrified. "How big *was* he, back then?"

Cherry collected herself and continued. "At first he was the size of a small hen. But he ate anything he could reach, and especially"—shifting in her seat, she gulped, visibly uncomfortable—"and especially meat. Before we knew how bad he could be, we started seeing the remains of small rodents, or we'd hear him ripping across the house even to catch bugs. When stray animals began to disappear, I already knew why, even if I couldn't bring myself to admit it. Then a neighbor's pet dog disappeared, and that's when we stopped letting him outside except on a leash. That was back when a leash could hold him. Then he got too big to control even if you *could* find a way to leash him.

"Mister had always slept under my bed during the daylight hours, which at least kept him locked up, even if he spent the nights staring hungrily at me or throwing my things around. He terrified me, but at least I knew he couldn't hurt me. Not much, anyway."

Otter cocked her head curiously. "But he could hurt you *some*?" That an imaginary could do such a thing had never occurred to her before. Now that it had, the disconcerting notion caused her to shift uncomfortably in her seat.

Cherry nodded, her expression flat and distant. "Some. He would nip at me or claw me here and there. But Mister's teeth and claws are not like a puppy's or a kitten's. I would sometimes wake in the morning after crying myself to sleep and find spots of blood crusted between my arm and my sheets." Cherry let out a long, exhausted sigh. "But it was never more than that.

Not to me. I think he couldn't do more to me without hurting himself. Other people though . . ."

Otter inhaled sharply, dreading the story's progression.

"Some nights, I heard my parents whisper about him. And I could see the worry on their faces all the time. Once I heard them talk about whether to get rid of him. But that was when they still had hope that he'd grow out of it." Another bitter chuckle punctuated the narrative. "Not long after that, it was too late. He was too big and vicious to grab hold of, and too smart and wary to sneak up on. Eventually, Mister realized this, too, and he went from being a problem to being a danger.

"The evening he attacked my mom, I was sitting at our table, which was a lot like this one, but smaller." Cherry gestured at the dishes and table scraps sitting before them. "I usually kept him closed up in my room so he couldn't cause trouble. But when he awoke that day, I guess he figured out how to open the door, because he came out.

"Mister has no problem being loud and fast, but he's at his worst when he's slow and silent. We never heard him enter the kitchen until my mom was screaming to get him off her leg. I screamed and jumped to help her but . . ." Cherry wiped her eyes again with a sniffle and looked up at the ceiling to clear her eyes before continuing. "Once he grabs on, getting him off is not easy. Even back then. I realized I had only one way to stop him. So I threw myself onto them, between them as much as I could, so that he was clutching and clawing at me with every effort to keep his hold on my mom. I got pretty scratched up, but it was enough to peel him off.

"My dad had come in during the struggle. I was so frantic to get Mister away from my mom that I hadn't even heard him enter. He grabbed Mister, threw him forcefully into my room, and slammed the door. He ran back to my mom and held her as they both cried. And I just stood there watching them, and I remember thinking how none of it seemed real, how it couldn't be real. But of course, it was . . ." Cherry absently stirred her tea, which had long since stopped steaming and grown cold. Her brow and lips pinched as she fought back more tears.

Otter sat silent, struggling to comprehend Cherry's life. Cherry had been a child with everything Otter had ever wanted: a lovely home, a loving family, human connection. And then she lost it all because of an imaginary, the one thing Otter wanted and could someday have. *Or at least I think I could.* These thoughts pressed down on her almost physically with their weight. Neither girl said anything for a long time.

When Cherry cracked the silence, her tone was controlled but oddly hollow. "I knew then that I couldn't stay. Later that night, when my parents' talking and crying had finally ended, I rose from bed and began to pack my things. I needed some clothes and some essentials, a pocketknife, a sewing kit, things like that."

A chill shimmied up Otter's spine as Cherry's recollection echoed Otter's own nighttime escape.

"I know he's your imaginary but"—Otter thought hard before continuing—"but wouldn't it have been better, um, not to let him, you know—live?"

Cherry's wry smile returned. "Wouldn't it ever! But he's strong, fast, and tough, and he's smarter than you might think for such a brute. By the time the thought occurred to us, it was too late. No one ever said it outright, but occasionally some-one would sigh and say something about how different things might have been if we'd only known earlier. If only we'd known we'd never get another chance to undo what my imagination had conceived—but we didn't."

Otter cringed at Cherry's sad, matter-of-fact response. She had felt callous for asking the question, yet the answer did not ease her discomfort. "So you came here?"

"This was a few years back, and I didn't really know of anywhere else I could go as a little kid and not be noticed but still be safe. So I came back, set up the perimeter, and settled in. Part of me thought my parents might still come looking. And I always hoped to see them again. But if they did follow, they never went beyond the warning signs. Sometimes I'm sad they never came. But most of the time I'm relieved. Mister only got bigger, and I'm not sure they'd have survived. Honestly, I'm surprised you did! I have never had anyone else inside the cabin since I got here, which was a while ago now. It's been nice to sit and talk and not worry about being seen and having to try to answer inconvenient questions about being a kid alone in the woods." Cherry smiled again, this time without the wryness.

Otter had so many questions, but she couldn't bring herself to interrogate the girl further in the wake of such candor, despite Cherry's barely knowing—and having no obvious reason to trust—her odd guest. Instead, she said simply, "I'm sorry." Her hand, she realized, had again crossed the small table, but this time it met Cherry's hand, which embraced her own with a warm squeeze. The girls sat without speaking for a long moment, smiling, hand in hand, neither wishing to end such a rare moment of heartfelt connection. Then Otter made a decision.

"Let me help you," she said.

Cherry's smile changed to a quizzical frown. "Help me? There's no way to help me." Her hand withdrew and returned to the invisible spot in need of further scratching.

Otter persisted. "What if there were?"

"There isn't," Cherry said, exasperation sharpening her tone. Abruptly she changed course: "I guess you'd probably better be on your way." She braced herself on the table as if to rise.

"Wait," Otter implored. She realized she had seized Cherry's hand again. "First I want to tell *you* something."

Cherry searched Otter's face and seemed to sense her guest's earnestness and urgency. Her arms relaxed, and she slowly settled back into her seat.

And then Otter began. She told Cherry everything—Junkton, the factory, her escape, her quest, the woods, the noises in the night, Eliza and Desdemona, Melvin, the Farm, Luna, everything. She told Cherry how she'd never known her family or where she came from or how she ended up in a place where everyone she met looked so different. Everything.

Cherry sat silent throughout, her eyes widening at a detail here or there, and she seemed to grow especially thoughtful when Otter's story closely paralleled her own.

"And that's why I want to help you. Together, I think we can do it." With that, Otter concluded. By then, the morning had bloomed into afternoon and bold beams of sunlight streamed deep into the room. The thoughtful expression remained on Cherry's face after Otter's final word dissipated into the room's warm brilliance.

"But," Cherry began before pausing, as though examining what she would say from all sides before it left her mouth for good. "But *how*? Even with your help, there's nothing we can do about Mister."

"When I left Junkton, I knew I would face hardship and maybe worse, all in the hope of finding the perfect imaginary friend. I never expected to also find *real* friends along the way. But I have. When I left the Farm, I left behind real friends for the sake of my quest. But I would have stayed and done anything if those friends needed my help. Now I've met you. You saved me without knowing anything about me. You gave me food and comfort, knowing I probably had nothing to give you in return." She smiled and squeezed Cherry's hand gratefully.

"And then I learn that you too are alone in the world, surviving without help, in need of a real friend. Well, if you'll have me, you've found one. When I leave here, it will be because you have made me leave or because we have figured out a way to stop Mister once and for all." The dishes before them clinked resolutely as Otter's tiny chestnut fist thumped on the table's wooden top.

For many seconds, Cherry peered silently into Otter's eyes as if examining a gem she suspected of being glass. Then she blinked, and her jaw set in that seemingly familiar way once more.

"Okay," she said, her voice resolute. "But we're going to need a plan."

# CHAPTER 10

# THE PLAN

AND SO THE girls set to work.

Most of the remainder of their first day together was spent seated at the same table, or clearing and resetting their places in the transition to subsequent meals, while Cherry educated Otter about all things Mister.

The more Otter learned, the more battered her confidence in their mission became.

Mister was a formidable beast. Even Otter's own terrified imagination, extrapolating from only the thunderous noise when Mister charged down the wooded path and then through the cabin's front door, did not do the creature justice by even a fraction of Cherry's account. Cherry described a massive monster that could run like a horse on sixteen thick, segmented legs, with each spidery limb terminating in a vicious, pinching claw. One whip of his long, stout tail could devastate even without the cruel barb that crowned it. "As he grew, the tail grew, too, and developed venom," she said matter-of-factly. "I've seen him stalk as silently as the breeze and use his tail to poison his prey before it ever sees him coming. So dealing with his tail might be our biggest problem."

Otter could not restrain a shudder at the thought.

Cherry continued. Mister's legion legs grew from a body linked with many segments, like those of a centipede. Glistening black hide made nearly every inch of the monster's long, sinuous form impenetrable. From Cherry's description, Mister was all but perfectly imagined for both defense and attack.

Most disturbing of all, though, was Cherry's depiction of Mister's face. "He has so many jaws that they overlap in layers of sharp-toothed mandibles, right in the middle of his face. He has lots of eyes too. They surround his mouth on all sides of his head. Some are like a bug's eyes. Some even look almost human, and you can see his intelligence and cunning in them."

"Doesn't he ever sleep? And why doesn't he come back during the daytime?"

Cherry shrugged. "He sleeps during the daytime, but not here. He can tolerate daylight, but he hates it, so he spends his days somewhere it doesn't intrude. My guess has always been that he's found a cave somewhere. But I've never exactly missed his company, so I never followed him to find out for sure."

Otter grew thoughtful. "Didn't you ever wonder whether you could, um, do something about him while he's asleep?"

Cherry laughed wryly. "Didn't I ever? Yeah. Plenty. But you can't sneak up on him. He seems to sense whenever someone approaches him in his sleep. And if you think some *people* wake up in a bad mood, you can't even imagine waking Mister in the daytime. Even when he was newly hatched, he always needed to sleep and"—a brief shudder interrupted her explanation—"and to feed," she finished. "So he spent the days hiding out of the way as much as possible, and I spent the days letting him. But at night, that's when he's active."

Listening intently, Otter tried to hide the terror these descriptions inspired.

If Cherry intended to allay those fears, her words gave no indication. "He can't seem to smell, and his hearing is rather poor. I guess I didn't really think about those things when I imagined him. Also, he doesn't have proper hands. So he hasn't found my hiding spot because he can't see into it, and I don't think he could claw it open if he did. He'd have to break in if he wanted to get into the cellar—" The word seemed to catch in her throat as her eyebrows raised in alarm. Her chair nearly fell backward as she bolted upright from her seat. "*The cellar!* You have to go. *Now!*"

Startled, Otter froze for a moment, unable to respond. Looking over Cherry's shoulder, Otter saw the sinking sun's pale light receding through the window. The shadows had grown long and together. That meant darkness would soon arrive. And Otter now understood that night in this part of the woods belonged to Mister.

Dawning realization forced these thoughts through Otter's head in a flash. But moments might as well have been weeks if she didn't rise and hide where Mister wouldn't find her.

Leaving their forgotten dishes and lost time behind them, the girls raced in unison to the cellar's hidden hatch and practically jumped into the open space revealed below it. Otter watched as the warm rays of the late afternoon were severed by the quick but quiet closing of the hatch now above them. Cherry fastened a small latch on the underside of the closed trapdoor and then scurried down the ladder to the floor.

Otter sat panting. "Did something hap—"

The words broke off at Cherry's sharp glance, accompanied by a stern, shushing finger at her lips. Leaning close to Otter's ear, but still barely audible, she whispered, "He's too clever. He saw you come here last night, and he knows I have a hiding place, even if he doesn't know where. He sometimes comes back early to see if he can catch me opening it and find it. He's never come back this early, but we were getting close. Our only choice now is to wait him out in silence."

Quiet and darkness enveloped them like a cocoon. For a time, fear and anxiety huddled with them, keeping their eyes and ears straining for any sign of Mister. But the terrifying hush and darkness persisted without further addition. Exhausted from the prior night, Otter's eyelids grew leaden, and her chin began to sink rhythmically toward her chest.

A low thud from above snapped her eyes and head to attention. A silent hand squeezed her shoulder. Squinting toward her friend in the hideout's negligible light, she made out the vague shadow of a single finger extended upward toward the cabin above them. Otter allowed her gaze to follow the pointing digit. Her breath caught in her throat.

The pale, flagging light of late afternoon was barely visible through the slight cracks between the floorboards. Where it penetrated, it hung like gauze or cobwebs just beneath the cellar's ceiling, never reaching the subterranean chamber's dirt floor. But the light didn't hold steady. Otter focused through squinting eyes, but the light was interrupted, as if something above them undulated silently through the beams to cast slices of shadow and glow onto the cellar's ceiling.

Otter realized she was holding her breath and exhaled as softly as possible, forcing herself to breathe naturally. Her hand found Cherry's, and the two of them sat trembling in the darkness.

Mister took his time. The shadow crept and crawled across every inch of the cabin's floor, as if inspecting it for clues. Otter knew from the stampeding roar in the forest and the wake of shattered branches on the path that Mister was enormous. But it was not until now, seeing his sinuous shadow cast in relief above her, that she appreciated just how *long* he must be as well. Despite such mass, however, her friend's dark imaginary moved without making a sound. Had his forcing the door not wakened, they would never have heard him at all.

The thought of being hunted by such a creature squeezed her throat with apprehension. With difficulty, she gulped.

Once Mister had canvassed the entire floor, the undulation slowed and eventually stopped. Otter's breath halted as well while she waited to see what he would do next. Then, when she began to think he would stop there and wait out the night, the shadow surged toward the center of the room and emitted a roar that froze Otter's blood and set both girls trembling in their shared embrace. Seconds later, with the silence and dust still settling back over the cabin, the creature seemed to decide that nothing was there for it before skittering noisily back out of the cabin.

By that time, the darkness in the cellar was nearly complete, and Cherry was a mere shadow despite Otter's eyes having grown accustomed to the lack of light. The girls sat entombed in the hollow silence, adding to it only their own subdued breathing, which the silence impassively swallowed. An unsettling expectancy hung about them in the quiet, as if the air itself was waiting for further disturbance. The progression of tension—from the cabin's initial calmness, to the creeping quiet of Mister's entry and inspection, to the beast's terrifying utterance and its audibly insouciant departure, and finally to silence again—left Otter feeling as though anything might yet happen, and she dared not make a sound.

Cherry seemed to sense the tension as well. Barely visible now, she once again placed her finger to her lips and shook her head.

Cherry's meaning was clear, and Otter had no intention of defying the command.

Sight had long since failed when sleep finally came for them, surrounding them like an army laying siege to their cocoon of quiet dark. Otter fought against the crushing onslaught of exhaustion and tense boredom, but to no avail. Just as consciousness slipped from her grasp, she realized she had neglected the one weapon she had. She only hoped she would remember it in the morning.

"Your libertyslippers?"

Otter had the eerie sensation that this was not her first time living through this very day. After a night of frightened huddling and restless sleep in the hideout, she sat at the cabin's scarred table across from Cherry and ate breakfast in the mid-morning sunlight that bathed the room through the windows, much as she had the day before.

She nodded patiently. "Right. There has to be a way to use them to defeat Mister."

Their return to the surface had come with unsettling news. Mister had somehow removed the door from the frame without it falling to the floor, which was how he had made so much less noise during his most recent intrusion. Worse still, he had removed the door from the cabin altogether, taking it with him when he left. Eddies of leaves swirled into the open doorway from time to time and skittered across the floor upon gaining entry. That, at least, was different from yesterday, although not in any way Otter liked.

A small gust of wind sent a curly strand of Cherry's red hair flying, and she absently tucked it behind her ear as the words wrinkled her brow: "But how? Wouldn't wearing libertyslippers mean you couldn't touch him at all? That seems like we'd be even more helpless against Mister than usual."

Otter was growing uncharacteristically excited, and her feet bounced on the floor as she inched forward in her seat. In her brief period of freedom, Otter had received a great deal of help from the few friends she'd made along the way. The idea that she might now be the one to help her new friend was exhilarating. "Right, but he wouldn't be able to touch *you* either. Or maybe me." She frowned slightly from the difficulty of working out how to deploy the libertyslippers as a weapon. "Well, whoever is wearing them, anyway. And the best part is that he won't know that until he tries." The frown transformed to confidently pursed lips as she finished her sentence with a triumphant nod.

Cherry's face suggested that she found any triumph premature. "I don't know, Otter. He's so smart. And what good is it that he wouldn't know about the libertyslippers? How do we use that to get rid of him?"

Otter's pensive frown, never far from reach, had returned. Staring out over Cherry's shoulder and through the rectangular hole where the door had been, Otter scratched her head, lost in thought.

"Maybe we could lure him into a trap. What if I wore the slippers and acted as bait? Could anything hurt him? Is anything dangerous enough to work as a trap for something so big and strong?"

Cherry opened her mouth as if to protest, but no words came, and slowly her mouth closed. It was her turn to frown. After a moment's thought, she said, "You know, maybe something is."

Looking over the ledge of a yawning chasm that cut the forest in two, Otter felt her head swim and her stomach lurch. Dizzy, she stepped backward and gulped down the icy knot in her throat. "Do you think it could work?" Despite the earlier enthusiasm, her ears found that her own voice had adopted Cherry's doubtful tone.

Cherry's clipped laugh made it clear that her own doubt had gone nowhere. "I really don't know. Until yesterday, I had never even considered that I could somehow get rid of Mister. And maybe even together we can't. But if anything could stop him, I would think it would be a fall from up here."

Otter took a discreet step back from the ledge and felt immediately better. "So we lure him out here, he finds me cornered on this ledge and when he pounces, he goes over the edge and down to the bottom of the ravine?" She paused as Cherry confirmed this understanding with a nod. "But how can we be sure he comes at me fast enough to go over?"

Cherry's smile was devoid of mirth. "That is an excellent question. He will be suspicious if we make it too obvious. He's clever and cunning, and he won't be easily fooled. So getting him over here is the first problem. Getting his guard down is another."

Otter held her chin in her hand, and her fingers drummed thoughtfully against her cheek. "What if I looked as if I were armed? What if we made it seem as if I were luring him out to fight him? Or capture him?"

Cherry's face grew still with thought. After a moment, she blinked as if shaking off a daydream. "I just don't know, Otter. I just don't know. I've never even considered anything like this before. So maybe it works. But maybe it doesn't." The two of them stood looking into each other's eyes, the silence crystallizing into tension. At last, Cherry broke her gaze and the silence with a long, deliberate sigh. "Okay, Otter." This time the smile conveyed warmth. "Armed with *what?*"

Otter smiled back. "I don't know. Maybe a knife? Or a big stick?"

Cherry rubbed her chin. "Maybe. But probably the best way to get him running in the first place is for him to be chasing you. Maybe he could find you a short distance from here and you could run to the ledge with him in pursuit."

Just the mention of running in the libertyslippers was enough to freeze Otter's blood. "Cherry, I don't know about that. What if I trip while I'm running? I would fall into the ground and be gone for good."

"If Mister is chasing you, that would be the case regardless of the libertyslippers. But yes, that's a problem." Cherry pondered for a moment. "What if he were chasing me instead?"

"But you said he can't hurt you. Why would he chase you?"

"He might do it if he thought I would lead him to you. I could pretend to be running to warn you, and you could pretend to only be looking over the edge when he arrives. Maybe the excitement of the hunt would keep him running at full speed . . . over the edge?"

The question mark in Cherry's voice betrayed a lack of confidence in the plan. But it also spurred Otter on. A plan was their only hope, so if the plan didn't inspire confidence, it meant they just needed to keep working on it.

Planning continued in snips here and there throughout the day. Cherry was committed to completing the chores she'd neglected the day before, and much of the girls' conversation was occupied by Cherry's coaching Otter in the basics of living alone in the cabin. Still, whenever more pragmatic talk died down, Otter returned to the plan.

"What if I ran only a little way, to make it seem as if I wasn't waiting there for him?"

Each suggestion garnered the same dubious response from Cherry: "Maybe."

Yet Otter persevered. And each "maybe" seemed to carry just a shade more confidence. At least Otter thought that's what she heard when she listened closely.

With the dishwashing from their last meal done, and the doorless cabin tidy except for whatever forest debris the wind carried in at random through the rectangular hole that was the entrance, the girls filed into the hatch for another night huddled in the darkness.

In the morning, they stood gaping at the spot where the table and chairs had been.

Mister was clearly trying to make their lives more difficult in any way he could, all while making sure his presence could not be forgotten. The girls had never been in any danger of *that*. But they certainly had more Mister on their minds than usual as they stood and ate their breakfast in sullen silence.

They brushed the crumbs briskly from their hands, and then their planning resumed with a renewed sense of urgency.

The details had now begun to take shape. Behind the spot they'd selected, the ledge took a nauseating plunge into a ravine whose floor of jagged stone teeth all but vanished in the distance. Otter would wait, libertyslippers off, near the ledge, but not so close that it would raise suspicions. She would pretend to be working on something, distracted. Upon hearing Cherry's warning cries, she would wait until Mister drew into sight, run to the edge of the chasm, and then don the libertyslippers, as quickly as she safely could, while he charged at full speed. She would then stand up as if to face him and, if all went as intended, he would continue his charge straight through Otter and perish in the depths below.

Cherry gulped audibly as they peered down on the place where they hoped soon to be looking over onto Mister's still form. "I know it's for the best, but I still feel guilty. After all, it's my fault, right? I made him this way. And now I know I made a killer. And if we don't do this, it's only a matter of time before it's you, Otter, or eventually someone else."

Otter didn't know what to say. She couldn't imagine how Cherry must feel. Having never had an imaginary, she had nevertheless devoted a great deal of thought to imagining the perfect one, and the idea of having a truly horrid one, of having to choose between its life and that of others, was simply unfathomable. Yet here they were, and Otter was helping Cherry make exactly that choice. Without thinking, she reached over and placed her arm around Cherry's shoulder. She felt her companion stiffen momentarily at the contact. Then Cherry seemed to alight upon a decision and relaxed, tilting her head until her temple touched Otter's.

The girls stood there like that, looking over the ledge, for several minutes without speaking. Then the tension built up in Cherry's shoulders and communicated through Otter's extended arm, and Otter sensed another decision in the making.

Cherry lifted her head and turned to face Otter. A firmness had taken hold in her voice. "Well, we had better start practicing if we want to get this right."

"'Practicing'?" Otter turned her head quizzically.

Cherry smiled firmly and nodded. "Practicing," she repeated. "I don't know about you, but I sure wouldn't want my first time trying to rush a pair of libertyslippers onto my feet to be the exact moment when Mister is actually barreling down on me. So unless you don't need the practice . . ."

Otter needed the practice.

For the next several days, the girls rehearsed their eventual showdown with Mister, simulating their worst expectations as best they could. Taking up her post where they'd decided she would await Mister's charge, Otter began tending a small new patch of garden. After a time, Cherry ran shouting from the woods—the signal that Mister was coming. Otter bolted to her feet and ran to the spot near the ledge designated for her final confrontation with Mister. Stopping just shy of the edge, she quickly but carefully pulled the libertyslippers onto her feet, all while Cherry counted off the seconds.

The first attempt did not instill much confidence.

"That was well over half a minute," Cherry said, her doubt weighing down her tone and expression. "I checked my own speed from the woods to the ledge, and it took me almost exactly half a minute. Mister runs much faster than I can, even accounting for any element of surprise when he sees you."

Otter had doubts of her own. But she resolved not to succumb to discouragement. "Well, it was only the first time. How long should we take to be on the safe side?"

Cherry shrugged. "Twenty seconds?"

"Then we had better get back to it."

Improvement came, but slowly. They broke for meals and any time the frustration grew intolerable. By the time they returned to the cabin for dinner on the first day, they had shaved several seconds from their initial run.

"We'll do better tomorrow," Otter assured Cherry as she used a heel of crispy bread to sop the last dribbles of sauce from her plate. She had even improved at eating while standing.

Cherry nodded but still looked dubious.

They retired to their hideout for the evening while the sun still shone. That night, the darkness above rattled with unusual noises as Mister implemented whatever new annoyance he had contrived. They woke in the morning and ascended to the cabin, which was oddly bright and devoid of shadows. Mister had somehow removed the shutters.

Otter and Cherry ate their breakfast on the cabin's squat stoop, their plates perched on their laps. Neither uttered more than a sigh until they were done and had returned to practice, which they undertook with fresh urgency.

That second day of practice saw their technique advance and their time shrink. It also invited a phenomenon to which both girls had grown unaccustomed: play. As the tedium of their repetitive practice wore on, their frustration mounted, and their patience wilted in the sunlight. This led to a proliferation of breaks, giving the pair such free time and young companionship as neither had experienced in ages. Cherry had been almost entirely alone since leaving her family in Harborton. And Otter had not enjoyed the company of "peers" since her time in the Home's dreary nursery. But despite the maturity their adultlike duties had imposed on their lives, both girls were quite young, and play came back to them as though they were greeting an old friend.

"Throw it to me while I run!"

Otter looked at the specterine in her hand. Its red skin already sported multiple darkening bruises, and in several spots the pale flesh beneath its skin shifted squishily beneath her fingers' casual probing. A mischievous grin curled Otter's lips as she wound up to catapult the battered red fruit to her speeding friend.

Her aim was true, and Cherry deftly seized it from the air. But the specterine could take no more. A dramatic splattering sound accompanied a sudden gush of sticky juice and pulverized fruit flesh, coating the startled child as her run slowed to a bewildered halt. For one stunned moment, she looked down at herself and the mess that coated her, and then she and Otter broke into simultaneous peals of laughter. Cherry sat down with a thump and laughed from her spot on the ground, while Otter rolled about as if she were being tickled. Cherry could hardly remember the last time she'd laughed so hard; Otter could not remember ever having done so. By the time their giggles had subsided, they were both ready for lunch, and they walked hand in hand back to the cabin, still wrapped in the glow of their frolic.

As Cherry cleaned herself off, Otter prepared their modest midday meal, deep in thought. Even her time on the Farm, when she was surrounded by friends imaginary and real alike, had been solitary in a sense because the others were all adults, and Otter, despite age beyond her years, remained a child. She found herself counting off events on her fingers in an effort to calculate the passage of time in her life. "So—eleven years, I think," she mumbled to no one. Yet the youngest people on the Farm were imaginaries, and they all belonged with adults, which meant the imaginaries themselves were essentially adults too. Even Melvin and Luna, as close as Otter had grown to them, were not the kind of friends with whom she could find herself tossing distressed fruits and falling into fits of giggles. Cherry, she realized, was the first friend she could relate to, who understood not only her hardships, but also how those hardships appeared through the eyes of a child who was afraid and alone.

Birdsong and the rustling of leaves in the arid afternoon breeze supplied the only sounds on the stoop as Otter and Cherry ate their lunch without speaking. But Otter no longer sensed in the silence between them any trace of the tension that had strained the lulls in their earliest conversation.

With their meal reduced to erratic constellations of crumbs on their plates, Otter hurried them through cleanup and all but pushed her friend off the porch to resume practice.

The final run of the day dipped below a half minute for the first time.

The cycle repeated for days. The girls rose in the morning to find some freshly missing convenience, they practiced and played between meals, and they retired to their subterranean refuge when the afternoon grew short. Each day they shaved a few seconds from Otter's run-through of the plan. Each day Otter grew defter with her rehearsals. Each day they lost something that made life easier or more pleasant.

On the fourth day, it was their food.

The night prior had been unusually noisy, with Mister neglecting to sneak about in his thievery. That morning, the girls peeked up into the cabin and found a cataclysmic mess. Virtually every item that wasn't part of the cabin itself was scattered on the ground. The cupboards were bare. Breakfast was late that day, postponed until they'd foraged more food from the forest.

Otter chewed a mouthful of specterine in silence. Cherry, eating just beside her, attempted to stifle her sniffs and sobs, occasionally wiping at her eyes or nose with the back of her hand. But Otter could only pretend not to notice.

Their first practice of the day was several seconds worse than the day before, and they made scant progress from there. As the day wore on, they exchanged few words beyond what their practice necessitated. There was no playing.

That night, for more than an hour, the cabin shook like thunder, and dust sifted down on the huddled girls from between the floorboards above, each falling cloud coinciding with a boom from above. When Mister had tired of his havoc, he emitted an unearthly roar that rattled the girls' bones, forcing them to bury their faces in each other's shoulder to suppress the sounds of their mutual weeping.

Sleep took its time coming that night, and it settled only uneasily upon them. They awoke exhausted and in poor spirits.

The sight that awaited them when they emerged from hiding was almost beyond comprehension. The wall beside where the door had been was a wrecked mass of splinters and space, crushed by the force of Mister's repeated assaults. The roof sagged dangerously where its former support lay ruined. Pieces of timber and plaster littered the floor, and thick dust coated every flat surface.

"He's going to tear down the cabin," Cherry said flatly.

Otter looked at her friend. She had heard Cherry's words, but she felt slow in understanding them, as though she were thinking through molasses. All she could say in response was a confused "What?"

"He's done waiting for us. He's going to tear down the cabin. He knows we'll have nowhere to hide once the cabin is gone. He'll tear it down. He'll find us. And he'll . . ." Cherry seemed to choke on the words, and she looked at Otter with tears in her eyes. "We can't stay. We have to go."

In all her tribulations, even when she had held in her hands the libertyslippers that had doomed Crim, Otter had never felt so helpless as she did in that moment. "Go where, Cherry? Where else is there? You came to the cabin because you knew it before. Do you know someplace else you could retreat to? Someplace where Mister couldn't hurt anyone else? And if you did, what would stop Mister from following you again?" Otter inhaled deeply and chose her next words carefully. "Cherry, this is all my fault. If I hadn't come here, none of this would be happening. You would still be surviving just fine, your things would be here, and your home would be intact. I think—I think I should go. I can't fix what I've caused, but I can save you from any further pain on my account."

For a moment, Cherry's tears had stopped, and she looked expressionless at Otter. Then Cherry's face contorted with strong emotion. Otter didn't realize until after the words began that the emotion was anger.

"After all of this"—Cherry gestured expansively around her, her words rolling out in a swelling crescendo—"after all of this, you're just going to leave me alone again? You aren't the only person who's been friendless and frightened in this world, Otter. You aren't the only one who was desperate to escape long before your journey began. Yes, I was *surviving* out here, with Mister posing no life-threatening danger to me. But I was in constant terror of what else he might do to me, or what he might do to someone like you, passing through unsuspecting. Many days I wished I *wasn't* surviving at all if this was how it would be. I can't tell you how often I thought about how I could end Mister's reign in these woods. In this world. In my *life*. I can't tell you how many times I thought how nice it would be to have rest, how I would pay almost *any* price."

By now, Cherry's face had grown white with rage and, it seemed to Otter, profound sadness, as she spat each staccato pronouncement at her companion. She had not seen such fire or felt such heat from her host since that first morning when Cherry had shouted at Otter about Mister and about how Otter could not possibly understand. And she had been right. Yet she was surprised by this barrage, and she flinched as Cherry's finger rose and jabbed in accusation toward her.

"And then *you* came."

Otter hung her head slightly, shamed by the truth, the truth that her coming had destroyed what little serenity Cherry had enjoyed. It was right that she should leave, and it seemed she would not be missed.

So she was surprised to feel her hand being gently taken up in Cherry's, and to hear the suddenly softened tones replace her former fury.

"You came, Otter. And for perhaps the first time ever, I had a friend. And I had hope. And I had a mission, Otter, just like you."

Otter blinked, surprised by her friend's kind words—not that Cherry had given any reason to doubt her kindness, but Otter was surprised by the depth of emotion Cherry was expressing so openly to her. She felt her eyes welling up and wiped wetness from her cheeks with a sniffle.

Cherry continued. "And yes, Mister made my life even worse when you arrived. But if he can put me through this because you are here, he could do the same at any time. And you understood the danger but stayed to help me anyway. If I have to choose between danger and terror with a true friend, or only the illusion of safety alone, I choose you, Otter. If you leave, I leave. Unless"—here a hint of doubt seemed to weigh her voice down—"unless you *want* to leave without me . . ."

Otter sat stunned. No one had ever expressed such feelings for her, even during her extended stay on the Farm. And she had never felt such fondness for someone else as she did in that moment, despite the girls' short time together.

Almost without experiencing the space that separated them, Otter found herself embracing Cherry, who let out a mild squeak at the sudden contact. Otter was reminded of her tearful farewells with the denizens of the Farm. Yet somehow this was deeper, as if their shared struggles had connected them in a way she did not know a person could be connected to another. And this was no goodbye. For a moment, doubt nagged at her as well, with Cherry standing stiff and surprised in her arms. Then Cherry returned the embrace, and they stood there in each other's arms for several minutes with their muted sobs the only sound exchanged between them.

When they stepped back to clear the tears from their faces, each girl seemed to the other to stand a bit taller, their backs a bit straighter, their jaws more firmly set.

Cherry broke the silence first.

"You're right. We can't run. And if we can't run, we have to stay. I think we have some practicing to do." She flashed a smile and squeezed her friend's hand a last time before turning to the woods in search of breakfast.

The day's foraging was surprisingly good. Mister's furious rampage had extended beyond the cabin and into the forest, where he had collided with various trees and dislodged plenty of fruits. Summer was teetering into autumn, leaving the specterines at their sweetest ripeness, and nudging the first sweet acorns of the year, usually still out of reach in the tree-tops, into the dawn of their edible youth. The girls' scavenging also yielded a surprising cache of wild mushrooms of a type prized regionally for their meaty texture and flavor.

Wiping specterine juice from their mouths, they leaned back in the morning sun, oddly rejuvenated despite their ordeal.

Practice went well that day. By lunchtime they had regained their losses from the prior day, and then some. Their moment of shared openness spurred them on even as their mutual fear of Mister could not, and the day seemed to speed by so that, when late afternoon approached, they found themselves push-ing their practice as late as they dared. The last run of the day was barely two seconds over their goal.

"That time was so close!" Cherry's red curls bounced with her strides as she ran to Otter in excitement.

Otter felt her dark cheeks flush, either from her exertion or from the compliment. "I think by tomorrow we'll have it!" Her smile was nearly ear to ear.

Hand in hand and laughing, the girls walked back to the battered leaning cabin in the reddening rays of the low after-noon sun. Side by side they walked, as if by habit, where the doorway had been. Then Cherry's laugh was abruptly severed, and her face blanched as if Mister were there waiting for them.

Alarmed by the sudden shift in her friend's demeanor, Otter squinted into the cabin, searching for the cause of Cherry's alarm.

The cabin was a wreck. But it was no worse than when they had left it that morning. The cupboards laid bare, the furniture stolen, the dust that had settled from Mister's violent assault on the cabin's structure, covering every flat surface except—

"The hatch . . ." Otter's voice sounded distant in her own ears, as though she were calling out a warning to herself from far away. But even from across that great imaginary divide, she heard the fear in her voice, understood the imminence of the threat.

How many times had Cherry told her how clever Mister was? How often had Cherry warned her that they must be wary first and foremost of Mister's dangerous intellect?

And now she saw why.

The layer of dust had coated everything when the house was wrecked. But Mister had not merely been trying to demolish the cabin with his attack. He had looked everywhere in the cabin but had apparently been unable to discover where Cherry had been hiding her new companion. And not having seen Cherry for several nights since Otter's arrival, he seemed to realize that they must be somewhere beneath the cabin. The floor's old wooden planks, smoothed with age, offered little purchase for Mister's hard limbs to search and scour at random. But he must have realized that, if he could figure out where exactly to look, he could focus his energy on their escape route. By dusting the floor, he had laid his trap; the very act of the girls' exiting the cellar that morning had sprung it. Tonight, he would know where to find them.

The two girls stood there, Cherry gaping at the conspicuously cleared rectangular spot on the floor, and Otter looking frantically over her shoulder and anywhere else she could, alert for any threat. An impulse deep within her, the primal feeling that had fueled her endless hours of tedium at the factory as they mounted in daily increments toward escape, the basic instinct that had kept her moving along on her journey, the one intense need that superseded nearly every other in the face of danger, had settled on her as thoroughly as the dust should have been settled on the floor: the need to *run away*.

"Cherry, we have to *go. Now!*" She turned to flee the way they had come. But she stopped short when Cherry didn't budge and didn't release Otter's hand.

"We can't" was all she said, a whisper that barely reached Otter's ear.

"What do you mean? We have to! We can't stay here anymore, Cherry! It's over!"

"No, Otter. You said it yourself. Where would we go?"

"I don't *know*, Cherry! *Somewhere*. But we need to do it now, before he returns!"

A strange calm had settled over the other girl. "We can't," she repeated. "We have to run the plan now. No more practice. This time will be for real." And through the fear that was plain on her face, Cherry smiled reassuringly. "We can do this."

And in that moment, despite everything, Otter believed it. She inhaled deeply and squared her shoulders, lifting her chin to meet her friend's level gaze. She waited a moment to give her faith time to dissipate. When it did not, she nodded firmly. "Okay. Let's do it."

They bolted in unison toward their practice spot, Otter drawing the libertyslippers from her pocket as she ran, balling them up in her hands to carefully keep her fingers from entering the foot holes.

They barely made it. Just as they emerged into the clearing where they'd spent days preparing for this moment, a tremendous noise burst forth from the forest, like the sound of trees being thrown aside with some great force.

"He's here!" Cherry's urgent tone rose in pitch as she veered toward Otter. "He must have risen early today to check on his trap. I'll try to slow him down," she shouted, panting from the exertion.

Otter ran frantically as she tried to regain and sustain the momentary confidence that had surged with Cherry's encouragement. The effort was complicated by the inhuman roar where the crashing sounds had only just subsided, and she felt herself turn involuntarily to look toward their source as she ran. Even Cherry's terrifying descriptions could not have prepared her for what she saw.

The roar itself had emerged from a face dominated by myriad slavering, sharp-toothed jaws, set about a single central gaping maw. The mandibles were layered in a way that resembled the unfolding of rose petals, with each opening and closing on a separate hinge and studded with its own glistening, pointed teeth. The head itself was oddly oblong, like a disc that bulged at the center where the mouth protruded. A ring of many wildly varied eyes encircled the head, running along the edge of the disc at regular intervals. Each eye was part of a pair, separated from its mate on the opposite side of Mister's head, and orbiting the vicious blossom of jaws like planets around the sun. One pair was like that of a cat, another was like the faceted domes of a fly, and still others were unlike any eyes Otter had seen. Most unsettling, just as Cherry had explained, one pair looked distinctly human, albeit larger than any actual person's eyes, and possessed of unmistakable intelligence as they scanned the scene before seeming to lock onto Otter as she ran.

Mister surged forward, thrashing aside any smaller trees or branches that remained in its way. Undulating forward at nearly the speed of a horse in full stride, the beast's body was no less frightening than its head. Cherry had compared his likeness to that of a centipede, and Otter's mind had formed the image of an oversized version of that common creeping bug. Her imagination had not done Mister's hideous but awesome power justice. He was easily the largest imaginary Otter had seen, and yard after yard of his body followed his head over the terrain at breakneck speed. His midnight-hued segments flowed one after another as the late day's orange light glinted off his armored hide. When fully extended toward his target, Mister covered a massive stretch of ground, eating away voraciously at Otter's slender lead with every forward stride.

Glimpsed from the corner of Otter's eye as she raced to the cliff's edge, Mister was more terrifying than any nightmare, and certainly the most terrifying being she had ever seen in the flesh. And he was barreling toward her at an alarming pace. Looking from Mister back to the ledge, Otter realized she could not beat him to the finish. By catching the girls off guard, he had all but finished her. Otter's feet began to feel leaden with the dread of her inevitable demise.

Suddenly Mister drew to a short, scrabbling halt, the front half of its sinuous form rearing up to tower several feet over something that now blocked his way. His enraged roar raised the hairs of her arms as if they were electrified. Distracted by the spectacle, Otter looked over and saw that the obstacle was not some*thing* but some*one*: it was Cherry!

Seeing Otter slow to stare, Cherry screamed urgently at her friend. "Run, Otter! You have to keep going!"

Cherry didn't have to say it twice. Finding within her legs a sudden burst of energy, Otter renewed her push to beat Mister to the designated spot beside the ledge. Mister's early arrival had rendered the subterfuge of gardening irrelevant. Arriving at the ledge, she immediately doubled over and carefully donned the libertyslippers while Cherry occupied Mister's attention. With a speed to rival any of their practice sessions, she had pulled the magical slippers on and now stood ready to face her friend's horrid imaginary. She inhaled deeply, only then realizing she'd been holding her breath. In that moment, she thought again of Cherry and looked up to scan their former practice yard for her friend.

Otter's sight alighted on the other girl, who was still fending off the increasingly frustrated beast, whose unnatural and spittle-flecked roars were growing more frequent and—although Otter could scarcely believe it—louder. Mister feinted left and right to get himself around Cherry, the one person he could not merely plow through, as she raced back and forth to block his way. His link to Cherry had in all likelihood saved Otter, but even from her distant vantage, she saw his impatience whittling away at his caution. Each successful block elicited another furious howl and a slightly more aggressive push, and each time Cherry would block all the more dramatically, jumping into his path or grabbing onto a foreleg in such a way that, were he merely to push past her, she would as likely as not be crushed by his great weight. Mister knew he could not afford that risk.

Still, as his ire boiled over, his caution evaporated. After one particularly exaggerated block left the nightmarish creature's real unbalanced, Mister's body surged abruptly toward Cherry and grabbed her entire body in a swarm of his frontal limbs, lifting her from the ground as she screamed. Otter saw him rear up again and contort into an improbable backward twist, allowing him to toss Cherry roughly but safely behind him, and clearing the path between him and Otter's perch.

Unfurling from his twisted orientation, he turned back to Otter and looked at her for a long moment. He roared again, as loud as ever, but this time Otter did not feel the fear rise in her throat. She knew herself to be safe, the libertyslippers having taken her beyond Mister's sinister reach. The bulging disc of his head turned on his neck as if to give all his many eyes a better look at what must have seemed like cornered prey, but its rotation paused as the strangely human yet inhuman eyes narrowed to inspect her. Satisfied as to his triumph, Mister took up his charge once more.

Otter closed her eyes and waited for him to go crashing through her and onto the floor of the chasm so far below her

feet. She opened them at the sound of Cherry's frantic shouting. "Otter! It didn't work!"

What Otter saw froze her terrified scream before it could
leave her throat.

Mister's strange, ravenous head was mere inches from her
face. He had not run through but had instead stopped to examine this curious brown prey that did not run or panic when
trapped. His vast array of quivering, dripping jaws pulsated
with each breath, but neither its wind nor its teeth touched
Otter in her libertyslippers, even to rustle the tiny hairs on the
edge of her forehead and scalp. Seeing this oddly placid child
in such proximity was apparently too unusual for Mister to
take at face value. Again, he turned his head at a sharp angle
as each set of eyes ringing his jaws examined her more closely.
Again the almost-human eyes seemed to tarry on her to get an
especially good look.

Otter jerked in alarm as Mister roared without warning.
From this distance, the unearthly howl was nearly deafening,
and it left Otter's ears ringing painfully even as the torrent of
breath carrying the sound blew through her unfelt. His inspection continued, with the eyes of one side of his head mere
inches from Otter, and the eyes on the other side of his head
facing away. After a moment, the beast undertook one final
experiment with this odd child, and he swiped his foremost
monstrous limb through Otter's torso.

If she had been solid, the blow would at least have pushed
her to a jagged death below. But it was delivered with such
speed and such force that Otter was unsure she would even
have been alive to experience the fall.

Each of Mister's eyes blinked in surprise at the unexpected
result. He took a few steps back as though to reassess, and his
head moved in a slow vertical rhythm as he examined Otter
from head to toe and back up again.

Cherry had picked herself up and come running toward the ledge where her imaginary had now cornered her friend. Otter saw that Cherry intended to come between her and Mister as she had done so long ago to remove him from her mother.

But Mister was no hatchling now. Without taking his attention from his cornered prey, a single eye rotated to track the incoming child. As soon as her feet touched the ground within his reach, his barbed tail whipped out and looped around her feet. She would have tripped and fallen, but Mister used his thin tail to lift her from the ground where she dangled with a frightened squeak while the monster continued working over the puzzle before him. Then his many eyes blinked in unison, as if he'd reached a conclusion.

Mister began to dig.

The creature seemed to understand that Otter couldn't be touched. But he also grasped that she somehow stood upon the ground, and that this particular ground, projecting as it did over the cliff, was precarious. If the ground fell, so, too, would the girl. And since he could not eat her if he could not touch her, he seemed to prefer her demise to her escaping. His great, shining limbs went to work, digging his claws into the ground, tearing into it as if the rocky soil were mere cake.

All the while, Otter stood frozen in terror, uncertain of what to do next. She considered running, but she dared not while wearing the libertyslippers. And anyway, she realized, she could not run forever. She considered retreating by walking through him, but she knew this was at best a temporary solution. He would follow her until she inevitably had to stop to remove the libertyslippers. And now that he had Cherry, Otter would not abandon her friend.

Having found all other options lacking, Otter realized that her only hope was to conjure an imaginary even more fearsome than Mister, a protector who could save her from having him literally remove the ground she stood on. Because libertyslippers or not, she could not survive this fall. So she closed her eyes and tried to ignore the violent sound of Mister's digging as she began to conceive of the kind of formidable features her imaginary would need if she were to be saved. At that moment, she thought she detected a faint shadow of the tingling she'd first felt in Eliza's cage.

Just then, an oddly familiar rumbling from the forest combined with the noise of Mister's determined digging and drew Otter's eyes open, interrupting her feverish imagining. Moment by moment the rumbling grew, until even Mister could no longer ignore it. By the time he looked up from the deep gash he had cut in the earth and cocked his head to allow each of his eyes to better examine the source of the low-pitched crescendo, Otter had recognized the sound.

It was the same guttural, growling din that had prowled the dark nights throughout her journey. She had been too distracted to notice the twilight enveloping the three of them as they struggled, but now she saw that the day had dwindled nearly to nothing. Evening had apparently brought with it the beastly noises Otter had avoided in the nights she'd spent with Cherry. And judging by their rapidly increasing volume, the sources of the noise seemed to be quickly converging on the spot where Mister had ensnared the girls. Otter was relieved for anything that offered a respite from the digging, but the return of the mysterious beasts that had haunted her through so many tormented nights, at exactly the moment she was already in the clutches of another terrifying beast, seemed a mixed tiding at best.

Suspended above the ground by Mister's serpentine tail, Cherry paused in her frustrated effort to wrest herself free, her curiosity arresting her struggles. "Otter, is that the noise you told me about?" Her voice was tight with fear, and loud so she could be heard. Otter could tell from her tone that Cherry had never encountered such sounds before.

"Yes," she shouted back. "Those are what I thought were, um, you know." She meant Mister, but she dared not speak the creature's name, lest doing so might draw his attention back to her.

Cherry just continued staring, upside down, as the roaring rushed toward them like a great wave, its source racing unknown in the shadows of the forest. "But—but what *is* it?"

They found out soon enough.

From the edge of the forest a beast sprung, its massive paws propelling it off the trees' vertical boles as if it had come by bouncing through the forest without touching the ground. A mane of thick, matted fur lay sleek against its head and neck, flattened by the rush of the wind as it bounded toward them. Its huge mouth, full of shining white teeth bared by snarling lips, was open wide and emitting one note in the chorus of roars rushing toward them.

*Right* toward them, Otter realized. This new creature was fast closing the distance between itself and the three of them as they stood—and hung—by the cliff's edge, perplexed by this shocking spectacle.

Then another of the gigantic beasts leaped from the forest. Then another, and another. Soon it became clear that an entire pack of these creatures was emerging from the forest, and all of them heading straight for her and Mister.

Mister sprang into action. His tail tossed Cherry aside like a rag doll as he turned his back away from his cornered prey. Cherry shrieked at the sudden acceleration and let out a grunt as her body hit the earth with a dull thud. She recovered quickly enough, though, and rolled beyond his reach.

Next Mister's segmented body surged upward, and dozens of limbs with their claws and shining armor spread as if inviting an embrace, but he was bracing for battle, anticipating the impending onslaught. His tail flicked irritably back and forth, and Otter flinched as it whipped through her intangible form.

Mister's venomous tail was not her only concern, though, as more of the shaggy beasts surged from the forest and through the rapidly descending night. She began to shake as their approach grew closer. In mere seconds they had halved the distance from the forest to the cliff. In only a few more, they would be bearing down directly upon the girls and the rearing imaginary.

Though only scant light now remained in the shroud of darkness around them, Otter found herself squinting at the blur of creatures hurtling her way. Something nagged at her memory in that moment, and she could not shake the sense that she had seen these creatures before. Then, just as their leader had nearly reached Mister and lunged toward his weaving, menacing massiveness, her jaw dropped open with sudden recognition.

These were the same animals that had been held captive in Junkton on the grounds outside the factory. The same creatures she had fed from the towering wheelbarrows of fruit as she was making her escape. Not just any fruit, she now realized, but specterines. And these were not just any animals, she saw as they piled one after another onto Mister, whose roars blended with theirs in a chorus of dueling battle cries.

These animals, Otter realized, were libertylions.

And this time, *they* were rescuing *her*.

~ CHAPTER 11 ~

# A FRIEND FOR OTTER

OTTER STOOD IN astonishment as, perhaps only ten feet from her, half a dozen libertylions collided at full velocity with Mister while his sinuous body whipped about to confront them with ferocious speed and strength. The giant cats were almost as big as horses. But Mister was bigger. Still, with six libertylions already set upon him and more on their way, he struggled just to emerge from their assault.

Mister was not the only one reeling from the libertylions' emergence from the tree line. Otter thought back to the sleepless nights accompanied by the chorus of menacing, feral sounds. But they had not been a menace at all; they had been an escort of libertylions, apparently following her ever since the night of her escape. She thought back to what Cherry had told her about libertylions drawing their ability to dematerialize from the specterines, of which their keepers in Junkton fed them only enough to ensure the magical properties of the libertyslippers. Her feeding the animals, then, had freed them. And their nocturnal nature had put their devotion to good use by guarding her nights. Now they were doing it again, and that devotion had landed them in a fight where even their great size and numbers could not guarantee victory—or survival.

Still, the libertylions held their own pretty well.

Repeatedly Mister lashed at the pouncing cats with his wicked tail, but each time its venomous barb passed through them without contact. Otter's eyes widened as the furious flurry of libertylions phased in and out of substance while they fought their single foe. She saw one libertylion lunge at him and, upon his turning toward the incoming attacker with his many-eyed, many-mandibled head, pass through him, so that his jaws snapped shut on empty space, only to receive a jarring blow to the back of his neck as the same libertylion emerged from behind him. He spun about and roared in frustration, already too late to avenge the blow.

Still, Mister was taking his toll on the beasts, and with such a mighty adversary, even their great size, speed, and magical abilities could not keep them all from harm's way. Otter gasped as one libertylion fell to the ground with a nauseating noise, its neck turned at an odd angle after it materialized too soon and was rammed by Mister's flailing head. Another had wandered from the fray, staggering and disoriented after taking the barb of Mister's tail across one wide flank.

Yet for each libertylion removed from the fight, others came in as reinforcements. Otter counted more than a dozen that had joined in the melee, and a few stragglers stood aside, wagging their haunches as they searched for an opening in which to pounce.

But Mister was clever, as Cherry had often reminded Otter, and he quickly seemed to realize that he could not dislodge the pack by fighting on their terms. So he changed tactics. One moment he was towering over the earth and striking like lightning at the throng of cats bearing down on him; in the next he had curled into a tight, armored ball, buried beneath the fur and fighting, made impervious to attack by his impenetrable hide. Then, like a giant compressed spring he erupted from the pile of libertylions, sending some of them flying even as some doggedly hung on, with jaws and claws sunk in to their quarry. Otter let out a dismayed squeak as two of the libertylions were propelled over the cliff by this tactic.

"Otter!" Squinting into the deepening night, she barely made out Cherry's outline waving frantically for her attention. Cherry's face made it plain that she, too, was surprised and shaken by the spectacle before them, but her composure remained intact nonetheless. "Don't move! I'm going to get a lantern. We can't do anything in this darkness." And with that, she was off.

Otter tried not to let panic carry her after her friend. The risk of retreating while wearing the libertyslippers was too great, especially with all the distraction from Mister's mortal combat with the libertylions. Still, as her friend faded into the darkness, Otter could not keep her heart from sinking at least a little.

For better or worse, she had little time for such thoughts now as the fight began to creep toward her. Mister's tactic had done more than dislodge some of his attackers. It had also given him space to regroup and adopt a new strategy. Withdrawing again into his carapace, Mister used his alternating maneuver of contracting and surging to fling off libertylions here and there. But then Otter realized Mister was not merely shrinking and rising but was also using his rhythmically alternating positions to move the entire battle toward the ledge—and right toward Otter.

This was a disconcerting revelation. That approach not only seemed to be working at thinning the libertylions' numbers, but it was also increasingly shrinking the space where

Otter stood between the fight and the chasm below. Alarmed, she tried to edge farther in from the ledge by going through the fighting. But a momentarily dematerialized libertylion's tail smacked her hard across the cheek and caused her nearly to lose her balance. Peering over the chasm's depth, she gasped with fright even as her mind raced to comprehend what had just happened. Unlike all the rest of the world, the libertylions could physically interact with her while she was wearing the libertyslippers. But it seemed only to happen when the cats were in their phased-out state. She shuddered to contemplate her fate if a libertylion collided full-on with her should she attempt another escape. Otter decided the peril was too great a risk.

The lions seemed to understand Mister's ploy as well. By then, all the remaining libertylions had joined in, having stepped in for their comrades who had fallen to Mister's thrashing. The group of them began to focus their attacks on one side of the monster in an effort to push him back inland, but not before several had gone over the ledge and fallen to the depths below.

Mister responded to their attempted compensation by alternating his expansion and contraction with sudden lateral attacks. He would lash out suddenly as the libertylions poised to pounce, catching one here with his nightmarish maw, another there with his deadly tail. Despite the libertylions' numbers, the tide was turning slowly against them.

"Otter!" Cherry was panting from running. She had returned with a lantern, which she held aloft several feet from the battle. "Are you in there?"

"I'm here," Otter shouted back. She struggled even with the lamplight to see her friend through the tumult that cornered her on the chasm's lip.

"Can you use the light to see your way out?"

Otter again assessed her situation. The libertylions seemed not to be using their phasing abilities as much, but occasionally she felt a breeze as one moved violently past her. "I think my best chance is not to move. The libertylions' bodies can interact with mine when they pass through Mister. They know where I am, but it will be harder if I move."

Cherry's mouth was tight with anxiety, but she nodded her understanding, and Otter turned back to her bizarre confines.

Squinting at the battle blurring before her, Otter realized that Mister was not the only cagey combatant here. The libertylions had changed tactics in the face of Mister's methodical gambit, and now it was they who were inching the fight toward the ledge, having abandoned their powers in lieu of raw physical force. Otter's eyes widened and her breath caught as the battle crept closer and closer to her. And then it was upon her. She tried not to panic as the storm of combat between Mister and the libertylions came to occupy the very ground on which she stood. Where Mister and her body overlapped, she felt nothing. But where the libertylions passed through her, even in their solid form, she felt a gut-wrenching pull. It was as though the beasts' substance, endowed with the same powers that rendered her insubstantial to all the rest of the world, stuck to her own being and dragged at her as the cats ferociously flew away from and back toward their enemy.

Otter was not the only one who had noticed the libertylions embracing Mister's creep toward the precipice. Too late he seemed to understand they had co-opted his approach, apparently with the same intent—to force their adversary over the cliff and to his demise.

But that plan had a problem. The libertylions may have had superior numbers. But Mister had the advantages of size, strength, and armor, to say nothing of the swarm of insectile limbs that would allow him to hang on even as he flung the cats violently from him. The libertylions were not similarly equipped. Their giant paws hid powerful claws, but they were poorly suited for hanging on to a cliff's rocky face.

Otter stood, in the eye of this bestial storm, occupying the same space where Mister lashed about to inflict as much damage as he could on his way to where the land suddenly fell away, and she realized with despair that the libertylions who remained in the fight had determined to finish Mister here, even if it cost them their own lives.

The wrenching in her gut now was from more than just the discomfort of solid libertylions passing back and forth through her body. It was also from the nearly incomprehensible realization that these creatures, freed from their captivity all those months ago by her hand, had so dedicated themselves to her survival that they would now sacrifice their own to save her. Otter wondered how terrible their lives must have been that an isolated act of kindness had inspired such loyalty. She could not imagine, even knowing as she did the cruelty that pervaded the factory and its environs.

But more immediate concerns brought her back to the present. The fighting was now terribly close to the ledge. In fact, the cloud of striking and leaping animals had moved nearly completely through Otter, and she finally saw an opening to move out of its way. Letting the pale light of Cherry's lantern guide her, she stepped delicately across the ground, away from the ledge and the ear-splitting clash now teetering upon it.

Reaching Cherry, she immediately bent over to remove the libertyslippers and tossed them to the ground as though even having them near her was too great a danger. She had never worn them so long before, let alone in such perilous conditions, and she felt certain she'd rather face Mister on his own terms, should he survive, than risk another second with those *things* on her feet. Then, having rejoined the material world, she crashed bodily into her friend's arms. The two of them stood there a moment, oblivious to the roaring and teeth gnashing mere feet away from them.

The embrace lasted only a few seconds, but it felt like an eternity had passed by the time the girls, tears streaking their cheeks, returned their attention to the deadly fray on the cliff's edge.

Five libertylions remained attached to Mister by little more than force of will. Four had each snared a cruel, segmented limb, each of which groped viciously but ineffectively about, in search of a libertylion's soft hide to grab and slice. The fifth great cat had caught onto Mister's tail, whose wicked barb hung mangled and limp, even as the tail itself writhed to inflict its whipping wrath on its captor. Several libertylions lay around unmoving—perhaps, Otter feared, unbreathing. Still others were unaccounted for completely.

Mister roared in frustration and fury. His oblong head swiveled about so that his many eyes could better examine the foes who had him pinned. Occasionally, having found a slight opening, his sinuous neck would spring forth and his layered jaws would snap hungrily at one of the libertylions. But they held him so that, each time, the jaws closed on air only.

More pressing than these intermittent attacks, Otter realized, was the libertylions' slow but steady march over the tiny and shrinking space to the ledge. Inch by inch, they tugged and pushed, with Mister fighting them for every step. One moment he was lashing out in search of any opening to strike at his opponents, and the next moment his rearmost legs found that the earth beneath them had disappeared and they dangled helplessly over the lip of the chasm.

Only then did the cunning monster seem fully to comprehend the degree of his peril.

Madly he jerked about, searching for purchase beneath him. Forgotten were his attacks on the libertylions. His only focus now seemed to be his mad scrambling to remain atop the cliff as his feet scrabbled and clawed at the air for solid ground.

That's when the first of the libertylions' final company went over, leaving only four for their last topside stand.

But the massive feline had hung on in its fall, refusing to release its grip on Mister's tail. Staggering, Mister lurched backward as gravity and the libertylion's plummeting weight yanked him violently toward the ledge. A piercing, shrieking roar escaped from his many furiously trembling jaws, conveying for the first time not only his rage, but also a hint of fear. Otter could not help but wonder whether the monster's panic was amplified by his unfamiliarity with the kind of terror he routinely inspired.

In either event, his panic seemed justified to Otter. Several more skittering, flailing legs were forced over the cliff. The libertylions remained doggedly attached, unfazed it seemed by their quarry's violent thrashing. Then another reached the chasm's edge and took the plunge without ever relinquishing its hold on Mister's black segmented leg.

Again Mister lurched backward, and again came his screaming roar. But before its piercing echo had faded, another libertylion went over, pulling almost a yard of Mister's snaking length after him. Barely a third of his body still clung to the earth, and the rest of him flailed helplessly above the vast drop below. Only two libertylions remained above. Clearly neither intended to let go while their enemy hung on.

And hanging on he was.

Mister threw himself forward with all the force he could muster, and with a sudden, violent burst, he drew back his head and then plunged face-first into the rocky soil. His multitude of mandibles had bitten into the earth in a desperate attempt to anchor himself against the libertylions' relentless pull.

Otter realized she had been holding her breath as she watched this spectacle unfold in the harsh shadows cast within the lantern's flickering cone of light. Her hand reached out in search of Cherry's. She found it quickly; apparently Cherry also sought a comforting hand, and their fingers interlaced as they both looked on in suspense. Helplessly they watched, unable to affect the titanic tide of the battle, and hoping desperately that at least these two remaining allies, who had come to the girls as strangers to rescue them in their time of need, might survive it.

The last two libertylions continued their tenacious pull against Mister's new tactic. His ring of eyes peeked hatefully out at his tormentors from barely above the ground, as if daring the cats to dislodge him. Even as his head and mouth seemed to burrow into the ground, his captive limbs continued to fight. They jerked and seized against the powerful jaws, which stubbornly refused to let go.

Still the libertylions continued their march to the ledge, albeit slowed significantly by Mister's attachment to the ground. He was showing signs of fatigue, though, and his reliance on a single point to anchor his mass was taking its toll. From their vantage, the girls saw Mister's armored body stretching unnaturally, its hard black segments slowly pulling away from one another and on the verge of tearing.

The libertylions, too, seemed to notice their enemy's increasingly desperate predicament, and they began whipping their heads from side to side as if to hasten the effect.

Slowly, Mister's embedded head emerged from the ground as his grip and the earth began to fail. His many eyes shifted momentarily to the girls, and his two disconcertingly human eyes locked with their gazes, as if to save his final hateful glare for them. The girls could not tear their eyes away from Mister's as he abruptly released the earth with a roar. Striking like a bolt of lightning, he snapped his head around in one desperate attempt to inflict suffering on the libertylions, even in the face of his inescapable defeat. But relinquishing his hold on the earth released all the resistance at once, and like a spring they snapped back with all the force that had built up between them.

And with that, Mister and the last two libertylions still atop the ledge descended over the cliff as one.

Otter and Cherry stood there in stunned silence, mouths and eyes unable to widen any farther. Around them lay libertylions, some barely moving, others showing no signs of life at all. A rustling near the forest's edge drew the girls' eyes to a smattering of cubs and elderly libertylions emerging into the open, having hidden out of the way while their able-bodied compatriots did battle. Slowly these newcomers shambled over to stand with the girls and join them in silently staring out from the lantern's flickering glow after those who had fallen into the deep blackness below.

Cherry broke the silence first. "I guess I thought I would feel it."

Otter looked at her friend, unable to respond. So she simply stood there and gave Cherry's hand a gentle squeeze.

"He's been with me for so long. How could I not feel it now that he's gone?" Cherry didn't sound sad. To Otter, she sounded—confused.

A memory tickled Otter's brain. She recalled Luna explaining the bond that existed between herself and each imaginary she brought into being. Luna had spoken of feeling the bond to a new imaginary disappear when it passed on to the intended real. She supposed Luna had never said so expressly, but Otter would have expected a real to feel the bond disappear in the same way if the imaginary were to meet an untimely end. And Mister's end would certainly seem to qualify.

As she chewed nervously on this puzzle, an odd glint of reflected lamplight from the cliff caught Otter's attention. She squinted, trying to make it out. It almost looked like—

"Cherry! It's him!"

A shining black leg, battered but intact, had clawed back over the ledge. Somehow, Mister had survived the libertylions' onslaught *and* his tumble over the cliff.

The girls froze in place, horror-struck. Cherry's grip clamped Otter's hand until her fingers began to hurt.

Slowly, Mister's mangled form emerged from the chasm and onto level ground. Within a few seconds, he had heaved the rear of his massive carapace over the edge and announced himself with a roar of undefeated ferocity. When the unearthly sound had finished cascading against the chasm's stone walls, the beast's odd, oblong head swiveled, so that his eyes, shining in the reflected lamplight, could better regard the girls where they stood. The eyes narrowed at the corners, as if Mister were smiling at the girls with triumphant malevolence.

Then he came for them.

Mister's speed was not what it had been. The fight had left him wounded and limping, and some of his rearmost segments dragged limply behind him. Still, many of his powerful append-ages remained intact, and he surged fitfully forward. His most disturbingly humanlike eyes seemed to bore into Otter as he moved, and she had the sense that the creature, having endured such violence in trying to finish her, had resolved not to let that task go unfinished and pay the price in vain.

The pressure on Otter's fingers vanished, leaving them throbbing. She realized with alarm that Cherry had released her hand only to run ahead and confront the charging beast.

The lantern sat on the rocky soil beside Otter in the space where Cherry had been.

"You can't have her! Why can't you just let me have a friend?" Her shouts were punctuated by sobs of frustration and anger. She planted her feet and stood firmly athwart his path. "You have taken everything and everyone. You won't have Otter!"

Jerking unsteadily but unrelentingly forward, he quickly covered the ground to where Cherry stood. Never slowing or taking his eyes from Otter, he swatted his defiant real aside like a bug and staggered ahead toward his intended target. Cherry fell to the ground with a frightened but angry yelp.

Ravenous and determined, Mister bored ahead. Otter had only seconds. Desperately she searched about for cover. The woods, she thought, might be her only hope. Had he been in his normal condition, the woods would do little to shield her. In his current state, though, perhaps the woods would give her a fighting chance. Certainly the motley pride of libertylions that remained could not mount the kind of assault that had already postponed this showdown.

She reached down for the lantern and ran for the tree line, trying to steer clear of any helpless libertylions who would otherwise end up in Mister's path. The lantern, she realized, would make her easier to track. But she was hopeless without it, the night's curtain having descended completely around them.

Mere seconds later she had reached the trees, and she turned to assess the width of her lead.

It was not enough. A startled gasp escaped as she realized how close he had already come. Despite his condition, Mister was still strong and fast, and he had covered more ground than she had in the same time. *Now or never*, she grimly thought as she pivoted back to the trees. The lamplight infiltrated only a few feet into the forest's impenetrable darkness. Taking a deep breath, she braced herself for the plunge into the woods.

*"Mister!"*

Cherry's furious cry behind her carried a strange weight. It commanded attention and would not be ignored. Otter turned to see what had prompted her friend's shout. In the lantern's pale light, she saw that Mister, too, seemed affected by the tone in his real's voice and had stopped to assess the situation.

"This has to stop," Cherry yelled, and she held something aloft.

Otter and Mister both squinted to see, Otter with two eyes and cocking her head to one side, Mister with his many eyes and his oblong head swiveling for the best vantage. Despite their straining in the dark, they were too far away. Whatever she held was small, no bigger than Otter's—

Otter's hand jumped to her pocket with alarm in search of the discreetly folded bulge. Nothing was there. She had thrown the libertyslippers to the ground upon taking them off. And now Cherry had them. But why?

Otter's mind raced to fit the pieces together. When Mister pushed Cherry aside, Cherry had grabbed the libertyslippers from the ground. As Mister had been about to chase Otter into the woods, Cherry shouted to get Mister's attention. When Mister turned, she held the libertyslippers up as if Mister should pay attention. Not only could Otter not see how the libertyslippers changed anything, she was concerned with Cherry's cavalier handling of them.

That's when it dawned on her. Cherry had not shouted only to get Mister's attention. She had shouted to get Otter's as well. So that she could say goodbye.

"Otter, he'll never stop. He'll never leave you alone. And—" An impassioned sob caught in her throat. Mister watched closely, his head still shifting, as if trying to sniff some understanding of the situation on the wind. But Cherry kept speaking, and the monster that lay between her and Otter, unsure of the girl's gambit, kept listening. "And just as bad, he'll never leave me alone. He'll never let me have a happy life. He won't—he won't even let me have a friend, Otter."

"Cherry, no! We'll find a way!" Desperately Otter racked her brain for a way to stop her friend. Haunting memories of the factory and her brief introduction to Crim, whose sudden end Otter had witnessed, ran through her mind. She thought again of imagining a beast that could best Cherry's terrible imaginary and, closing her eyes, she returned with terrible desperation to the imaginings she had entertained when Mister had her cornered on the cliff.

"Otter, I can't let you do what you're thinking."

Cherry's tone and words were so matter-of-fact. Otter knew she had almost no time. Furiously she imagined with an urgency she had never felt before. In her mind, a monster of terrible feature and tremendous proportion took shape. Again the indescribable tingling sensation came. But instead of creeping upward, it surged from her toes and through her small body like a tidal wave as her face contorted with grim concentration. The tingling flooded her being with a chill and violent current, which seemed to squeeze through her essence from bottom to top until it could eventually do nothing but emerge whole from her mind.

Mister, too, understood that something had changed. He may not have understood how, but he had somehow sensed that the source of his anxiety hinged on whatever Cherry was holding. Slowly he brought his sinuous body fully about, as if any sudden movement might trigger whatever plan his real had in store for him. His mouth opened, but instead of the usual roar, it made a soft, almost soothing clicking sound, as if to convince Cherry that he meant no harm—as if she didn't know better than anyone that he did.

"Otter, no."

Cherry's seriousness was more pronounced this time. But Otter would not stop. The tingling continued to surge up her legs and into her body as if she were a vessel into which a torrent of icy liquid was being poured.

"Otter, it's more than just losing the chance to imagine the perfect friend. If you imagine a monster, you will be responsible for it. Its monstrosity will not only be *from* you but a *part* of you. If we make monsters to fight monsters, we are still making a world of monsters. I can't let you do that. Not for me, Otter. Not for me." Cherry choked on another sob, and Otter's imagination froze. The rising sensation vanished all at once, as though it had never been. Her lower extremities, where the feeling had seemed to occupy her every fiber, now felt only fatigue and numbness. She opened her eyes so she could see the truest friend she had ever known or could ever have imagined.

Mister had crept closer, but he continued to advance carefully, unsure of what might come next.

"You were the only friend I ever had, Otter. I am sad we didn't get more time to get to know each other. But I am so happy to have known you. Thank you for all you have done for me and meant to me."

"Cherry," Otter sobbed. "Please, don't do this. Let me. I can stop him. I can do this. I can't go from having you as a friend to not. Please. Please let me help."

Mister seemed to sense his time to act slipping. He surged forward at an unreal speed given his condition, so that he would soon be upon his real and the lethal libertyslippers she held in her hands.

"Goodbye, Otter," Cherry said. Otter could barely hear over the pounding and dragging of Mister's legs across the ground. "I love you, friend."

"NOOOOOOO!" Otter screamed. But to no avail.

Otter could not see Cherry's face as the girl slipped her fingers into the openings in both libertyslippers. Like a sack of grain, she sank into the ground, disappearing from sight in an instant.

Mister's legs buckled and ceased moving, as though an internal switch had been flipped. He crashed into the ground with the phenomenal force of his forward momentum and slid half the remaining distance between himself and where his real had disappeared. Not a hair of him so much as twitched.

Otter's shout still reverberated in her own ear as her feet took flight toward the spot where Cherry had stood. She paid no mind to Mister's crumpled body, which she trampled over like so many mounds of dirt.

Arriving at her destination, she slid to her knees, sinking to the ground. She dropped the lantern blindly beside her, and it illuminated the inhospitable, rocky soil where she knelt. Before her lay two motley, makeshift libertyslippers, stitched together what seemed a lifetime ago from the scraps Otter had slowly collected, their soles turned blankly to the sky. Otter had made these. And now they had taken her friend. She grabbed the libertyslippers and clutched them in her fists, which she raised to her face as sobs shook her. A guttural, tortured moan escaped her throat, and Otter knew sadness as she had never even imagined.

The remaining libertylions who were still capable of unassisted movement, drawn to her mournful wailing, crept toward Otter and surrounded her as she sat huddled over the spot where her friend had been. Seeming to sense that she could not be consoled, the cats lay down around the crying child but left a few inches of space between her and themselves on all sides.

Otter had survived every hardship, escaped every peril, overcome every odd, all in pursuit of the perfect friend. And now, here, she knew she had found that friend. But not in any imaginary. In a real little girl, just like her, born from flesh and blood and not by anyone's whim. A girl who, like Otter, had experienced profound pain and fear in her short life, but who had never lost hope for a better day. Cherry had been the friend she had sought long before she even knew it, when setting out from Junkton on her quest. Even earlier, since she had been waiting all her conscious life for the perfect friend. And now, here, just as suddenly and unexpectedly as Otter had found her—

She was gone.

Otter wept harder and more bitterly than she had in her entire life. Because every other time she'd shed tears, she had saved for herself a hope, if only a glimmer, of a future when she would be with the friend she was always meant to have. And that hope, like her friend, was now gone forever.

A stray libertylion cub, lacking the restrained wisdom of its older peers, nuzzled the weeping girl's arm with its nose. Otter peeked out from her arms and, seeing the cub, who had surely lost as much today as she had, took it under her arm and pulled it close, so that its warm, thick fur absorbed the tears as they streamed down her face.

Cherry's face hovered before Otter's mind's eye, as if Cherry refused to relinquish her grip on Otter's imagination. Or as if Otter's imagination refused to relinquish its grip on Cherry's image. And as Otter lay there, crying and destroyed, she felt in her toes the same odd sensation that overtook her moments ago, just before she had been distracted by Cherry's shout, and that she'd first felt while imprisoned in Eliza's shack. The disembodied face of her fallen friend grew so large in her mind that it seemed to displace everything else—Mister's monstrous corpse, the libertylions assembled at her sides, her quest, even her own existence, all of it was pushed from her mind with her singular, devastated focus on the likeness of her friend.

The tingling sensation grew and spread throughout her body, rising from her feet and her legs, until eventually it engulfed every particle of her being even as it drew from them. And then it filled her head as well, and it was as if she were a vessel filled nearly to overflowing by this unknown feeling. The only things left in all existence were this electrifying, overflowing feeling and the unshakable image of her friend in her mind.

And then it was over. The tingling was gone. Cherry was gone. Otter was back in the moment, exhausted as she'd never been before. And the darkness of night, unaltered by any happenings of the living world, had shrouded her and the libertylions once more.

The stillness seemed almost too complete to Otter, who was briefly disoriented by the night's strange quiescence. The shock of it interrupted her weeping as abruptly as it had begun. She looked around in the lamp's flickering light as if these strange feelings might produce some physical effect on the world. But all she saw were the gathered libertylions, Mister's mauled and fallen carcass—and Cherry, who stood staring at her hands while she slowly flipped her palms up and down again, as if she were seeing them for the first time.

Otter's jaw dropped. She was unable to form even a basic word. A whispered gasp was the best she could muster.

Cherry looked up at her. "Otter?" She sounded every bit as confused as Otter felt. "How am I here?"

Otter did not recall jumping to her feet or crossing the couple of yards separating her from her friend. When their embrace finally ended, both girls' ribs ached from the squeezing, and the lantern light shined reflectively from their tear-soaked faces. Barely daring to believe what they saw, they stood, staring at each other from mere inches away.

Otter spoke first. "But—I saw you disappear. And"—looking over her shoulder, she could do no better than to gesture at Mister's lifeless form—"and *him*. What did you do?"

Cherry looked hard into Otter's eyes without saying anything for a long while. When she spoke, her voice was solemn, weighed down by the seriousness of the words. "Otter, I didn't do anything. I died." She paused, looking at her hands, and repeated, "I *died*. I decided it. I *felt* it." Her shoulders shook involuntarily. "I *remember* it. *All* of it. So you ask me what *I* did, Otter. But I think the real mystery may be what *you* did."

Otter leaned back, mouth wide open with shock. "What *I* did? What do you mean?"

"I don't know why. I certainly don't know *how*. But you—"

"I *what*?" Otter demanded.

"You . . . *imagined* me."

"But that's not even possible," she spluttered. "Luna told me imaginaries can't be people except . . ." Her mouth peeled back from her teeth and she stood aghast at the memory of Desdemona, whose nearly human features accompanied a twisted nature and a stunted mind.

Cherry seemed to hear Otter's unspoken concern. "Otter, I'm not like Desdemona. I'm not like *anyone* except *me*. I *am* me. When I say I remember everything, I don't just mean everything that happened in the fight with Mister. I mean everything. My entire life. All of it. *Everything*." Otter's horror slowly eroded as Cherry spoke, and her skepticism gave way to wonder. "I don't know how you have done it, but you have somehow imagined me back from the dead. I was here. Then I fitted the libertyslippers over my hands, and I sank into the ground. And then—and then it felt as if I was flying, as if I was being drawn somewhere. Then I felt myself returning, as if something was pulling me right back to here. And right before I appeared, it was as though I flowed"—Cherry's brow furrowed as she formulated the words—"as though I flowed *through you*, Otter."

"But that isn't how it's supposed to work, right?" Otter realized she didn't really understand how imaginaries were "supposed to work." Still, she had thought she understood at least that it didn't work like *this*.

Cherry's words echoed Otter's thoughts. "I guess I don't really know how it's supposed to work. All I know is that I died to save us both from Mister, and it worked. And now I'm here, and he's gone. And"—she seemed overwhelmed again by emotion, and her lip quivered to hold back more tears—"and I'm here with you. With my friend. And for the first time in so long, I'm relieved, and unafraid, and happy."

With that, she reached out to take Otter's hand in hers. Her smile invited Otter to return the gesture.

Otter realized that she, too, was happy and unafraid in a more complete way than she had ever known. And for the first time in her memory, she felt free. Free from the need to escape or flee or persevere. Free from fear and sadness and torment. But most of all, free from her quest, her singular drive to find that one perfect friend. Because she had found her. Cherry was all the friend Otter had ever hoped for.

Hand in hand, the two friends looked around in the lamplight and surveyed the pride of libertylions that had saved them in their hour of need. Some had injuries needing attention after their encounter with Mister. The girls realized they had, in these great cats, gained some additional friends along the way.

As she and Cherry made their way in the dark to tend to the wounded libertylions, Otter smiled. Her quest had been for the perfect friend. Otter had found her. But she had found many other friends along the way as well—including now these creatures that had come to her aid. With her difficult journey at an end, she was happy to replace her *search* for a perfect friend with the next stage of her journey: *being* one.

# ~ EPILOGUE ~

*ECSTASY.*

No matter how many times they emerged into a new form, Magnar still felt the same intense rush of pleasure, the sensation of every fiber, every particle of their life and body and mind flowing into a single vessel and taking shape around their thoughts and desires. The incarnation never ceased to produce this thrill, and Magnar never grew weary of it.

For many decades now, the incarnation had been more or less the same. This one was no exception. From a featureless central trunk that would be their torso, Magnar's arms coalesced as two nondescript cylindrical appendages, lacking even fingers or discernible joints. Next came their legs, materializing from the bottom of their torso and then extending down as a single pillar of malleable flesh. As the lower extremity reached the chamber's floor, it split into two sturdy limbs to distribute and support Magnar's mass as it seethed into existence. Although they could not see their face forming before them as they could their limbs, the familiarity of the process told Magnar that the same nearly featureless visage they'd formed time and again—the same large, round, lidless eyes; the same flat folds of ears; the same lipless mouth—had emerged once more in the incarnation they'd perfected over the course of near countless centuries.

Even the place was the same. The incarnation chamber's familiarity contributed to Magnar's comfort and pleasure. With its flickering candlelight and the curve of its stone walls encircling the entire room and disappearing into shadow, the cavernous incarnation chamber was the closest thing to home Magnar knew at this point. They allowed their gaze to wander about the room, orienting the senses of their new flesh to the hallowed space, until their eyes came to rest admiringly on the device occupying the chamber's center.

The soul spout was complex, beyond most beings' ability to comprehend, but its only visible feature was simple enough, at least in appearance. That lone feature, a glowing orb suspended aloft beneath the ceiling's tallest point, dominated the room. Even with their fully forming height, Magnar had to raise their eyes to behold the orb and the pearlescent mass of miniature storm clouds swirling with untold energy within it. Reflecting on its elegant beauty, Magnar mused that the soul spout was as much their own heart as it was the heart of the room. And like the body forming around them, it was a creation almost entirely of their own imagination.

Yes, the incarnation chamber was home. And the soul spout was its hearth. And this was just as Magnar liked it.

As the incarnation drew to conclusion, Magnar felt their weight coalesce until, with one final push, all their being had solidified into a single mass, born again of little more than will-power and the souls that powered their divine manifestation.

And with that, it had ended. The ecstasy faded, disappearing into the eternal essence from which it had sprung.

"Mirror," they commanded, with the simple authority of those in the habit of having absolute obedience.

A black-cowled figure came silently forth from the chamber's shadows and extended a mirror to them from a smooth pale hand that had been concealed beneath its robe. The shapeless end of Magnar's arm reached out, articulated into digits, and grasped the mirror in their newly formed fingers to raise it before them. They regarded their divine face.

*Perfection*, they thought, with faint echoes of vanity and relief—feelings rooted in a former life. Just as expected, the face they beheld was neither animal nor human, neither real nor imaginary. It bore no trace of the weak, imperfect form they had abandoned so long ago, but also no suggestion of the feeble humans and imaginaries that now surrounded them as servants. It was, they thought, the undeniable face of a deity.

A distant knock echoed unexpectedly through the vast incarnation chamber, interrupting Magnar's self-adoration. A hint of a frown, like the expression of a vague memory of emotion, bent the face in the mirror.

"Come, child." Their flat, unnatural voice resonated in their own flat, unnatural ears. Something seemed amiss, although they did not understand how. *Not yet*, they thought, with the certainty of a being that had long grown used to understanding anything they might encounter.

A sharply dressed figure, not nearly as tall as Magnar but only slightly shorter than the average adult male human, glided into the chamber, his fur-lined cloak and shoulder-length blond hair flowing gently behind as he advanced. The newcomer kneeled when he had reached a respectful distance from Magnar and gently cleared his throat.

"Lord, we have a report from Industriopa." Skylar's voice usually flowed from his mouth like honey, exuding the same beauty and elegance he cultivated in his appearance. He was among Magnar's most trusted followers. He was, in fact, their longest-serving imaginary. Now, though, Skylar's velvety voice was uneasy.

That made Magnar uneasy.

Like all Magnar's closest confidants, Skylar was not easily shaken. One could not unquestioningly serve at the pleasure of a living god and retain a sense of casual unease. Skylar's unease, they reasoned, must not be casual.

Magnar extended the limb that held the mirror, and the cowled servant retrieved it without a word before disappearing silently back into shadow. Upon releasing the mirror, Magnar's massive form imploded into a nondescript mass, which surged in a nebulous wave toward Skylar. In a heartbeat the wave had covered the few yards of distance that Skylar's deference had left between them. When Magnar took solid shape again, they stood immediately in front of Skylar, so close they could feel their servant's breath upon them.

Skylar didn't so much as flinch. Sudden displays of Magnar's power were nothing new to their truest devotees, and Skylar's many battles had left him steady in the face of even the gravest peril. Few could have served as Skylar had and retained the ability to be startled or astonished.

When their head had fully resolidified and their eyes emerged from its forward aspect, Magnar looked for a long time without speaking into the downturned face before them. Magnar gave imaginaries of Skylar's rank significant discretion over their forms, and Magnar had always found amusement in Skylar's choices in this regard. Skylar had been a homely man in his own flesh. When given the choice, he had crafted delicate, noble features after the human ideal of handsomeness. A sloping nose ending in a finely upturned point. High cheek-bones framed eyes that were blue as sapphires and cold as ice. But his vanity was nothing to his loyalty, and Magnar would not begrudge him such silly flourishes.

Having observed a sufficient degree of deference in their servant, they finally deigned to speak.

"Report," they commanded simply. Nothing more was necessary.

"Lord, we have lost two of your vanguard children under suspicious circumstances, and in proximity to each other."

Magnar felt their face draw involuntarily taut. "'Suspicious circumstances'?" Dispassionately they noticed an all-but-forgotten tone of tension in their voice, such as they had not heard in many lifetimes. "Explain."

Skylar continued without hesitation. "Within a span of a few months, we have lost both a scout and—" Here he paused.

Already on edge from the tenor of this report, Magnar was annoyed at Skylar's sudden timidity. They did not care for mysteries, let alone unpleasant ones. "And what?"

"And a marauder, Lord."

For the first time in ages, Magnar felt genuine shock. A sickening chill tingled throughout their being. Scouts wandered into trouble here and there. They were none too bright and were prone to biting off more than they could chew. Sometimes they sought prey where they shouldn't, attempting to take on a large predator or a well-equipped human. It was not even unheard of for one here or there to get into a bind and die from starvation, dehydration, or exposure. Indeed, they were ultimately quite fragile despite a sometimes-menacing appearance. But a marauder—Magnar could scarcely remember the last time they had lost a marauder.

"Show me. Begin with the scout."

The bottom of Magnar's form deconstructed and then realigned into a sturdy base to support their frame, as though a blocky throne had grown out from under them. Simultaneously Skylar moved to obey.

Without speaking a word, their loyal servant glided to a console a few yards away in front of the soul spout and manipulated its controls. As Skylar worked, a beam of dull light emitted from the soul spout's crystalline core and projected a series of images flashing in front of where the throned deity sat. These were the last several days of the deceased scout's memories as seen through its own eyes. It was by all appearances a typical life for a scout—albeit a more leisurely existence than many settled into.

The large, unblinking orbs of their eyes took the images in, scanning them as they raced by at an accelerated pace. "Faster," they quietly commanded. The projection sped up until each hour of the scout's life cycle of hunger and feeding and transformation and sleep raced by in seconds, as it was cast before Magnar. And then, the end. The scout had gone to sleep a final time, never to awaken.

The silence in the chamber was absolute until Magnar, after a moment's contemplation, broke it. "Again." The toneless voice demanded obedience, and Skylar never failed to heed.

Magnar moved closer to the speeding images, examining their every detail.

"Hold." Again Skylar's obedience was instantaneous, and the memory froze in midair, as if preserved in amber. Magnar examined it with curiosity, scanning the suspended image up and down. "Now the marauder too."

Skylar's limber arms and nimble fingers moved skillfully over his work as he continued to manipulate the device's controls. The orb emitted a second beam of light. Like the first, this projection, too, bore the speeding memories of one of Magnar's distant servants. Magnar smiled in a lipless grimace at Skylar's anticipation of his request. *After millennia together*, they thought, *he well ought to anticipate me.*

These were the last days of the marauder's memories. Magnar watched them unfold with interest at their artificially enhanced speed, standing in frenzied contrast to the adjacent image, the frozen frame of the scout's projected recollections. *Nothing unusual so far—*

The thought was interrupted as something *quite* unusual, in fact, caught their eyes, and their initial shock only increased as the scenes progressed before them. "Hold," they said again, this time in barely a whisper. Immediately the images halted before them.

The silence stretched across several tense minutes. Magnar sat comparing the pair of frozen scenes, separated here by only a few inches, but having originally occurred months and miles apart from each other, and halfway across Imbria from where Magnar now sat.

"My child," they intoned to Skylar, though their voice had taken on a quiet, ominous depth. "Who is *this*?"

"I do not know, Lord," came Skylar's contrite reply.

Magnar glanced back and forth between the two images, and their throne-like mount merged into their body once more as they moved deliberately toward the memories where they hung suspended at the end of the soul spout's beams. Magnar drew closer until their face nearly touched the ethereal projections, until they could almost smell their servants' final impressions of the diminutive figure cast in duplicate before them.

"Well," they declared at last, "it seems high time you found out."

Skylar stood at attention. "Understood, Lord." And without another word, he turned from the soul spout with a whirl of silk and fur and departed swiftly from the incarnation chamber, leaving his master to continue their examination of the twin images.

And as they peered ever more intently at those images, Magnar, the unchallenged god of their domain, the future ruler of all Imbria, committed to memory every detail of this mysterious person who had interfered with that future, who had escaped the scout—perhaps even poisoned the scout—shortly before it wasted away, and who had somehow also dispatched an exquisite marauder, the most capable variety of Magnar's vanguard children.

"Yes, child, we would very much like to know who you are," they said, speaking only to the incarnation chamber's echoing solitude, to the mute servants that lined the shadowed walls, to the glowing globe that pulsed within the soul spout—and to the twin likenesses of a small brown girl from halfway around Imbria, and apparently on the wrong continent, to boot. "Because we have many questions for you." The soul spout's light reflected in their great, lidless eyes, and their gaze grew ever more intense as every feature of this curious little girl seared into a memory longer than natural life. "And you will answer, child," they said. "You *will* answer."

# The End

# ACKNOWLEDGMENTS

Writing *A Friend for Otter* was a challenge unlike any that either of us has ever undertaken, and we could not have done it alone. We are immensely grateful to the many readers who had faith enough to preorder our book and stick patiently by us throughout this unexpectedly long journey. We are also grateful to Inkshares, whose innovative publication model made our mission possible despite our slow going, and whose team of consummate professionals provided insightful and practical guidance in this, our freshman effort. We must also thank Senetra Busbee, whose inspired illustration adorns our cover and capture's Otter's face just as our imaginations had. Finally, we owe a great debt to the friends and family who generously gave their time, interest, and intellect to help make the substance of this story what it is today. Particularly deserving of mention here are Kathy and Kevin Acre (Jesse's parents, and Ván's beloved Nana and Papa); our friend Robert Mitchell, whose love of adventure and head for science helped us strike the right balance of fantasy and reality; and Brianne McCarthy (Jesse's spouse and Ván's mother), whose feedback was so constant and crucial that she practically deserves credit as a coauthor.

# GRAND PATRONS

Alexander D. Jakle
Alice Bozarth Moore
Art Navarrette
Brianne Mccarthy
Byron T. Deese
Christein Aromando
Elizabeth Lemerande
George John Gigounas
Gloria M. Mc Carthy
Jamie C. Walker
Jamil Mcclintock
Josh Evans
Justin Cotton
Kathy Goldstein Acre
Kimberly Baird Mitchell
Laksmi Govindasamy
Luis A. Bonilla
Melanie Kim
Nathan Hagman
Scott Early
Thomas Turner

# INKSHARES